T0193403

BLACKLISTED

A Trail of Deception, Mystery and Love

DARLINE R. ROOT

authorHOUSE®

AuthorHouse™
1663 Liberty Drive
Bloomington, IN 47403
www.authorhouse.com
Phone: 833-262-8899

Published by AuthorHouse   08/02/2023

ISBN: 979-8-8230-1048-1 (sc)
ISBN: 979-8-8230-1049-8 (hc)
ISBN: 979-8-8230-1050-4 (e)

Library of Congress Control Number: 2023911283

Print information available on the last page.

Cover design and photography by Jennifer Pauly Peterson, owner of JP Creations.

This book is printed on acid-free paper.

This book is dedicated to
Daniel W. Root, my deceased older brother, who
loved the idea of my writing. One of the last things he
did before dying at the age of fifty-three of
kidney and bone cancer in 2005
was provide me with valuable advice for this second
novel in my series starting with my first Christian
fiction book, *Traces of Discernment.*
We hope you enjoy
Blacklisted: A Trail of Deception, Mystery, and Love.

About the Author

Traces of Discernment was Darline's first attempt at writing a fictional novel, in which she wove a story while teaching about complicated investigative processes in solving a string of cases derived from satanic activity. Now her second book in this adult Christian fiction series, *Blacklisted: A Trail of Deception, Mystery, and Love*, continues the story in a fun way with some of the original beloved characters.

Darline has always had a love of words but never thought in a million years she would be writing down the stories from her mind and sharing them.

Providing investigative instruction throughout the first book was only fitting since Darline served as a criminal justice and paralegal academic department head and full professor at several small private colleges and universities for numerous years. She is a graduate of South Texas College of Law—affiliated with Texas A&M University, University of South Florida, and Hillsborough Community College.

Besides a profession in the academic world, she has worked in several law firms and financial institutions. Presently, she pursues other professional opportunities and writes. She thinks becoming a successful full-time author would be nice.

As she gets older, Darline longs to experience more of nature and the artistic things in life and maybe work on a bucket list.

Darline now lives in the southeastern part of the United States, with her remaining family members, while handling the complications of multiple autoimmune diseases.

Character Dedications

1. Character Dedication for Midnight

The first character dedication is for the tiny black male kitten character found by Amanda O'Neal on her first evening near the manor of Huntington Hills College campus.

I fondly named the lovely creature Midnight after the real Midnight, a large, black male feline member of the Pauly Peterson family. They will always be in my heart, as they are some of my best friends. The real Midnight once lived a sad, feral existence until he was recused. Now, he lives a charmed life. Here's to you, Midnight. This character dedication is for you! Meow.

2. Character Dedications for Timothy and Karen Ruff

Two interesting characters introduced at Huntington Hills College are professors Timothy and Karen Norman. These are dedicated to my brother's lifelong friend Timothy Ruff and his beloved wife, Karen. My older brother, Daniel, and Timothy were always together when they were growing up. Since they were around our home, Timothy emotionally became like a second brother to me, someone I could always count on. He was fortunate to marry Karen, who likewise became a member of our family.

Timothy, you said if I ever wrote another book, you hoped I'd include your name in the story somehow, so, brother, this is for you. I hope you and Karen enjoy your characters. I love you both very much.

3. Character Dedication for John and Mary Ward and their son, Gregory J. Ward

The character of Chief Braxton Ward is dedicated to a deceased former law enforcement officer, John H. Ward, and his wife, Mary Ward. John started professionally as a motorcycle cop and then a patrol officer and finally retired as a plainclothes undercover police officer in New York City. Out of respect, I created the character of Braxton Ward to thank John and all those who have served, and continue to serve, to protect all of us.

Thank you.

Also, this dedication was done due to the kindness and friendship of their son, Gregory J. Ward, who professionally mentored me at a job I had never done before. Gregory and I remain friends.

Thank you, Gregory. I hope you and your family enjoy this character.

4. Character Dedication for Judith Louise Jewel Zimpher

Gena Jewel, the hospital administrator character at Huntington Hills Hospital, is dedicated to my cousin Judy Jewel Zimpher. Judy is one of the best people and truest Christians I know. As a teacher, she dedicated her professional life to enriching the lives of hundreds of students through education. Now, all her spare time is devoted to her family, husband, and faith. She is also devoted to her church as a lay speaker and servant, as well as involved in several organizations that bring young people to the Lord. She is presently serving as the office manager for Cross Road Farm Ministry.

This is for you, Judy Jewel Zimpher. You are an inspiration.

5. Character Dedications for Glen and Fern Root

The characters of Glen and Fern Beasley were named after my paternal grandparents.

Grandma, I remember.

6. Character Dedications for Michael and Christopher Ranly

Ryan's full name of Ryan Michael Christopher McFarlan comes from the combination of a deceased cousin's husband, Michael Ranly, and their son, Christopher. Both Michael and Sheila served in the US Navy.

Rest in peace, Sheila.

7. Special Thank You Dedication

A special thanks to all the members of Root's Revival Sunday School Group at a nearby traditional Methodist church, New Hope Methodist Church. Without all your love and support, this book would never have been written. You know who you are! You are my Christian family and greatly loved by the Root family forever. Thank you.

Root's Revival was named in honor of my father, Rev. Wayne G. Root, and my mother, Rachel E. Root. With my mother's constant devotion and help, he pastored many churches throughout his life as well as traveled the world spreading the gospel of Jesus Christ and taking medical assistance where needed.

Contents

Preface

Blacklisted: A Trail of Deception, Mystery, and Love, is the second series novel following *Traces of Discernment.* These Christian fiction books are considered for adult reading only. I recommend they not be read by children, adolescents, or young teenagers without parental approval, and the prologue should be read before chapter 1.

Although I have dedicated various characters in *Blacklisted* to people I know, the story comes purely from my imagination and research for detail. Some geographic areas are real, such as the Tampa Bay area in Florida and parts of Ireland, including Dublin and Mullaghmeen Forest, but all events at these locations are purely fictional. Although I never have been to Ireland, I have done my best to depict these beautiful locations and feel honored to utilize them throughout my story.

No aspects of *Blacklisted* may be changed or utilized in any way except for positive marketing purposes or with the legal approval from the author. All written work of the author is copyrighted and protected.

A great apology and thank-you go out to all the internet sites I visited to do research to obtain accurate information. When writing, I mentally get so into my stories that other aspects, such as research documentation, are neglected. I become so deeply involved in the story that the characters often take over. One publication I utilized for architecture research was W. Fleming's *Arts & Idea*, published in 1980 by Holt, Rinehart, and Winston.

Due to several years of unforeseen personal tragedies in my life, I was unable to write for a long time. But suddenly, I finally started to write again, and this story took off. The COVID epidemic and lack of finances delayed the publishing of this book, but I hope my readers can see that my writing has greatly improved compared to my first book in this series. I hope you enjoy the continuation of Amanda's story in this book.

I have always had all these stories running through my mind. Honestly, I thought everyone else had that happen too! Now, I just want to continue to write and get them out for others to enjoy and to share what I visualize, promoting the fact that everyone can have a more fulfilling life through Christian faith. Thank you for reading my work.

Please don't forget to rate this book on the website where you have purchased it, once you are done reading. Your encouragement and comments are welcomed. Thank you.

Book cover design and any photography are by Jennifer Pauly Peterson, owner of JP Creations.

Prologue

Before Huntington Hills College

Every year, Shawn and Amanda O'Neal had a community Christmas Eve celebration in their barn. When the Tampa Police Department and court system were fighting against a horrible crime spree and Shawn was viciously attacked in the barn, it made no difference at the O'Neal farm. As far as all were concerned, the annual celebration of Jesus Christ's birth would continue. Beautiful lights were strung all over the barn, and a nativity and manger were set up. The neighborhood children portrayed the night Jesus was born in Bethlehem, with a prayer or two, a little Christmas message, and wonderful music and food.

Once everyone had arrived, Amanda moved to the front, pushing Shawn's wheelchair.

"Shawn and I want to welcome as well as thank everyone for coming to the O'Neal farm this Christmas Eve. We hope you truly enjoy the rest of the candlelight service."

Shawn added, "May all of you have a very merry Christmas and a happy New Year. God bless."

Soon after, Amanda quietly sneaked out of the barn with Shawn. Detective Brad Conner viewed them from a distance in the crowd and went to help.

Since Shawn was still recovering from his right shoulder being shot as well as some unusual infection, Amanda thought it best to get him back in bed to rest as soon as possible. Besides, he had just had surgery a few days ago. Doctors had insisted he continue to use the wheelchair for a few more days, due to his weakness. Shawn, of course, protested, feeling a little humiliated. The only thing that calmed his nerves was Royal, their Labrador retriever, who stayed right by his master's side. Amanda got Shawn and Royal settled in their bedroom and then headed for the kitchen for refreshments.

Amanda and Brad Conner, a police detective and dear friend, sat on the farmhouse front porch, sipping on iced tea while watching all the happy activity in the barn. They spoke about many things that special evening, including her complete faith in Shawn's recovery. After all, he had always been positive and strong, serving as a pillar in his community and church as well as working hard on the farm and caring for everyone he loved.

To Amanda, Shawn O'Neal was her handsome husband, her best friend, and her whole world.

A few months had gone by, and spring was just around the corner. Shawn didn't want to admit that he was still fighting the dreaded infection raging in his body after the shooting. What kind of infection was it? Physicians had been having a difficult time determining its cause and any cure. He'd also had to endure quite a bit of physical therapy but insisted on still doing some of the daily farm chores. Amanda had hired some temporary help around the place to lighten his load, along with little José doing as much as he could to assist. José and his grandmother Soledad lived behind the O'Neal barn, in a tiny cabin that everyone had fixed up for them.

It will all work out, Amanda kept telling herself.

The months seemed to fly by, with the rainy season now upon them. Day after day, the storms seemed to come. Rain, rain, rain.

One Friday evening, Shawn and Amanda turned in early. Jasper, their cat, made herself comfortable in the living room, so Amanda left her to enjoy the cozy comfort of the house rather than the barn. She knew all the storms lately had kind of worn off Jasper's joy of staying in the loft. Royal, as always, lay at the end of the bed in blissful sleep on his back with all four paws stuck up in the air. Everyone seemed to be in a relaxed state but her.

She worried often about Shawn's slow recovery, wondering why doctors couldn't get the infection under control. After all, Shawn had always been perfectly healthy, due to being active in sports in college and always working hard on the farm most of his life. He never had gotten sick before the incident. In fact, she often saw other women of all ages checking him out. He was tall, lean, and muscular where it counted. Amanda often smiled to herself that she was a lucky gal.

Shawn was handsome inside and out. Most people didn't realize that he and Amanda had known each other since they were young children. They'd been childhood sweethearts, really, almost as if their being husband and wife had been preplanned destiny. Their love for each other had always been intense from the first time their eyes met, and he'd offered her a glance at a frog from the farm pond. She and her brothers had visited the O'Neal family often, and all the children had known every inch of the farm. For them, there was no other place in the world they could really call home.

Amanda lay on her side while moving her pillow around to get comfortable. The storm outside was raging like a wild beast. The wind and rain were slamming across the windows, and she could hear thunder coming from a distance. All of a sudden, there was a loud, thunderous crack, and the electricity went out. Amanda checked both their cell phones, and of course, they had forgotten to charge them after dinner.

Shawn, who was lying on his back, calmly grabbed her arm. "Amanda."

"Yeah?"

"You or José have to go get Ben."

"Why is that? We're OK."

Gasping for breath, he replied, "No, honey, something is wrong. I think I may be having a heart attack."

"What? Oh my God! Shawn!"

She bent down over him, feeling his breath. Even though it was dark, they looked into each other's eyes. A funny feeling went from the top of her head to the ends of her toes. They communicated without speaking. She kissed him softly. He kissed her back. Tears came to her eyes, and then just like that, her professional persona kicked in.

"Hurry, Amanda. I love you. Go as fast as you can. Be careful."

She jumped out of bed, grabbed her jeans on the nearby chair, and sank her feet into the only boots she could find were Shawn's boots. Her sleep T-shirt hung way past her knees, but she didn't give her looks a thought as she ordered restless Royal to stay with Shawn as she found a flashlight in one of the kitchen drawers and raced out of the house.

Unfortunately, her Jeep was in the shop to be fixed, and Shawn's truck seemed to be flooded. It wouldn't start. "Now what?"

The storm was too fierce for her to jump onto one of the horses or go the direction of the little cabin where Soledad and José were, so she ran for the fence and into the wooded area between the O'Neal farm and Corporal Ben's property nearby. Branches scratched her everywhere. Her wet hair kept getting in her eyes. The rain, wind, and thunder raged on as she kept going, stomping through muddy puddles and foliage.

Oh God, please get me to Ben's soon.

Finally, she reached the front door of Ben's house and started pounding on the door with her fist. "Ben! Ben! It's Amanda. Help! Something is wrong with Shawn. Help!"

He swiftly opened the door, standing there in his underwear. "Oh my God, Amanda. My electricity is out too. OK, don't worry. Let's get to my issued sheriff vehicle and call for backup, the fire department, and an ambulance. Don't worry. We'll get help to him as soon as possible. He is going to be OK."

After calling for backup, Ben and Amanda raced back to Shawn. She ran into the bedroom like a madwoman. Shawn's breathing was weak, but he was still alive. Amanda leaned down over Shawn to give him a quick hug and kiss as Ben swiftly moved her so he could immediately start CPR. She could see Shawn's eyes trying to focus on her face, but his vison appeared to be fading.

"I love you, Shawn O'Neal. Do you hear me? I love you. We need you. Don't you give up. Hang in there. Don't leave us. Ben is here. Don't leave us. Shawn!"

By that time, Royal was whimpering.

Soon the fire department and ambulance arrived, but with all the drama, it seemed forever before they got there, instead of just a few moments.

Amanda sat in the hospital chapel, waiting for Ben, feeling numb inside. She just wanted to go home. Maybe she didn't really know what she wanted. She sat there in unbelief. Her mouth opened for a few seconds, but no words of prayer came out. It seemed she'd been sitting there forever, but it had only been a few moments since she was by Shawn's side in the ER as they pronounced him dead.

In her mind, she kept hearing the words, *It will work out. It will work out. But Shawn died. We didn't even get a proper husband and wife goodbye! Oh God, he is dead. It's too soon, dear Lord. It is too soon. Now what do I do? How do I live on this earth without him? My Shawn. My soul mate. My better half. Oh God.*

Chapter 1

The Campus

The fall wind swirled and whipped around the old Gothic-style buildings as if it were running a race against time. Branches from the many aged trees that covered the campus like a blanket clicked together as the wind picked up speed around the building corners. Some of the colorful leaves remained attached, while others traveled with the wind like small ships being swiftly taken away by high seas. There was an endless variety of shades and tones in reds, golds, and greens. It was a spectacular sight, the type of view that perhaps a blind man would give a million dollars to experience in one quick glance.

If you paused for a moment and quietly stood glancing about, nature created a feeling as if you were in the middle of God's canvas, as if he had just dropped an array of autumn hues around you. The wind had a biting coldness to it, but none of that seemed to matter. If you let it, just standing there looking around caused your soul to feel consumed with the many elements of the scene before you. Amanda would remember that first sight of the campus for the rest of her life.

She stood at the door of one of the cathedral buildings with her arms crossed in front of her, rubbing her hands up and down her arms to keep herself warm. Thank goodness she had worn her wool tweed pantsuit. It felt as if the wind was going right through her as it slipped by, sounding momentarily like a train. The tall buildings had something to do with the noise, but Amanda's mind wasn't on the sound of the wind. She was too busy knocking on the door, hoping someone would hurry up and unlock the entrance so she could swiftly slip in.

OK, Lord. Here I am. Now what? Right now, I'm freezing my Florida you-know-what off, wondering why I agreed to this sabbatical at Huntington Hills College in North Carolina. I must have lost my common sense for a few moments when I agreed to this! Can't believe I've left the farm in the hands of José, Brad, and Henry. Shawn, my deceased husband, is probably looking down from heaven at this very moment, yelling about how I've left the family inheritance in the hands of a group of greenhorns. My husband. My husband.

Just as she was controlling a feeling of grief, the small, square peephole in the door opened, and a smiling elderly man looked out at her.

"Nice to see you, Dr. O'Neal. Frankly, we all were not sure you would actually come!"

"Well, I'm here. I don't make promises unless I intend to keep them."

"Excellent indeed. The dean will be most pleased to hear of your arrival. Please let me direct you to his office, where you can comfortably wait by the fireplace with a spot of tea before he returns."

"Thank you. You are very kind."

"You're welcome, madam. If I may say, it is my pleasure and duty to assist such an attractive woman."

2

Amanda glanced at the diplomatic elderly man and gave a warm smile like only she could give. She thought to herself how funny it was that he referred to her as attractive. After all, she knew her age was beginning to show through small age lines and a few extra unwanted pounds. No telling how old this guy was! He probably viewed Amanda as young. Oddly, that was a comforting thought.

"If you don't mind me asking, what is your name?"

"Of course, how rude of me. My name is Covington Strongwell III. I am the butler of the campus manor. As long as Huntington Hills College has existed, there has always been a Strongwell seeing to the comfort needs of the administration and faculty here within the walls of the manor. My father and his father before him worked here. The manor is kind of a home away from home for those of you who require it during your stay here on campus."

"I see. It is really quite lovely here. Very nice meeting you, Strongwell."

"My pleasure, Dr. O'Neal. My pleasure indeed."

"Do I detect a tone of English in your voice, Strongwell?"

"Most assuredly, madam. It is quite true. I am a blue blood most assuredly."

With exact precision, Strongwell led Amanda down the long, gigantic hallway filled with enormous oil paintings, tapestries, and museum-like statues.

Amanda smiled to herself, thinking the dark hall needed only cobwebs and spooky music to be a proper setting for a horror movie. It was a beautiful place but also a mysterious sight. The view brought a chill through her. Strange. Still, there was also a feeling of pride in every aspect of what she saw. The architecture itself showed a form of artistic pride and artisan skill usually unique only to late-twelfth- and thirteenth-century cathedrals like those in France. Most spectacular.

Suddenly, her attention was interrupted by the voice of Strongwell.

"Dr. O'Neal, I can see that the darkness of the hall concerns you. Fear not, for the darkness comes soon to this geographic area when late fall arrives. I suspect a good storm in the form of rain is soon to present itself. Just wait, madam, until the morning light comes in. See the pointed arches and ribbed groin vaults fundamental to Gothic architecture? Such a design makes it a light and flexible building system that permits generous openings in walls for large, high windows."

Strongwell held his right arm straight up, pointing to the windows, as they continued to walk. He slowly moved his arm in a half-circle sweep to demonstrate where the sun might shine in. "Wait until you see the early morning light illuminate this whole area. The view these stained-glass windows project is something to behold when light comes through. I have studied these windows all my life but never grown tired of looking at them. There is something almost hypnotic about their arrangement. Well, here we are. Please, Dr. O'Neal, seat yourself in front of the huge fireplace while I depart for a spot of tea. The academic dean has been informed of your campus arrival and will return to his office shortly."

Looking about while she spoke, Amanda replied, "Thank you, Strongwell. I don't mind if I do take a seat and relax awhile. Hot tea will be most appreciated at this time. You are very kind."

"It is no fuss, madam. I am just doing what my position requires. Duties are very important here at Huntington Hills College. It is my pleasure to serve you. My pleasure indeed."

With that, Amanda sat comfortably on the soft brown leather couch in front of the enormous black granite fireplace. She glanced backward over her right shoulder to give Strongwell a soft and kind smile.

The dean's office was almost overwhelming. The room was so huge and spectacular that there was no way a person could take everything in during one visit. It was as if time stood still for a few seconds, or it possibly moved in slow motion. It was something she would never forget. Not ever.

When Strongwell initially had led her into the room, she hadn't had time to really examine how tall and thick the wooden double doors were. There was so much to take in all at once. Artfully, it appeared as though the doors instinctively leaned against the walls, as if they knew their proper place when forced to stay open. An architectural eye might have immediately recognized how the doors appeared to be guarding the room with eloquence and strength— quite threatening at first sight. Still, the most impressive thing in the room was the gigantic black fireplace she sat directly before. The fire burning within the framework of the magnificent structure was equally intimidating, but Amanda had to admit to herself that the warmth it produced was welcome.

There was a long, narrow wooden table directly behind the couch, with a lamp standing atop it on its far-right corner. Just a few feet beyond the table was a window with a spectacular view of the campus. A few feet from the table stood one of the largest desks Amanda had ever laid eyes upon, even bigger than the one Judge Walter E. Pace II had had when she visited his court chambers back home. It was hard to believe her supposed good old friend Walter had been found to be responsible for the horrible chain of satanic crimes in Tampa, Florida. Well, that was the past, and now she could look toward the future. Maybe a few months of working at Huntington Hills College would help her heal from all those past pains.

Oh God, she thought, *how I miss my husband, Shawn. Why did he have to die?*

The warmth from the fire as well as deep thoughts made her miss the fact that Covington Strongwell III had returned holding a tray with a teapot and two teacups.

"Here is your tea, Dr. O'Neal."

"Thank you, Strongwell. You are ever so kind. These teacups are very eloquent looking. Oh, I know these! They are part of the Dimension collection from Lenox. Very plain with the cream-color china and a fourteen-karat-gold rim around the top of each cup and saucer. Plain but classic. I love it!"

"Dr. O'Neal, I see you are a connoisseur of detail in teacups."

"Actually, Covington, I'm a connoisseur of detail in almost everything. After all, I am a lawyer and investigator. Unfortunately, I was born with these traits, rather than solely acquiring them by training. Sometimes I have trouble turning my brain off due to always zoning in on everything around me."

"Well, this tea is sure to relax you. It has been served here at our manor since the beginning of time. It is a secret blend of green tea with natural herbs and spices said to be picked atop the hills just beyond the campus. Gossip about town is that the herbs and spices were left long ago by American Indians. The faculty around here swear it relaxes them at night when nothing else will and rejuvenates them during the day. My mother, God rest her soul, used to tell others that her youthful skin and beautiful hair were due to this tea. Legend has it that no one truly becomes part of Huntington Hills until they have partaken of the legendary tea."

"Is it safe?"

"Of course, madam. Probably purer than most water people drink. Trust me. Between the warmth from the fireplace and the tea, you will forget all about that cold fall wind that followed you to the main door, where I promptly welcomed you. Now, you just sit here and relax. The academic dean will be with you shortly."

"Thank you, Covington. I will just sit here quietly until Dean Russet arrives."

Amanda slowly sipped the delightful tea, every once in a while leaning her head on the back of the couch. She soon drifted to sleep.

Chapter 2

Dean Russet

Amanda had no indication how long she had been out while sitting in front of the dean's fireplace. It was a little disconcerting, wondering what had happened while she was blacked out. She swiftly checked her clothing with her hands to see if everything was in its proper place, fighting to become more alert.

"Sorry to have taken so long, Dr. O'Neal. I was in the midst of a faculty meeting, and time just got away from me. I trust you enjoyed your first experience with our wonderful tea here at Huntington Hills College."

The screechy tenor tone of the dean's distant voice sounded a little villainous for a second, but Amanda ignored it as she became aware enough to respond. "Yes, thank you, Dean Russet. This green tea does have a very unique flavor, to say the least!"

With a little, sinister laugh almost too soft to catch, Dean Russet responded, "Yes, very unique."

Amanda finally had enough visual focus to look over to the dean, who was sitting at his desk. For a second, she felt like laughing out loud, but she controlled herself as she gained composure. It was entertaining to see the little, pudgy Dean Russet sitting behind the enormous desk. Like a beach ball bobbing near a pier.

Professionally trained to observe, Amanda moved her eyes secretly up and down to take in as much as possible. She forced her face to show no emotion as she unconsciously worked to store details.

The dean's thin ash-brown hair was in a short, choppy style that circled around the ears and straight across the back of his short neck. His skin was beardless and extremely pale, with red patches, especially across the nose and cheeks. His small, beady eyes were framed by gold-wired glasses, while a thin-lipped area seemed unnaturally close to his large nose. Dean Russet almost appeared to be slightly larger than one of the munchkins introduced in the classic *Wizard of Oz* movie.

For a second, Amanda wondered in her subconscious if he was really a she, but that flash of a thought quickly left. *A supposed respectable academic dean certainly wouldn't portray himself as being something other than what he truly was. Would he?*

Dean Russet wore a navy-blue JCPenney suit with brown lace-up oxford shoes that presently failed to touch the floor by about six inches.

Amanda's first thought after a glance was *Where did they get this one? Sure hope he has the credentials to hold the position of academic dean!*

Now that Dr. O'Neal was looking directly at him, the dean proceeded. "Well, I suppose you are worn out from traveling all day. It must have been difficult to leave the balmy Florida weather. I'm afraid your destination of North Carolina in the fall has presented you with our cold and unpredictable elements to contend with. I trust you have brought enough warm clothing to help with such extremity."

"Your concern for my well-being is graciously accepted and touching, Dean Russet. I have brought enough warm clothing to last a few days. Any additional items I might need can most likely be purchased in the shops around the center of downtown, near the campus. At least that is what I was told when I accepted this sabbatical."

"Yes, I am sure you will enjoy the shopping our quaint little town has to offer. At least I have on many an occasion! Perhaps I can show you around our township sometime when we both have a few moments to spare."

"That would be nice. Thank you."

Amanda hadn't quite figured this person out yet and, therefore, didn't want to go anywhere with him until she felt safe. Despite her inner thoughts, she demonstrated to the dean an appearance of ease, smiling the brilliant smile that only Amanda could, despite all circumstances.

"Good. We will plan a community tour for the future. For now, though, I want to briefly inform you that we have assigned you to teach two classes this semester. One course is Criminal Investigation, and the other is Criminal Procedure. Details can be discussed once you have reviewed the material and gotten a better grasp of the campus and its policies. Classes will begin in about ten days. Until then, you will be required to attend all the faculty meetings. There will, of course, be other accomplishments we will expect from you—you know, such as publishing articles or books and guest speaking. This all can be explained later in more detail, but for now, I will have the butler, Mr. Strongwell, take you to your room. I am sure you are most anxious to get settled in your assigned quarters. Hopefully, you will find the faculty guest accommodations most comfortable. Please do not hesitate to inform me at any time if there is anything we can do to make your stay here more pleasant."

The dean's high-pitched voice paused for a moment when he said the words *at any time*, but Amanda was clever enough to appear as though she had missed his emphasis.

"Dean Russet, you are most kind. Yes, I would like to get settled for the evening in my assigned room and then perhaps get a bite to eat before retiring for the evening. Thank you."

Amanda slowly stood from the couch and extended her right arm to shake the dean's hand. His right hand was freely extended to meet hers, but it felt limp, lifeless, and sweaty during the brief physical connection between them. Still, it seemed to be a cordial goodbye as the dean swiftly left, and Strongwell entered to show Amanda the way to her room. She had no idea what to expect regarding the quality of lodging she would be assigned.

This should be interesting, Amanda thought as she trailed behind Strongwell as they left the dean's office into the great hall before them.

Strongwell handed her an old-looking skeleton key for the door. The key at first felt unusually heavy in the palm of Amanda's hand. Automatically, she looked down at the key before placing it into the door. It was surprising to see the intricate craftsmanship on its body. The key's detail was something she would surely study at another time, but for now, Amanda swiftly slipped the key into the old door's keyhole. The hall was growing darker as the sun slowly lowered behind the beautiful North Carolina mountains. She finally opened the door and momentarily stepped back in disbelief as her eyes grasped all the details of the room. Strongwell stood behind her, ready to give his usual historic tour of the room.

The large canopy bed was adorned with an elaborate deep burgundy bedspread trimmed with gold rope and tassels. Above the bed, the heavy velvet matching canopy hung down at each corner as if to dramatically connect with the bedspread below it. As the head of the bed faced the north wall, the east wall displayed a castle-like window at each end, with a reading table and lamp in the middle.

A small, slow grin formed on Amanda's face. "Strongwell, this reading table, or desk or whatever you call it, will be perfect for my studying and lesson planning. I love the fireplace on the south wall of the room! It will be great to feel and watch the warm flames as I drift off to sleep on these cold nights. How perfect to have a vanity and armoire on the west wall that leads to my own private bathroom. These quarters will be lovely while I'm here at Huntington Hills College. Thank you."

"You are most welcome, Dr. O'Neal. I am so glad that our selection of accommodations for you at the manor fits with your approval. Many a scholar has graced the walls of this room. Legend has it that a princess once occupied this room as she waited for her prince to return from battle. There is, of course, much more to the story, but I shall save that tale for another time. For now, Dr. O'Neal, please get settled and rest. Dinner will be served at eight o'clock. If you need anything at all, feel free to ring for assistance by dialing six on the phone. A menu has been left for you beside the phone."

"Oh. Yes. Thank you again, Strongwell. I will try my best to dine with the others later. If not, I'll just ring for something to eat in my room."

"Very well, madam. Someone will be by shortly to start the fire and turn down your bed."

Amanda sat in the chair by the desk, dreamily looking out the window. She was beginning to feel tired for some reason and in need of some peace and quiet in her room. Without delay, one of the maids knocked slightly at her door. Once in the room, the maid, in an exquisite uniform, started the fire in the fireplace and turned down her bed.

"Will there be anything else to your pleasing, madam?"

"Yes, I think I'll skip dining with the others this evening and settle for a couple of those homemade biscuits that Strongwell bragged about with butter and honey. Oh, and some tea as well. Is that something you can provide?"

"Of course, Dr. O'Neal. It is my pleasure to assist you. I'll be right back with your request."

Happily, the maid was true to her word, and Amanda enjoyed every sip and bite as she sat by the fire, going over the day in her mind. She then turned the water on in the huge tub that adorned the breathtakingly beautiful bathroom to her suite, and she added some lavender bubbles for comfort. Once tucked in bed, Amanda hardly got time to voice her prayers before she drifted off to sleep.

Chapter 3

Déjà Vu

Surprisingly, Amanda woke up early the next morning. She gradually sat up in bed and plumped up the pillows behind her. After lying there for a while, contemplating the possible activities for the day, she finally got up. Amanda combed her fingers through her hair as she noticed she could still feel heat from the fireplace nearby. The sun was shining from one of the windows, which made her curious about outside. There was something lovely about her image draped in a long, flowing silk nightgown while standing by the window. At home, she might have slept in one of Shawn's old T-shirts, but not there. She calmly stood there for quite some time with her arms folded across her chest and her hair cascading down her back.

Hm, Amanda said to herself. *I can't really see that far, but it looks like there is a wooded area beyond those campus buildings. Guess I'm up for a little stroll before breakfast. Now, if I can only find my jeans, sweatshirt, and walking boots.*

Before long, she was out the main door of the manor and heading for the trees. A welcoming warmth came from the sun.

Thank goodness the wind was down. Hardly a breeze could be felt. Suddenly, she saw an image of the back of a man among the trees.

OK, either my senses are off, or I'm having a déjà vu moment. The back of that man can't belong to Ryan McFarlan. Why in the world would he be here? Suddenly, her stomach felt sick, and her forehead was hot. *OK, remain calm. Get it together. Act calm! Breathe. It can't be him.*

"Well, saints preserve!" Ryan yelled out. "If it isn't Red herself. So what brings you to the forest of Huntington Hills College? Guess Shawn finally decided to let you off the farm for a short sabbatical."

"Very funny, Ryan. Believe it or not, I had this suspicion that the back view of the man I saw was you."

Before her was a heavier Ryan with slightly graying, wavy hair instead of his signature penetrating dark brown. Like years ago, he still wore blue jeans, a long-sleeved light blue shirt with the sleeves rolled under, and a thermal coat vest for warmth. He still was a solidly built, good-looking, tall guy with a touch of sexual appeal—aged but handsome. Of course, he firmly held a camera, as she always remembered him carrying, clicking one image after another, all the while making comments to the dozen or so students grasping every word out of his mouth as if he were a god or something.

Unbelievable, thought Amanda as she stood there glaring at him with a straight face. At that moment, she wished he'd wipe that smile off his face as he pretended to ignore her, getting closer.

"And it is auburn, not red. You never could get that right!"

"Red, you always were a pain in the ass when it came to details. Lighten up, and enjoy the sunshine. OK, class, that will be all for today. Your project will be due next Friday, so get busy, guys. Oh, and enjoy! Don't photograph just to take pictures. Think about what you are doing, and then click. You're dismissed. I think I'll chat with Red for a while since we haven't seen each other for about twenty years."

"The name is Dr. O'Neal, and I sure am praying right about now that after this inappropriate introduction, none of you will be in any of my classes this term."

The students snickered and laughed among themselves as they drifted off toward the dorms in the distance. Amanda and Ryan stood there for a moment, looking at each other. She felt the energy between them like warm liquid moving from the top of her head to the tips of her toes. For a moment, Amanda thought she was going to pass right out. Finally, Ryan moved slowly toward her and hugged her like a long-lost friend. For a few seconds, not a word was said. It was just them and their memories.

"Let's go for brunch, Red. My Jeep isn't far. I'll drive you into town."

"I sure hope it isn't the same Jeep you had when we were in college together."

"No, actually I destroyed that one."

"How surprising!"

"Yeah, a lion came after me in Africa, and I crashed while trying to get away."

Amanda laughed. "Yeah, it probably was a woman's husband chasing you after finding you with his wife."

"Now, now, we don't need to get testy right off the bat! You can at least give a guy a break during brunch. After all, we haven't seen each other for quite some time."

"Well, actually, I didn't think I'd ever see you again."

"OK, so view me as a blast from the past. Don't get all tied up in knots, Red. We've only been together for fifteen minutes. Try to hold your temper toward me for at least another hour."

Amanda couldn't help but laugh at that remark as they walked to his Jeep. She had forgotten his sense of humor—his sometimes-nonstop sense of humor. Inside, though, Mr. McFarlan was an old soul like herself. She hadn't forgotten that.

He walked over to the passenger's side of the Jeep and opened the door for Amanda as if she were a princess and he were her chauffeur. A boyish smile came to his sculptured face as he looked deep into her eyes. "McFarlan at your service, my lady."

Not able to help herself, Amanda laughed again. "You haven't changed at all, McFarlan."

He breathed a deep laugh back and replied, "I'll take that as a compliment, my lady. I'm just happy you haven't cleaned my clock yet. Well, I think that is what you used to say to me back then, or maybe it was knock my block off. I'm not sure."

"OK, Ryan, enough teasing. You make it sound like I was horrible to you."

He turned the Jeep toward the road to town and responded, "Oh yes, a lioness in disguise. Horrible indeed! I think it best that I feed my lady before she attacks."

They both laughed while looking at each other as they drove down the road. After all, the morning was much too beautiful to waste.

After parking on the street, they walked into the Corner Café and sat at a small table near the front window. Outside, the wind appeared to be picking up. Fall leaves whipped past the window as if they were doing a ballet dance for the customers. It felt good to be inside, sipping a hot cup of coffee, as they faced each other in silence for a moment. Ryan took a menu and handed it to Amanda without saying a word. He nonchalantly pulled out his black-rimmed glasses and put them low on his nose before reading the breakfast selections. Amanda covered her mouth with her hands as she quietly laughed.

"What is so funny, Red? Oh, I see. You are getting great pleasure in seeing me wear glasses. I forgot that when you last saw this handsome face, I had no need for assistance in the vision department."

"I'm sorry, Ryan. Don't worry. I'm in the same boat when it comes to needing glasses. In fact, I can't read a word on this menu. So what is good here? I guess I'll just tell the waitress what I want and hope for the best."

"Here, Amanda. Take my glasses, and see if they help."

"Wow, I haven't heard you say *Amanda* in a very long time. It is nice to hear your voice say my name, Mr. McFarlan."

"Happy to oblige. It is nice to see you again." With that, his left hand softly grabbed hers. His grasp didn't last long, but the warmth of his masculine hand over hers went straight down to her toes. "So how did you know it was me by simply viewing my better side? I didn't realize you had memorized the identity of my butt so profoundly."

"Ryan, when you've cared about someone as we did for each other, you just know. No matter the length of time or number of years, I would know you. It was just always that way between us. You know that. We were the best of friends."

"Yeah, friends," Ryan replied while rolling his eyes.

She didn't notice. "To tell you the truth, I felt like I was having a déjà vu moment when I saw you standing there."

"I know, something familiar. Not unpleasant, I hope."

"You know better than that. Not unpleasant at all. Just a little bit scary. It has been a long time."

"Yeah, sorry about that, Red. I had my reasons. You know that."

"Yes, of course."

Just then, the student waitress approached with her small pad and pencil. Ryan proceeded to order. "Red here will take one egg over lightly, hash browns, two pieces of bacon well done, and corn bread. I'll take the same, except give me two eggs scrambled. Anything else, Red?"

"No, just keep the coffee and cream coming. Thank you very much."

Looking over his shoulder, Ryan said, "Thanks," as the smiling waitress rushed to hand in their order. "So, Amanda, how are Shawn and the farm?"

Amanda looked down, trying to hide the tears coming to her eyes. She paused for a moment, thinking she might choke.

"What? Amanda, tell me!" His hand reached for hers again, staying there for a while.

Finally, she whispered, "Ryan, Shawn is dead."

"What? Oh, Red. I'm sorry. I didn't know. Honestly, I didn't know. What happened?"

It remained quiet for a moment, and then Amanda spoke. "Well, it is kind of a long story. I'm not sure I can discuss all the details right now, but basically, he got sick due to an injury and died. Everyone thought he was getting better. Doctors thought they'd gotten the infection with antibiotics, but somehow, some remained in his system and hit his heart. It was hard, Ryan. I still can't believe it. Guess I'm kind of in an emotional fog right now. If I hadn't had my faith in God, I'd probably have gone crazy and died with him. Anyway, that is why I took this sabbatical. I had to get away. Thankfully, some friends are staying at the farm. They are family, really. Sorry to go on so. I didn't mean to bring you down."

"No, Amanda. Don't worry. I'm glad you told me. I'm so sorry. I didn't know. I've been gone a long time. Man, I just can't believe Shawn is gone. You were such a great couple. Like soul mates."

Ryan's and Amanda's eyes met as his hand moved from her right hand to her shoulder. He rubbed her shoulder for a second, and then he reached up and wiped tears from his eyes. "Life on this earth can really suck sometimes. Come on, Red; let's get out of here. We need to get back." Ryan quickly paid, and they exited the café.

Amanda requested that Ryan let her off about a block from the manor. She wanted to walk a bit and think before going inside.

Just as she neared the edge of the building, she thought she heard a tiny meow.

"Oh, poor kitty. Where are you?"

Looking underneath a bush that had tall grass around it, she saw a frail, furry little black image. The wind was picking up, and when Amanda reached for the little feline, it shook while crying.

"Don't worry, little fellow. I'll help you." Holding the furry black ball near her face, she whispered, "Now, you have to be quiet, so I can sneak you into my room."

The tiny black fluff began to purr as she placed it under her sweatshirt. Amanda then moved quickly through the manor's back door and slipped in unobserved.

Chapter 4

Class in Session

"Well, class, we have officially completed our first week of Criminal Procedure. Let's take a few moments before class ends to review. Close your textbooks and notes. See if you can answer from memory. Ms. Vivian Smith, which early code was the foundation of Judeo-Christian moral teachings and the basis for the US legal system?"

"The Code of Hammurabi."

"Mr. Albright? Daniel Albright."

"Here, Dr. O'Neal."

"Yes, I see that. Tell us why you laughed to yourself when Ms. Smith replied with the response of the Code of Hammurabi?"

"Because I think you are trying to trick us. I think the correct answer is the Twelve Tables."

"OK, Mr. Dembe Luganda?"

"Dr. O'Neal, I am here."

"Yes, I also see that. Mr. Luganda, please tell us what you believe to be the correct answer to this question."

"Dr. O'Neal, I believe the correct answer to your question is the Mosaic Code."

"And, Mr. Luganda, why do you believe this is the correct answer?"

Just as Amanda asked the question, she thought she saw, in the back of the room, a dark figure in the last aisle, but she couldn't quite make out who it was. The person seemed to be frantically taking notes or something. Amanda swiftly worked to pull herself emotionally together to ensure that all appearances showed she was in control. She sensed a strange feeling in the air. Amanda wondered if Dean Russet was already sending one of his alleged classroom spies, or was this merely a mystery visitor sneaking in without permission? Suddenly, her thoughts were brought back to reality to hear Dembe.

"I believe my response is correct because the Mosaic Code is an ancient legal code still surviving. A code from the Israelites. As a basis of the US legal system, the code concerned such things as prohibitions against murder, theft, perjury, and adultery. This Mosaic Code preceded the same laws now found in the US legal system by several thousand years; therefore, this is why I think the Mosaic Code is the correct answer, Dr. O'Neal."

"All right, Mr. Luganda. Can you remind the class when this code came into being?"

"Yes, Dr. O'Neal. The Mosaic Code of the Israelites is said to have come about around 1200 BC."

Amanda could see that the dark figure was moving from one end of the back of the room to the other. The person seemed agitated and angry. *Stay calm, and keep going,* she told herself.

"Your answer to the question is correct, Mr. Luganda. Very good. OK, students, please see that you read Exodus 20:1–3, 7–17 before our next class. If you do not have a Bible, you will find a copy in the college library. Also, if you do not believe in the Bible, it does not change the fact that our laws in this country come from the Bible, which is one of the oldest historical writings known to man. This is not a religious course, ladies and gentlemen; this is Criminal Procedure. Further, keep in mind that the concept of crime was recognized in early codes developed around 2000 BC. Such content is known today because it was later adopted by the Code of Hammurabi around 1792 to 1750 BC. Also surviving is the Roman law contained in the Twelve Tables, 451 BC. Study, people! We will have a short quiz next class on these topics. As always, thank you for your time, and have a great weekend."

Just as she was about to end the class, the dark image from the back, looking to be a young man, appeared to trip in the aisle as he tried to make a swift exit. His body fell across one of the chairs and made a sudden slamming sound, and then he regained his balance and ran out of the room. The students turned in their seats to see what was going on. To prevent any scene while the students began exiting to the hall, Amanda called out, "Class dismissed."

Almost like clockwork, Ryan popped his head in through the right entrance.

For a few moments, Amanda stood in the front of the classroom, holding her right hand to her chest. *Man, what just happened there in the back of the room? Should I tell anyone or what? Course reviews aren't until the middle of the semester. What was that all about? OK, just stay calm, and think this through.* She picked up her book and notes to leave as a familiar voice was heard from the door.

"Hey, Red, want to go grab some lunch? Man, you must have scared the hell out of your students today!"

"Oh yeah. Why in the world would you say a comment like that?"

"Well, from the conversations in the hall, they are pretty much afraid of you."

"Well, don't worry, Mr. Ryan McFarlan. Their fear of me will soon pass. They'll find out that I'm a softy soon enough."

"Hm, softy? I'm trying to figure that out about you myself."

"Oh, please. You make it sound like I'm a hard-ass or something. You know me!"

"Yeah, that is why I'm confused."

"Hey, I thought you were my longtime friend."

"I am one of your long-lost friends, but that doesn't mean you haven't always kept me on my feet trying to figure out what is going on in your mind. You can be complicated to figure out, Red. Now, that doesn't mean I don't love you. It just means you are a pill!"

"Thanks a lot! I'll remember that the next time you do something ridiculous, and I have to stop from going crazy."

"Who? Me? Remember that I'm a lover and not a fighter."

"OK, whatever you say. Let's go grab a bite to eat."

"Fantastic. I knew I could persuade you to grab some food."

"Right," Amanda responded as she rolled her eyes with a smile forming on her face. "I swear, Ryan, you will never change. You are still a boy in a man's body."

"Pretty nice, don't you think, Red?" They both laughed as they exited the lecture room.

"Hey, this cafeteria burger and fries are pretty good. How is your healthy chicken Caesar salad, Red? Man, it is going to be tough for me to try to get you to live a little dangerously. Don't you want some ice cream with that salad?"

"Honestly, Ryan, what do you have to worry about? By your appearance, you are still in pretty good shape for your age, despite the fact it has been quite a few years since we've seen each other. You probably don't have to watch your diet at all. If I ate everything I wanted all the time, I'd be four hundred pounds by now. Actually, I feel like I'm four hundred pounds most of the time."

"Oh, you women. All you think about is weight. What are you—about one twenty-five or thirty-five? One forty? Never mind. A stupid question. A man should never ask a gal her weight."

Amanda just continued eating her salad as Ryan rambled on. She was used to his ways.

"By the way, on Friday night, the faculty is to have dinner with Dean Russet in the dining room at the manor. I want to sit by you or across from you, so I can study your face when all the bull crap is discussed."

"Very well. Suit yourself, Mr. McFarlan. And if I may ask, what do people at these faculty dinners usually wear?"

"Oh, Dean Russet thinks he is the king of England, so faculty are expected to dress in their finest. Men usually wear a dark suit or tuxedo, while the ladies wear something formal or semiformal. These famous dinners usually occur about once a semester."

"Great. I didn't bring anything formal."

"Well, you have a few days. Guess you'll have to go shopping. You could just come down in your jeans and say that no one informed you of the dress code. No, honestly, there are a few unique shops in the center of town. Everyone goes there to get clothing advice for such occasions. Regarding the dinner, I'm always most interested in the unusual conversations that go on around the table. Believe me, it is better than any TV show."

"Guess I have no choice but to spend a few bucks. I wanted to really watch my spending here too. The farm back home is really costing a lot these days, especially since my husband, Shawn, is no longer around to handle things. Anyway, I would like to respond to your last comment by saying that I am sure you are entertained at these supposed mandatory formal dinners, but I know you well enough to realize your photographer eyes don't miss a single visual detail. You like all this high-drama stuff, especially if the high drama is some beautiful woman."

"Why, Dr. O'Neal, are you suggesting I am a womanizer?"

"If the shoe fits, then wear it. I don't know how you are now, but I sure remember how you were in college."

"What do you mean? I was one of your best friends, and you know it."

"Yes, you were and are one of the best friends I've ever had in my life, but the whole study group knew you were a player."

"I never lied to anyone. I didn't hurt anybody. I was just sowing my oats, sort of speaking. For goodness' sake, I was just a kid! You may not believe this, Red, but I am a man now. I kind of grew up since you crossed paths with me last."

"Really! Good to hear. I didn't mean to condemn. I was just stating some history. Sorry."

"Apology accepted. You've got a lot of catching up to do regarding my life since college."

"I guess so."

"Let's get the hell out of this populated student cave before they all gang up on us and decide to attack with a food fight."

"That doesn't happen here, does it?"

"Red, you are still as gullible as ever."

"Well, ditto when it comes to you having a lot to learn about how I've changed also. See you later, McFarlan." Not wanting to spoil the mood, Amanda decided not to mention what had occurred in the classroom. She would save that conversation for another time.

"Yeah. Later," Ryan replied as he darted out the door to his next class.

Chapter 5

The Dinner

The formal dining room of the manor was even more spectacular than what Amanda had already seen of the place. A fire glowed from the enormous gold-framed fireplace positioned in the center of the north wall. Across from the fireplace was a long table also centered perfectly in the middle of the room.

Above the eloquent table was one of the largest crystal chandeliers she had ever seen. Light from the chandelier was dim, which made the flames from the fireplace flicker off each individual crystal that hung brilliantly over the table. Chairs placed on each side of the table appeared to go on forever, with only one larger chair placed at the west end. Everything was decorated exquisitely: the beige, cream, and golden marble floor; the large gold-framed mirror above the fireplace; and various seventeenth- to nineteenth-century paintings displayed throughout the room. Everything was enchanting, something usually only envisioned in a museum or palace, an unbelievable spectacle.

Slowly walking into the room was like stepping into a movie scene. Most of the seats at the table were already occupied by various members of faculty and academic administration. For a moment or two, Amanda held her breath at the splendor of everything she was seeing. As she walked toward the table, she failed to see Dean Russet take his place at the end chair. She also failed to see that almost everyone was looking at her.

One of the unique clothing shops in the center of town had done her well. The deep burgundy velvet empire-waist gown flowed around her as Amanda slowly walked toward them. The gown's long sleeves were perfect for the cold air, but such could not be said for the low-cut front that tastefully displayed just a glimpse of her chest and neck, which were adorned by a single diamond on a delicate chain. A diamond comb was artfully positioned in a loosely pinned-up hairstyle, complementing long diamond-drop earrings. Amanda looked like a beautiful middle-aged woman that night, but she was unaware of the presence or impact she was making on the crowd.

Ryan was so stunned that he stood there for a moment with his mouth open. He then suddenly displayed one of his boyish smiles and walked toward her while offering his arm to escort her to the table. Once they were seated, Ryan leaned over and whispered in Amanda's ear, "Mrs. O'Neal, might I say that you are looking very beautiful this evening. I would also like to make it be known that Dean Russet hates to be outdone, if you know what I mean. You missed his grand entrance. Tread carefully, my dear."

"Mr. McFarlan, I have no intention of making a scene. I'm just here for the show."

"Well, there is no denying that, Red. God help us all or anyone who tangles with you tonight."

Amanda glanced back at Ryan as if to say, "Be a good boy." Ryan, of course, was smiling his usual masculine smile with a deep, soft laugh that only she could hear. Her eyes immediately reverted toward Dean Russet just as he began to speak.

"Dr. O'Neal, glad you could take it upon yourself to join us for this traditional gathering of faculty and administration." Sarcastically, he said, "Your entrance was something truly to behold. We welcome you."

"Thank you, Dean Russet. You are much too kind. Thank you for your warmth and generosity."

With Amanda's flawless reply, Ryan almost spit out the drink in his mouth. He could see fear in the other guests' eyes but not hers. *What a woman,* he said to himself. *Sure wish I had a camera right about now.*

The dean seemed perturbed. "Tell us, Dr. O'Neal. How are your classes coming along?"

"Quite well, Dean. At least to my knowledge. Have you heard differently?"

"Dr. O'Neal, surely you are aware that at Huntington Hills College, we do not do classroom course reviews until the middle of the semester."

"Of course."

"No news of inappropriateness has been heard as of yet."

Amanda held her breath, thinking of the incident at the end of her last class, and replied, "I should think not."

The room remained quiet for a few seconds. Their conversation occurred as though only the dean and Amanda were present; therefore, others around the table were feeling a bit uncomfortable, to say the least.

Ryan was enjoying the whole thing much too much. As the salad was being served, he gallantly looked to the couple sitting across from him and Amanda and said, "Dr. Norman, have you met Dr. O'Neal?"

"No, Mr. McFarlan. I don't believe my wife and I have had the pleasure yet."

"Well, Timothy, let me do the honor of introducing a very old and dear friend, Amanda O'Neal. From Florida she is and here for a short sabbatical."

Dr. Norman reached over the table to take her hand. "It is a pleasure meeting you, Mrs. O'Neal. My wife, Karen, and I often travel to Florida to get away from the cold weather."

"Very nice meeting both of you. Yes, Florida can be a nice escape from the cold. Tell me, Dr. Norman. What departments do you and your wife work in at Huntington Hills College?"

"Well, I myself teach in the engineering department, while my wife shares her artistic flair in the art department."

"Very good indeed," Amanda replied. "Such a wonderful thing for both of you that as a couple, you can share professionally in academic endeavors."

"Yes, working at the same institution has surely been a benefit to our lives both professionally and personally. Our true love is a small family farm farther up north."

"I likewise share the love for a small family farm in Florida. It was passed down from generation to generation to my deceased husband, Shawn O'Neal. God rest his soul."

"Land is a wonderful gift."

"Yes, for some reason, land gives you a sense of security. Stability of life in a fast-paced world, despite how small it might be."

"I totally agree. We are not like our friend here, Ryan McFarlan. Ryan is, thus far, a free spirit waiting to be tamed."

"How funny. The thought of Ryan calming down can hardly be imagined."

Ryan smiled, paused for a few seconds, and then responded, "All of you give me too much credit in being an interesting character. It is our Dean Russet whom I seek to learn more about."

Just as the second course was being served, Amanda looked toward the front of the table at Dean Russet. She saw the butler, Covington Strongwell III, whisper something urgently in the dean's right ear. The dean's face immediately turned stark white and then as red as a tomato. He quickly wiped his mouth with his elegant cloth napkin and stood to make an announcement.

"A most grievous event has just been brought to my attention. Another female student on Huntington Hills campus has just been recognized by our law enforcement security as missing. Please feel free to enjoy the rest of your meal as I speak to the authorities in my office. I bid you all good night."

As fast as the announcement was made, Dean Russet scurried from the room and down the hall.

Amanda heard gasps of fear in the voices of those around the table. "Strongwell, please tell us who they believe this student to be."

"Her name is said to be Miss Vivian Smith. Missing from her dorm room, where traces of blood and signs of a struggle were found. Very unsettling! This is the third missing girl from campus this year. No doubt a sign of something sinister occurring."

Amanda carefully leaned toward Ryan so only he could hear her. "Ryan, Vivian is one of my students. Quick—you and I must head for your Jeep and camera. We've got to preserve evidence prior to someone destroying the scene. Hurry!"

Before anyone else could comment on her inquiries, Ryan and Amanda left. Amanda stopped briefly at her room to swiftly change clothes and pick up an unusual black bag. They raced down the hall and exited through one of the back doors. Ryan firmly held Amanda's hand as they ran toward the Jeep. Mr. McFarlan jumped into the driver's seat and drove like a bat out of hell toward Vivian's dorm. He and Amanda had to get to Vivian's room before campus security, and possibly the dean, destroyed evidence.

Chapter 6

Dormitory Dilemma

Ryan parked the Jeep in the back of Vivian's dormitory so as not to create a scene. He and Amanda did not want to be immediately detected. He checked the back door, which was unexplainably unlocked. "Hm, that is unusual."

"What do you mean?"

"Well, the back door of the dormitory is unlocked. Good for us but against the usual protocol. All dormitory buildings have to be locked up by ten o'clock, especially the back doors."

"The campus rules certainly make sense; however, how are you so informed about these rules?" Amanda looked over at Ryan suspiciously with a little smirk-like smile.

"Never mind, Red. We've got work to do. Here—let's run by the information desk to check the computer for what room Vivian was assigned to. Be careful; we don't want one of those campus security, like Barney Fife from the *Andy Griffith Show*, to see us."

Amanda and Ryan ran down the hall as quietly as possible. He motioned for Amanda to stay put and duck down as a campus officer walked by the front door. Ryan slid over to the front desk and clicked on the computer to examine the room Excel chart to locate Vivian's assigned room. "Got it. Let's get the hell out of here!"

Amanda winked at Ryan while replying, "I can tell you are kind of enjoying this."

"I'm used to sneaking around to take photos for stories. The only difference here is that I'm doing it in my own country and with you."

"Well, we'll save that for another discussion. Where do we go to get to Vivian's dorm room?"

"Come on, Red; we'll take these stairs rather than the elevator. Don't want to give anyone cause to suspect something is up if they have emptied the whole dormitory. We're going up to the second floor, room 214. Hurry!"

Surprisingly, the hallway was eerily quiet.

"Man, where is everyone?"

Reaching room 214, they saw yellow security tap across the door.

"OK, Amanda, now what do we do?"

"Don't be silly, Ryan; we get in and check things out without anyone knowing it."

"Oh yeah, I forgot. You aren't one to give up."

"Not when it is a life-or-death situation. Vivian didn't come up missing for no reason. Neither did the other two girls. Something isn't right here at Huntington Hills College, and I intend to find out what that is. One way or the other."

"Yeah, it is the 'one way or the other' that scares me."

"Sh, we don't want to cause a commotion, Ryan McFarlan." Amanda reached into the curious black bag and pulled out some strange paper objects. "Here—put these paper boots on your shoes. Oh, these rubber gloves too. We're going in. Quietly, of course."

"Man, the woman comes prepared."

"Stop joking around and hurry up."

"OK, got it. Let's get in there before anyone detects us. May I ask what exactly is that medical-looking black bag you are carrying?"

"A crime scene technician kit from one of my dear friends back home, Henry Brooks. He is one of the best investigative technicians and detectives you'll ever meet. The guy is phenomenal with evidence. He sure has taught me a lot through the years."

"Yeah, that is what scares me! Once released, you are like a wild lioness looking for her prey. Maybe like a loose cannon. Whichever you prefer."

"Very funny. Come on; let's get in there and grab some good evidence so we can leave ASAP." They both sneaked into the room and began collecting.

"OK, Red, I'm walking around as carefully as possible. Now, what do you want me to do?"

"Well, carefully scan the room, and click as many photos as possible. Try not to miss anything. Then, I'll have you take some close-up shots of each piece of evidence I bag and label. We'd better hurry. For some reason, I think the dean and others aren't far behind us. Dean Russet probably told the campus officers to yellow-tape Vivian's room door so no one would tamper with the evidence before he got in."

"You're probably right."

Ryan skillfully clicked away, taking one photo after another, while Amanda searched for trace evidence.

"Are you pretty much done clicking photos?"

"OK, turn the light off, and I'll put this small alternative light source on, so we'll be able to see any evidence—you know, things like hair, fibers, drugs, paint chips, soil, semen, and blood. When the alternative light source, or ultraviolet, is on, you can often see such things as footprints, fingerprints, body fluids, and metal fragments that would be otherwise not visible to the naked eye. Oh, here—put these protective goggles on too."

They were an efficient team. The amount of evidence was amazing, but Amanda quickly picked up as much as she could by utilizing the appropriate tools from her kit. Each piece of evidence was properly bagged and labeled. Brooks had taught her well. Other skillful methods were used to preserve the footprints and fingerprints. Before they realized it, about forty-five minutes had gone by.

"Oh God, I hear something outside!" Ryan pointed to the window, where he and Amanda saw Dean Russet with some campus officers, walking toward the dormitory. "We've got to get out of here right now."

"Let's go."

They slipped swiftly out the door and between the yellow tape, which, unbelievably, remained in place.

Ryan looked back at the taped door as they ran down the hall toward the stairs. "Man, we are good, Amanda. Looks like no one even entered the room."

"Good job."

They raced down the stairs, out the back door, and into the Jeep before Dean Russet reached the front door.

Almost breathless, Ryan managed to say, "Wow, this investigation stuff can be exciting! I thought I was going to have a heart attack when I saw the dean coming up the path."

"Yeah, I thought I was going to pee my pants for a moment."

As the Jeep raced down the road past the campus, they both caught their breath and looked at each other with sighs of relief. There was silence for a moment, and then they burst into nervous laughter.

"Amanda, I'm driving straight to my cabin. We'll figure out what to do once we get there."

"Sounds good to me."

"Wow, you kind of look tired."

"Well, yeah! I'm not a spring chicken anymore."

"You mean a spring chick."

"Whatever. Let's just get there."

"Madam, your wish is my command."

Off they drove into the night.

Chapter 7

At the Cabin

The winding road to the cabin seemed to move up and down and around. For a few moments, Amanda felt as though she were on an amusement park ride at Disney as the Jeep continued to climb higher and higher into the mountains. They finally reached what appeared to be a small, wooded neighborhood consisting of several cabins scattered throughout. Ryan jumped out of the Jeep for a few seconds and punched in a code to open the large gate in front of them.

"Sorry. I forgot my opener for the gate," he explained, and then he quickly jumped in again and took off.

About half a mile down the road, she saw a small mailbox standing to the left of a dirt driveway. He turned sharply down the driveway, and as the foliage cleared, Amanda saw an adorable log cabin centered on a lot with beautiful trees encompassing it. It was dark, but she could see something like a garage or barn in the back of the lot, with a lovely stream behind it. It had a welcoming look and sound of flowing water as she exited the vehicle. Amanda caught herself breathless for a few seconds as she took in the beauty of the scene. *Unbelievable*, she said to herself as they hurriedly moved toward the cabin. The scene was almost magical.

They whispered back and forth while entering the cabin. Amanda didn't know why, but she followed Ryan's lead, due to wanting to get inside before the coldness of the wind froze her to death. Once inside, Ryan systematically took her coat, hat, scarf, and gloves. He stuffed the hat and gloves quickly into one of her coat pockets and hung the coat and scarf on a large hook near the door.

Well, looks like he has done that before, she said in her mind. Amanda set her black leather bag with all the evidence immediately down under the hanging coat and stood there for a few seconds, catching her breath, and looking into Ryan's eyes. Just as she opened her mouth to say something again, she heard a soft little voice.

"Da, is that you?"

Without thinking, Amanda responded, "What?"

"Oh, Da, do we have company?"

Just then, Ryan moved in swiftly and scooped the small boy into his arms. He hugged the child close to his chest and kissed him gently on his forehead while rubbing the top of the boy's head for a few seconds.

"Why in the world are you up, my little Ian, and where is Mrs. Beasley?"

"I not little, Da. I big boy!"

"Yes, of course. Well, big boys need their sleep too, so they can grow strong."

"Like Superman?"

Ryan smiled, trying not to laugh. "Um, yes, like Superman. Oh, hello, Mrs. Beasley. What happened here?" He pointed down toward Ian as he spoke.

"Sorry, Mr. McFarlan. I guess as soon as the lad heard the Jeep, he jumped out of bed like a grasshopper."

"Yes, it appears so."

Mrs. Beasley quickly grabbed her coat and headed for the door. "I'll be going now, Mr. McFarlan. My better half and grandchildren are waiting for me back at the house for movie and popcorn night. We can settle up later. Good night, Ian."

"Good night, Mrs. B. Love you!"

"Love you too," Mrs. Beasley said as she walked into the cold air and closed the door.

Amanda stood there motionless for a few seconds, feeling as if she'd just stepped into a fairy tale or something. Her head was spinning, and she was having a little trouble keeping up with all the events.

Ian now had his right arm wrapped around Ryan's left leg, with his left thumb comfortably placed in his mouth. His big hazel eyes were looking Amanda up and down, waiting for someone to say something.

"Ian, I would like you to meet one of my dearest friends, Amanda O'Neal. I've known her for a very long time. Say hello to her like a nice little gentleman."

"Hello, Amanda. Are you going to marry my da?"

Amanda glanced at Ryan, who showed a red face that could be seen even in the darkness. Smiling, Amanda bent down to the child and looked into his big, beautiful hazel eyes before responding.

"Well, Ian, that is an interesting question, but your father and I for now are just good friends. We've been that for a very long time."

"Oh, like me and Mrs. B."

"Yes, lad, like you and Mrs. Beasley," Ryan calmly responded.

"Well, I haven't heard about you before." With that, Ian ran to the couch in front of the fireplace, picked up his teddy bear, and skipped out of the room.

Amanda and Ryan stood there looking at each other and then busted out laughing.

"Oh my God," Amanda said. "What a surprise."

"I bet! Look, Amanda, I don't know about you, but I'd like to sit by a warm fire in front of the fireplace with a cup of hot chocolate." Ryan then yelled out, "Do you want some hot chocolate, Ian?"

"Yes, please. Marshmallows, please!"

"OK, marshmallows it is."

Ryan, Amanda, and Ian sat around the fireplace for some time, just enjoying each other's company. It made her think of José back at the farm and all the good times she and Shawn had had with him. She glanced at Ian in his cartoon flannel pajamas. His hair was thick, dark, and wavy like Ryan's used to be.

She thought, *Those eyes of Ian's are captivating, with sparks of gold, rust, green, and brown shining through. His little smile is something else! He couldn't be more than three or four years old.*

Ryan was now tickling Ian, who was rolling on the other end of the couch, giggling.

"OK, lad, off to bed you must go. Bathroom, potty, brush teeth, and bed, my little man."

"OK, Da, but piggyback ride first!"

"OK, OK. Jump onto my back." Off they went down the hall.

Amanda smiled, took another sip of her hot chocolate, and glanced into the fire while thinking.

Ryan finally came back into the room, plopped himself back onto the comfortable brown leather couch, and looked at her, smiling.

"Well, you could have at least warned me," Amanda mumbled.

"Red, it wasn't like I had a lot of time to do such."

"Ryan McFarlan, I've been here around a week, and we've seen each other quite a few times."

"Yes, I suppose. You see, no one really knows about him at the college yet."

"What!"

"I know what you are thinking, but Ian and I have quite a story, and I must protect him."

"Let's hear it, buddy!"

"Now? I'm kind of tired!"

"Give me the short version."

"Um, OK. Well, OK. About two years ago, I was traveling through Scotland and Ireland while working on an article for *Newsweek* magazine. The article dealt with political unrest there. Anyway, having a little time on my hands, I often traveled the countryside and got some awesome photographs. Basically, I was out and about one day and found this tiny lad out in the forest all by himself. He was crying louder than a foghorn. So dirty that all I really saw were those beautiful eyes piercing through his muddy, tearful face. He had on a nasty cloth diaper and torn shirt. God help him. Honestly, there was no evidence of homes or mankind anywhere near the place. It's a mystery how the child got there or how long he'd been there all alone. It was colder than Alaska that day and starting to rain harder with each passing moment. Not really knowing what to do, I gathered the little tyke up and took him to the authorities in the nearest village. They placed him in what we would call an orphanage, I guess. A terrible thing indeed. Every time I traveled, I would stop by to check on him, and still no one had claimed the child. The social workers at the orphanage informed me that several couples had come to see about adopting him, but he never responded to anyone. The babe would just lie there like a zombie, looking straight ahead. He didn't cry and hardly ate. As if a switch had been turned off. But each time I stopped to see him, the little guy lit up like a Christmas tree. He'd smile, play, and eat his food. We grew very close. Two buddies. As it was, I just couldn't get the little guy off my mind and heart, so to make a very long story short, I adopted him, and here we are."

"Wow, Ryan. Unbelievable. Maybe God brought you together."

"Maybe so. I know one thing for sure: no one could love him more than I do. He has become everything to me. Changed my life, really. That is why I pretty much took this job at the college—to be more settled for him. Give him a home. We've only been here a few months, but we're slowly feeling comfortable. He adores Mrs. Beasley."

"I can tell that. It is just such a shock to see you after all these years and then to realize you have a son."

"Oh yes, I'm sure. Especially with my age. He could be my grandson instead of my son."

Without their really realizing it, Ryan's head had ended up on Amanda's lap while he was talking, and she'd been stroking and softly twirling strands of his hair as the conversation continued. She was trying to ignore the heat between them, and it wasn't from the fireplace. She had always had an underlying attraction to Ryan, even though she had loved her deceased husband, Shawn, with all her heart.

Wow, now what? she thought as her hands still worked through his hair.

"It is getting late, Red. You are probably getting tired, and if you keep playing with my hair like that, the rest of my body might want to start engaging in a little foreplay, if you know what I mean. Anyway, we'd better decide what to do with that evidence from

Vivian's dormroom before someone catches on—that is, if they haven't already done so."

Amanda's senses finally came to, and she responded, "Oh, I'm so sorry, Ryan. Guess my hand was naturally moving, and I wasn't really thinking." Taking a deep breath in, she then added, "Well, I'll pack it up tomorrow and send all of it to my good friend Henry Brooks, who is an excellent detective and evidence technician back home in the Tampa Bay area in Florida. He and my friend Brad Cooper, a detective, can start on things for us without rocking the boat here. Can you save all the crime scene photos on a disk or zip stick so I can include them?"

"Tomorrow is Saturday, so that gives us time to get things sent off. You know, we can't speak to anyone about what we've done, or we could get into trouble. We'll have to be very careful where we talk about this."

"I know. Thank goodness Detective Brad had me get my license as a private investigator before I came. Maybe that will save us from some future trouble. I can say I saw the need for immediate investigation because the victim was one of my students, and as a duty as a lawyer and investigator, I took immediate action. I don't know. For now, let's just keep all this between us."

"Sure."

"Man, I'm suddenly extremely tired."

"You are welcome to sleep here on the couch. I have some extra pillows and blankets. Besides, I'll make some mean blueberry pancakes in the morning. Ian loves them."

"Sounds good to me! Do you have an old T-shirt or something I can wear?"

Ryan slowly got up while yawning. "Hold on. I'll bring one back with the pillows and blanket. Some old flannel pants too."

He was tired but didn't want her to know that her fiddling with his wavy locks of hair nonchalantly had made him start to get a hard-on. As he got up, he thought, *Lord, what is happening to me? Me and Red? Now, that is a thought I'll have to wrap my head around. I mean my thinking head.*

Ryan made her bed and got ahold of himself while she quickly got ready in the bathroom nearby. She jumped into the bed and sleepily said, "Good night. It's nice being around each other again."

In a low, deep voice, he kind of caught himself choking and replied, "Yeah, ditto. Night, Red."

Amanda heard Ryan quietly walk down the hall and swiftly close his bedroom door. The flames in the fireplace, like the ones throughout her body, were still flickering. *Good grief, Shawn. God rest your soul. Forgive my sensual reactions toward Ryan. A deceased husband shouldn't know about such things. Hope you don't. What in the world is happening here?*

Amanda smiled for a moment. Although a little frustrated, she felt safe and secure as she punched the pillow and laid her head down before drifting off to sleep, still feeling the warmth from the fire nearby.

Chapter 8

Office Agenda

Amanda quietly sat at her desk, sipping some tea that had been brought to her, while she enjoyed looking at the fruits of her labor. She had spent a good part of the morning hanging her diplomas and photos, as well as filling the bookcases with her own books, awards, and some personal mementos that had arrived there in some boxes a few days ago. As always, the tea had been delivered on a beautiful silver tray with an elegant teapot and china teacup. She laughed to herself as she slowly raised her right pinkie while taking another sip.

"Man, this tea is good. I've got to ask Strongwell again exactly what the ingredients of this tea are. So relaxing. I also feel happier after a sip or two. Probably due to the colder weather. I'm certainly not used to these low temperatures. Hm, maybe I shouldn't have any more. Guess I will just finish this one cup and then stop. I think."

The office walls were painted a pale green—just a kiss of color to accentuate the large windows framed in dark wood matching the bookcases, high ceiling beams, and wood floors. *It is a very comfortable, quaint room*, Amanda thought.

Unlike what others might have selected to do, Amanda had chosen to sit behind the desk with her back facing the window, rather than making it her view. With the beautiful North Carolina scenery right out her office window, she had determined that she would never accomplish any of her work if she was looking out the window all the time. Once her work was done, or when she needed a break, she could turn her desk chair around and have a wondrous glance out.

"Perfect," she whispered to herself as she had one last sip of the tea.

Amanda sat there quietly for a few moments as her thoughts drifted to the evidence obtained at the scene last Friday night. She and Ryan had carefully packaged all the photos and physical evidence at Ryan's cabin and then express mailed them to Henry Brooks, the Tampa crime scene specialist, on Saturday. She had also left Brooks a voice message on his cell, telling him that cookies had been sent to him and Pearl and that she would call him about the recipe on Monday. Henry, of course, would hear that message and instinctively realize something was up. Amanda never cooked much, and Henry knew that. After everything they'd gone through together with the Tampa, Florida, crime sphere they'd skillfully ended, she, Henry, and Detective Brad Cooper knew each other like the backs of their hands. They were a fine-tuned crime team.

"Oh, poor Vivian Smith," Amanda mumbled. *I wonder if anyone has gotten ahold of her family and what explanation was provided. Oh dear,* Amanda thought as she tried to adjust the strands of her semi long auburn hair that had fallen out of the tie and now flowed all around her face. *More importantly, though, where in the hell is the girl's body? What a mess! I've got to get ahold of Brooks and see what timeline we are working under regarding the evidence results.*

See if we can get some real answers. Not sure what the dean or campus police will have at this point. Unless they've actually located Vivian.

Just as Amanda lowered her forehead down to the palms of her hands for a few seconds of rest, Ryan popped his head through the doorway. He could see by the look of her that her mind was probably going a mile a minute. The word *stress* came to his thoughts.

"Well, good day, Red. Uh, I'm afraid to ask, but how is the day going?"

"Oh great," Amanda mumbled as she looked up at him. "I think I'm starting to feel a little stressed out after working on my office all morning, as well as thinking about all the events from the past few days."

Ryan quickly put a finger up to his mouth as if to say, "Sh."

She got the message immediately, and they stared into each other's eyes before he spoke.

"Well, I can certainly understand that. Sounds like you could use some lunch. How about we go somewhere for a quiet lunch and then come back and prepare ourselves for the next class? Nothing like feeling refreshed before speaking in front of a large group of somewhat eager students."

Amanda slowly stood while trying to smooth out her wild-looking hair. "That sounds good. Maybe it will do me good to get out of this office for a while. By the way, how does it look?"

"Very scholarly, if I do say—you know, all your diplomas, books, and such. By looking at all of this, I truly wonder if you ever learned how to have any fun."

"What a remark! Of course. Shawn, my beloved deceased husband, and I had all kinds of fun together. Living on the farm with all the animals and nature. It was great."

"Yeah, but that is just happy living. I'm talking about having fun. Like doing something crazy."

"Well, I guess that is what I'm doing now—having lunch with you."

"Oh brother, I think you need fun lessons."

They both laughed while Amanda grabbed her purse as they walked out of the room together, making sure the door was locked before stepping away.

It was a cold day, even though the sun was shining brightly. The wind swirled around like a whip in the hands of a trained cowboy and stung like a bee as it fiercely hit their exposed skin while they raced to the Jeep.

"Man, oh man, Ryan! Glad you put the top on the Jeep. I don't think I could have stood another second of that sharp, cold wind. Turn up the heat, please."

She shook as she clicked on the seat belt and rubbed her hands together as the warmth from the heater blew on them. At least she could feel her hands now. "Guess I've got to get a better scarf and gloves, which, by the way, I left in my room this morning. What? Why are you looking at me like that and shaking your head? Stop smiling!"

"Calm down, Amanda. Don't get all your feathers roughed up!" He reached over with his right hand and tried to smooth down her wild hair. "I don't know if you are just being bossy or simply crabbing."

"Ryan! What? It's cold, for God's sake! How about just shut up and drive?"

"OK, Red. You win. Good thing I like feisty women. Um, I said *feisty*, not *bossy*." They laughed together, looking into each other's eyes, as the Jeep continued onward up the mountain road.

Once inside Roosevelt's Lodge, they sat at a table right in front of one of the huge stone fireplaces. Amanda had her arms crossed while calmly rubbing her upper arms as she glanced deep into the flickering flames, watching the many colors.

"A penny for your thoughts, Red."

"Oh, nothing. I was just thinking it's nice feeling a few moments of true happiness. I haven't felt that much since Shawn's death."

"Well, that is good you're feeling some of that."

"Oh, I miss him, Ryan. It was like losing a part of my own body; and now I can't get back to normal. Whatever normal is. Kind of like walking around feeling emotionally numb."

"Yes, well, sorry for your loss, but I'm sure glad you're here now. Shawn was a good man. Better than most. I thought a lot about him. We had a few very good times together when we were in college."

"Oh really."

"Yeah. Did he ever tell you about the time the whole fraternity went out for a night in town, and he and I got so blasted drunk we didn't know what end was up? He was trying to bury his sorrows over you and him having some horrible fight between the farm and you going to law school. Anyway, we both worshipped the white porcelain god the next morning and vowed to never drink like that again."

"Well, at least I know why he would hardly drink during our whole marriage. I always thought it was his religious convictions;

now I wonder if he just never wanted to get that sick again. Hm, very interesting."

"Yeah, Shawn was a great guy. Probably one of the most real people I've ever met, excluding my present company, of course. If he said he was going to do something, you knew for sure it would get done. A very loyal and honest guy. He had a great dry humor that probably most people didn't get to experience. Glad I did! An old and wise soul he was."

There were a few moments of silence between them as they sat listening to the cracklings of the fire and feeling its warmth. The hamburgers and french fries were great. Amanda had determined it was too cold for a salad. It wasn't the time or place to discuss the crime scene and evidence. Perhaps Ryan knew Amanda just needed a few moments of peace before going back into the academic arena. He reached over and softly rubbed the top of one of her hands as they ate, and they glanced into each other's eyes occasionally, as if neither one of them had to speak to know what the other was thinking. Once done, they both ordered a large takeout hot chocolate and scurried out to the Jeep. Not only did Amanda have to teach Criminal Procedure that day, but she'd also have to address in class the disappearance of Vivian Smith to her students.

The lock to Amanda's office door clicked open, and Dean Russet, with campus security, entered.

"All right, boys, scan through everything without making a mess, and then plant the bug where Dr. O'Neal won't immediately find it. Remember, we are not dealing with an idiot here. Amanda is a lawyer and skillful investigator, so don't give her cause to contemplate even for a second that she is being monitored. In other words, don't move things around too much. Make sure you leave things exactly as they were once we leave. Don't be knuckleheads, and work smart and fast."

Dean Russet moved quickly around the room, looking at all the degrees, awards, books, and photos. His inner anger was ready to boil over as he thought about seeing Ryan McFarlan and Amanda O'Neal sneaking out of Vivian Smith's dorm after the alleged crime had occurred. "What are those two up to?" the dean whispered to himself. "Well, we shall see what they are up to. Sooner or later, they'll make a mistake. Come on, guys; get those cameras and microphones in place fast so we can get the hell out of here!"

Chapter 9

Secrets of the Morning

Amanda's eyes suddenly popped open. She waited a moment to realize she was in her own bed in her room at Huntington Hills College. The air felt warm and cozy as she heard the fire in the fireplace crackle. Amanda slowly rolled over onto her back and glanced up at the burgundy canopy above the bed. For some reason, it took her a while to sit up and realize she wasn't alone.

"Oh, good morning, Dr. O'Neal. It was quite cold this morning, so I slipped in to start the fire, hoping my presence wouldn't stir you from sleep. I'm one of the maids who takes care of the faculty who live on campus. Megan is my name, madam. We met the first evening you were here. Your room has been assigned to me to keep tidy. Whatever you need, like cleaning of the room, laundry, or food. I've also been caring for your little friend here as well. Some people back home would think unkindly toward the little fellow due to tales from long ago—you know, black cats and witchcraft."

Amanda glanced at the maid with a warm smile and then laughed as she glanced at the fluffy black kitten sitting in front of the fire while washing his paws and face. "Oh, how sweet! Having him in my room makes me miss my small farm back in Florida. Thank you for caring for him when I'm not around. He appears to be pretty content here."

"You have a farm, Dr. O'Neal?"

"Call me Amanda, please, when we are here in my room. *Dr. O'Neal* feels so formal. Yes, it's small. I inherited it from my deceased husband, Shawn. It's home to me."

"It must be a wondrous place, Amanda."

"Yes indeed. Megan, I detect a slight accent in your voice."

"I'm Irish."

"How lovely."

Just then, the small kitten moved over to Amanda's legs and started to rub himself against her. Reaching down, she picked him up and softly pressed his tiny face against her cheek. A rapid rhythm of purring started immediately. "Well, little buddy, I guess we should give you a name."

Megan and Amanda stood quietly for a moment, and then Amanda finally declared that he should be crowned with the name of Midnight. "I found him, you know, one night when I was coming back from being out. He was under the bushes nearest to the back door, meowing like crazy! It was as if he were telling the world, 'I'm cold and hungry, and please do something about it fast.'"

"How sweet, Amanda, that you came to his aid. Most people around here would have probably walked by. Indeed, it shows you have a good heart."

"Well, I don't know if it's that or that I'm a sucker for animals. Always have been. That is why my late husband, Shawn, and I loved living on our farm so much. I do miss it. Anyway, sometimes I think

I should have gone to college to be a veterinarian instead of a lawyer. Oh well. It is what it is."

"Well, pardon me for saying, Amanda, but you should be proud of all your accomplishments. You are helping a lot of students and people in general. It is for sure my pleasure to assist in making your time here as comfortable as possible. Oh, and Midnight's time here as well."

"Thank you, Megan. Your assistance while I'm here means a great deal to me. Know that for sure. Wow, look at the time! I'd better get cleaned up and off to my office. Unfortunately, time waits for no one. It keeps ticking away, whether we want it to or not."

"I'll bring you some hot tea and freshly baked biscuits with honey, so you can get ready swiftly and be on your way. A tray will be on your side table by the fire when you come out from the bath."

"Much appreciated, Megan. I've enjoyed our little chat."

"Likewise, Dr. O'Neal. Oh, I mean Amanda."

The women smiled at each other as Megan slowly turned toward the door and left. The investigative side of Amanda wondered for a moment if she should be a bit concerned that Megan had a key that allowed her to enter the room freely, but then the reasonable side of her brushed the concerned thought aside for the time being.

Amanda stood looking out the window toward the wooded area where she had first seen Ryan and his students taking photos just days ago. For a few seconds, she thought she saw someone glancing back at her from the trees, but that was ridiculous. Her thoughts traveled through recent events as she lifted her right arm toward her neck and shoulder to give them a few rubs. So much had happened in the last few weeks that it was a bit hard to take in.

Leaving the Florida farm as well as the law office for a teaching sabbatical in North Carolina. Being a professor again and all that entails and then something horrible happening to one of my students. Poor girl! Seeing Ryan after all these years and then learning about his precious little son, Ian. What happened to coming to Huntington Hills College for a little rest and relaxation? Boy, oh boy! And what in the world am I going to do about those strange feelings toward Ryan? Well, God, if ever I needed your direction, I think right about now would be a good time!

Her pale peach silk robe flowed softly off her cream shoulders as she quietly walked toward the bathroom to prepare for the day. It felt good to sink down into the luxurious tub as the hot water encompassed her body. As a rule, she was a shower gal, but now she could feel all her sore spots starting to relax as the lavender scent of the soap surrounded the tub. A little more of this, and Amanda would be napping instead of heading off to work in her office. She did one more delicious dip and then stepped out to her ringing cell phone.

"Hello! A good morning to you."

"Well, hello there, Amanda. Top of the morning to you."

"Now, there is only one person I know who'd be talking to me like that. Would this be the infamous Ryan McFarlan I am speaking to?"

"Of course. A bit late, aren't you, O'Neal?"

"Yes, I'm sorry. I was working late last night, and when I got back to my room this morning, I kind of crashed."

"Well, that is quite all right, but since I haven't heard from you for a few days, I thought maybe Ian or I had done something to cause you to run like the devil and never come back."

"No, nothing like that. Just being busy."

"Well, if that is the only problem, then how about you and I meet after your class today? I have a few photos I'd like to show you."

"Sure, sounds good."

"OK, then it's a date." His phone went silent.

Amanda stood there for a few seconds, and then his words hit her. *A date?*

"Hey, Red, why did you have me meet you at the back hall exit door of the manor, near your room, instead of just outside the classroom after class? Are you ashamed of knowing me, lass?"

"Heavens no! Since I didn't know what you were up to, I came back to my room to put my hiking boots on and grab my hat, scarf, and gloves."

Ryan looked at her with a crazy smile and then threw up his arms only to slap them back down against his hips. "You know me too well, Amanda. I can't surprise you with anything!"

"What in the world are you talking about? I thought you were just going to go somewhere to show me some photos."

He grabbed her left hand and dragged her toward him. "Come on, Red. We don't want it to get too dark outside and spoil all the fun."

A relaxed chuckle came from him as he continued to pull her to the nearby woods.

Chapter 10

The Woods

Soft snowflakes slowly fell as they walked together hand in hand beyond the campus buildings into the woods. The wind felt unusually calm and still, almost as if they were in a movie scene and everything were being controlled. Tree branches and leaves appeared as lace in the sky. There was a sensation that all the creatures were at peace and calm with their entering their domain.

Ryan pointed up high in the trees and whispered, "Oh, look, Amanda! There is a red robin just like you. The air feels so fresh and clean out here."

"OK, a few days ago, I was like a lion or black panther to you, and now you are comparing me to a bird?"

"Well, the color red always reminds me of you because I see you as spirited and mysterious. No one really ever quite knows what you are going to do. Like you have a little wild side hidden deep within. Like a feline, sometimes you circle your subject to investigate before making your move. On other occasions, you sit quietly contemplating just like the red robin over there. He is probably guarding his mate's nest. How do you see me, Red?"

Amanda pointed up to the sky, looking at an eagle flying by. As if the eagle were giving them approval to glance his way, the sound of the bird's call echoed through the trees. "I see you like that eagle. A world traveler. Strong and in charge but not afraid to just glide and enjoy sometimes. A protector and loyal."

"OK then, we are both a wee bit like birds. Well, enough of that malarkey. Let's just go a little deeper into the woods. I know you love trees most of all."

She smirked a bit and replied, "That I do." *Wow, funny that he remembers that after all these years. Man, what in the world is happening to us? Good thing Ryan can't always read my mind. I think.*

She gulped to clear her throat and then started walking again. Just when she thought all was right with the world, she heard the clicking of Ryan's camera.

"What in the world are you doing?"

"What do you think I'm doing? I'm taking some instantaneous photos of a beautiful woman out in this wondrous forest. Come on now, Red; let's do a selfie of you and me together."

Just as the camera began to click again, he pulled her into his arms with his back against a tree and kissed her. The kiss wasn't short, nor was it objected to.

"That was lovely," Amanda softly whispered.

"That it was," he replied with his eyebrows slightly raised and a tender smile. "Well, Red, though it may be improper to say, there is more where that came from." His full, moist lips met hers again, intensifying until his tongue entered her lips, exploring the depths of her mouth and soul. Their tongues battled, and emotions exploded as though they had waited a lifetime to do such a thing.

Amanda felt there wasn't a logical thought in her head at the moment and didn't care. She tingled all over as her legs grew weaker by the moment. She thought she would have fallen if not for Ryan holding her tightly. They played for a while, getting acquainted, so to speak. Finally, Amanda stepped back and looked into his eyes.

"Oh my God, Ryan. I'm older but not dead!"

"Well, thank God for that! It sure didn't feel like I was kissing a dead person."

"I know, but after Shawn's death, I just thought—" Tears started to run down her cheeks.

"I know, Amanda. You don't have to explain. I get it. Really. You know, I've loved you forever—and Shawn, of course—but in a different way."

"I know. Me too."

"You too? You don't say!"

"Don't be funny, Ryan. This is serious."

"Of course, it is serious, but I've never heard you say it before."

"It was buried deep, I guess."

"Well, I'm glad it's no longer buried. I'm hoping to love you for a very long time, Amanda O'Neal. I want us to kiss each other until our lips are so swollen we can't talk anymore and make wild, passionate love together until my best friend down you-know-where can't stand at attention any longer. That, Red, is what I hope for."

"Wow." Amanda slowly wiped the tears from her face as she reached for his hand that wasn't holding the camera.

"Wow is right! Now, let's go take some more photos and enjoy nature." His crystal-blue eyes met her rusty-hazel browns as he whispered, "Don't worry. I didn't take any rated-X photos of us."

As they walked through the woods, enjoying their surroundings and each other, it was as if they were separated from the rest of the world for a few hours. Like being in a fairy tale or something.

"Red, the sun will be going down soon. We'd best be heading back."

"Ryan, look. It appears to be a garden or something. Wonder who has this garden on campus property."

"Saints preserve. God only knows."

"They even have a small shack nearby. I wonder if this is where they get the ingredients for the tea the campus provides to all the faculty."

"That tea is strange. I drank it once, and it took me a while to drive home. I kept getting off on the wrong road."

Amanda and Ryan stood behind some trees and bushes, observing the area, for a few moments.

"Oh my God, look over there! There is Strongwell, the campus manor's butler, picking herbs or something over in the garden area to the left."

"Herbs my ass! That is marijuana! You know, weed, pot, dope, grass, reefer, Mary Jane."

"What! Let me adjust my glasses. What the hell? I've been drinking that tea for teatime at the manor. Good God, no wonder I've felt so crazy, relaxed, and sleepy sometimes."

Ryan couldn't help himself and started to laugh. "Well, Red, you probably didn't smell or taste anything because it was mixed with so many other things. Look at this garden. It's filled with all kinds of herbs and stuff."

"Sh, I don't want him to hear us with your carrying on over here. Are you kidding me? Look who is coming out of the shack!"

"Oh, the mysterious Dean Russet it is. Now, that is a weird bugger. He is walking toward Strongwell, who has a Red Riding Hood basket filled with marijuana and such. If you ask me, they look like a couple of cartoon characters."

"What in the world?"

"What?"

"Well, look what Dean Russet has in his hand. Looks like some kind of chain with a wrist brace or handcuffs. Ryan, are you taking photos of all this?"

"Of course, yes. My camera is clicking away as we stand here and snoop."

"Ryan, I've got to get into that shack to see what is going on. Maybe my missing student, Vivian Smith, is in there."

"Now, Amanda, don't get your panties all in a wad. It's getting dark, and we don't need to be snooping around when the dean and Strongwell are around. Besides, Dean Russet is probably asking Strongwell what in the world that thing is for. It could be some kind of harness for a horse. I don't know. We will have to come back another day."

"But that might be too late!"

"Late or not, I'm not letting you get yourself and me in danger. We need to think this over and make a plan. I've got Ian to think about." He quietly grabbed her hand and swiftly started back. "Time to get out of here as fast as possible."

Amanda kept talking as they hurried to get back to the campus. "Even if they had a license to grow marijuana for the college medical and science departments or whatever, that still wouldn't give them permission to be giving it to all the faculty in a mixture of tea without faculty members knowing it. Man, I sure hope there weren't cameras around the garden area that will show us viewing them."

"Stop worrying, Red. Relax. You don't know what Strongwell was gathering all the stuff for. I'm sure we are not the first to find this garden. If we were captured seeing the garden, then all we have to say is that we went for a hike together and stumbled into it. I will hide the photo shoots I took when we were standing there gawking, if that makes you feel better."

"No problem."

But Amanda couldn't help but think there would be problems coming their way.

God help us.

Chapter 11

Library Conundrum

Amanda was walking casually toward the library when Dr. Timothy Norman suddenly popped up beside her. "Oh, Dr. Norman, I'm sorry I didn't see you there. Guess I was deep in thought while heading toward the library for some research time."

"No problem at all, Dr. O'Neal. Please call me Timothy when we aren't around our students."

"Oh yes, ditto. Please refer to me as Amanda when under the same circumstances."

"Of course, Amanda. So how is the sabbatical coming along?"

"Well, honestly, it's been a little crazy! You know, with the disappearance of my student Vivian Smith and a bunch of other unexpected things."

Timothy glanced at Amanda with a concerned look, "Well, that is understandable. We are all worried about Vivian's disappearance. Hey, don't give up, though. I hear from the buzz of the students that they really like you and your lectures. I heard one young man tell some other students in the hall that finally he'd found a professor who

65

doesn't simply teach from the book but, rather, gives real-life stories and experiences. Especially in the Criminal Investigation class."

"Well, that is nice to hear!"

"Are you coming to the next evening faculty dinner toward the end of the week? My wife, Karen, and I would enjoy getting better acquainted with you and Professor Ryan McFarlan."

"Oh, good Lord, I thought we were only supposed to have one of those required dinners once a semester. Don't take that comment personally. Guess I'm not used to the dean's ways."

"No worries. My wife and I pretty much feel the same way. Well, apparently, Dean Russet feels we need another faculty dinner this semester due to the other one being interrupted by the horrid circumstance of Vivian Smith's disappearance. Guess the whereabouts of the student or her body are yet to be determined. So sad."

"Indeed, sad."

"As far as Dean Russet is concerned, I thought you handled his comments directed to you quite well at the last dinner."

"Thank you. I learned a long time ago if you don't stick up for yourself, who else is going to? In other words, don't let the monsters bully you."

"Well said."

"Thank you."

Dr. Norman gave her a smile and waved as he trotted off to an engineering lecture he'd almost forgotten about.

"Have a good day, Timothy! Please give Karen my best. Hey, make your engineering lecture exciting."

"Yeah right. Sorry, but I don't think I compete very well against criminology. If you ever need some help from an engineer and an artist, just let us know."

Amanda snickered to herself as she entered the huge, ancient library. In a world of technology, it was lovely to still be able to behold such a grand systematic display of books, some dating back hundreds of years. Even the library smell of old pages got her research skills itching to be used.

OK, I'm a nerd. There is no doubt about it. Definitely a nerd.

Much like the manor, the library had arches and ribbed groin vaults fundamental to Gothic architecture. The large, high library windows had stained glass, allowing the sun to shine or darkness to loom down through the rows of wooden bookcases. Every time Amanda entered this place, she felt as if she were stepping back in time. It was an eerie feeling at first, until one got used to the scholarly surroundings. As usual, students, faculty, and visitors were sitting around the library tables in the center.

Amanda quietly sat at a nearby table to review her notes prior to beginning the research she sought. She wanted to find out more history about the origination of the manor tea and campus traditions. All seemed mysterious. She walked through the rows of bookcases in the historical section and came across a few books that sounded interesting. One was titled *Exotic Veiled Pleasures of Huntington Hills College Tea*, and another was *Huntington Hills College Undisclosed*. Sitting back down at the table where she'd left some of her things, Amanda began to leaf through the book that had a specific section on the college's tea. Its pages were worn and aged. Glancing down, she began to read.

> The historic tradition at Huntington Hills College manor of serving our unique tea to faculty, some visitors, and those students who care to indulge gives the institution great pleasure indeed. The young green tea leaves, with our secret blend of herbs and natural elements, allow tea

drinkers to relax and enjoy any endeavor they choose to experience with themselves or with others.

Amanda quietly whispered to herself as she ran a finger down the page, "Hm, wonder what that means. Wish I could find out what the 'secret blend of herbs and natural elements' are. Guess I need to keep reading. Well, from what Ryan and I found back in the woods, marijuana might be one of the ingredients. What is this about 'enjoying endeavors by themselves or with others'? Good Lord! Is the writer referring to something possibly sexual?" She read on.

The origin of our glorious tea dates back to the very beginning of this college's existence. Cherokee Indians helped us perfect its blend, leading us to success. Few truly know the ingredients, and those who do seek to hide the sacred components so cherished.

Amanda stopped reading for a second. *OK, this book is like a puzzle. You must decipher every sentence. Do they mean academic success related to the college or something else? Seems like I could read this for the rest of my life and still not grasp what they are getting at. Wonder what Ryan would think of all this. I'd better check these books out and ponder them awhile.*

As Amanda glanced up, she saw one of her excellent students walking toward her. He was walking fast and sat across from her as quietly as possible. Nearby students studying glanced for a second or two, displaying disturbed facial expressions, and then went back to work.

"What can I do for you, Mr. Dembe Luganda? Are you ready for the Criminal Investigation quiz next week?"

Dembe sat there for a few seconds before speaking. He took ahold of one of her hands, which was resting on the table palm down, and swiftly moved it. Whispering so those around could not hear, he said, "Dr. O'Neal, I'm not here for that exactly. I've been looking for you all over campus. We even stopped by your office, but the door was locked."

"Dembe, you are kind of worrying me. What is going on?" She glanced into his eyes for a few seconds and then gave him a moment to respond. His fear and anxiety were evident. His eyes rolled downward to her hand and then immediately darted back to glance at her again in an urgent manner. Amanda then realized Dembe had slipped a small piece of paper under her hand.

Quietly, he said, "Dr. O'Neal, we need you to leave the library right now and review the message I've provided somewhere private. Please! Now!"

"No worries, Dembe. I will take care of that for you and the other class students immediately."

Dembe stood, placed his chair back under the table, and then left without another word. He moved at a fast pace out the front door and looked back but for a second.

Amanda quickly shoved the piece of paper into her sweater pocket, picked up her things, and went to the front desk to check out the two books she was studying. After swiftly exiting the library, she came across a bench camouflaged by bushes and sat down to read the note.

Dr. O'Neal:

Help us, please! Vivian Smith was found by the police early this morning, wandering the hillside road on the other side of the campus woods. She was extremely disoriented and covered with many bloody cuts and bruises. Word is she was almost unrecognizable. All we know is that she was taken to the Huntington Hills General Hospital, but we as students have not been allowed to see her. Police are keeping this all a secret. She somehow called Sarah, her campus roommate, asking that we find you and have you come to the hospital as soon as possible. Vivian sounded very scared and weak on the message. Please help us! Please!

Signed,
Your Criminal Procedure students

Amanda suddenly felt physically sick. Her face went pale white, and tears slowly filled her eyes.

God, help her. Make me not be too late.

She stood up too fast, and her vertigo spun out of control for a few seconds. Grabbing everything, she then raced toward her office to drop off the books and grab the keys to her rented truck.

She quickly called Ryan as she ran. "Ryan, Amanda here. Please meet me as fast as you can at Huntington Hills General Hospital. It's Vivian Smith."

Chapter 12

A Live Victim

Vivian was conscious, drifting to sleep on and off, as she heard all the hospital room monitors hooked up to her beeping. It was hard to stay awake. She looked to her left through the slits in her swollen eyes and, surprisingly, saw Amanda slumped in a chair, sleeping.

Slowly, Vivian attempted a raspy whisper. "Dr. O'Neal!"

Amanda suddenly jumped up and moved swiftly toward the bed. "Vivian, welcome back. You are awake! Do you want me to call the nurse or doctors?"

"No, not quite yet."

Time seemed to stand still for a few moments as Amanda grasped one of Vivian's hands and warmly looked into the girl's eyes. Vivian appeared completely bruised from all the swollen contusions from apparent beatings. There also was a large, deep laceration beside her left ear, but it already had been stitched. There were numerous other fresh and older scars on her arms and legs and probably over her whole body.

Amanda thought, *Man, are those cigarette burns on her arms, near the scars where she was chained on her wrists? What kind of animals would do this?* Amanda suddenly realized by the marks of the scars that Vivian had been restrained with a chain or belt around her neck and ankles as well.

Vivian whispered with difficulty, "You came for me."

Leaning down close toward Vivian so they could glance into each other's eyes, Amanda said, "Of course, my dear. I'd do that for any of my beloved students. Always, I want the best for you. Dembe found me in the library and gave me a tiny written message from all the other criminal justice students. Everyone cares about you." It was hard to keep composed, and Amanda couldn't help a few tears falling down her cheeks.

Vivian struggled to speak again and finally said, "Thank God."

"Yes, thank God. Let me tell the nurse you are awake now, and we can talk later once they've checked you out."

"No, not yet! I need to quickly tell you something."

"OK, what is it?"

"I'm in great danger. If you don't get me out of here soon, they will find a way to kill me to keep my mouth shut."

"What! Who? Um, wait. Before you say anything else, I must ask if you want me to legally represent you if needed. Do you trust me?"

While looking into Amanda's eyes, Vivian softly replied, "Yes, of course."

"Sorry, but I had to ask you that just in case there are any complications down the road. Now, whom are you speaking about?"

"The bad people on campus."

Just as Vivian whispered that statement, she drifted out again, causing the heart monitor to start beeping rapidly. As doctors and nurses ran in, Amanda slipped out of the room, which was being guarded by police. Glancing toward the waiting room, she happily saw Ryan. Before running to him, she spoke quietly to the police officer guarding Vivian's hospital room door.

"Officer, my name is Dr. Amanda O'Neal. I am doing a sabbatical at Huntington Hills College from my law practice in Tampa, Florida, as well as being a private investigator who sometimes works with law enforcement back home. The patient Vivian Smith is one of my criminal justice students, and she has just confidentially told me something I think the police chief needs to hear firsthand. Tell him to google me, and he'll see the horrible crime the Tampa Police Department and I solved a few years ago there. Please inform the chief of police of Huntington Hills that I need to see him personally here immediately, and it is a matter of life and death for Vivian that he and I meet with her doctors ASAP about a very pressing matter related to the case. Please help us if you can. Please! Please don't leave this door unattended for any reason. I will be in the room with her or sitting in the waiting room as directed. Thank you so much."

"No worries, ma'am. I will call to give him your message now. The chief does know that at this point, Vivian has asked only to see you."

"Thank you."

As Amanda turned to run to Ryan in the waiting room, he met her halfway. Ryan looked worried and folded her tightly into his arms as he whispered, "I'm here for you, darling. Are you OK? You scared the hell out of me with that phone message! What in the world is going on?"

Amanda leaned her head on his chest as a few tears streamed down her cheeks. He kissed the top of her head and rested his chin there for a moment. Finally releasing their hug, he looked into her eyes, and she whispered, "Come with me back into the waiting room, where I can speak to you privately."

In the waiting room, she continued. "Ryan, Vivian looks horrible. There is no doubt she was chained by her wrists and ankles and sometimes her neck. There are cigarette burns near where she was chained and multiple bruises and contusions. Cuts everywhere— some of them deep. It is a wonder she survived the beatings. Vivian told me in confidence that we must get her out of here, or the bad people from the college are going to kill her to shut her up."

"Good God! What kind of beast would do such a thing to an innocent lass?" Ryan was rubbing his chin and looked down into her beautiful rust-colored eyes as Amanda quietly gave him all the information she had. "OK, Red. You have dealt with this stuff before. What do we do to help her?"

"Well, first, you and I have to get back in there when things have calmed down in her room and take as many photos as possible without anyone seeing us do it. Then, when the chief arrives, all of us, including her doctors, must meet in a private room while I inform them of what she told me and then suggest that she and her mother be transported to a safe house where no one can reach Vivian. I'm going to suggest they be flown to Shawn's and my small farm near Tampa. At least until she gets better and it is time for a trial if one occurs."

"Well, I hope to hell someone pays for this!"

"Me too. Time will tell. For now, she is in great danger of being killed in here. These individuals will try everything to have her keep her mouth shut. One way or the other."

"Saints above us, please help us."

"Well, I think it would be best if we petition God Almighty himself for this job."

"Indeed."

"Yes indeed, for sure. Oh, there is the chief himself. Let me speak to him briefly for a few moments, and then maybe you and I can slip into her room to sneak some photos. Are you up for this, Ryan?"

"For sure, my love. I'm here for you. Sticking to you like glue."

"Good. I'll be right back." Amanda turned to walk to the chief, who ushered her into a small conference room the hospital provided for them.

The police chief and Amanda stood there for a few seconds, looking at each other in silence. Chief Braxton Ward was a handsome middle-aged black man who commanded respect just by his appearance, maybe due to his tall and slender but solid build. Without his saying a word, his presence projected complete confidence. Braxton stretched out his arm for a handshake and said in a low, deep whisper, "It's nice to see you again, Dr. O'Neal."

"Nice to see you again, Chief."

"Sorry we meet under these circumstances."

"Yes."

"I know we must talk about this particular incident, but I just want you to know that I miss Detective Captain Lukas Emerson. He and I went to college together and were roommates for a while. The world lost a great detective and friend when he was shot and killed in Tampa. Glad that horrible satanic criminal case there was solved. I followed the investigation and status of that case closely since Cap and I often talked. Especially when things at work got really stressful. So you see, there is no need for me to google to find anything about you or the case all of you previously solved."

Amanda answered softly, "Yes, we all miss him immensely and always will. That was one of the reasons I took the sabbatical at Huntington Hills College—to get away from Tampa for a while."

"Understandable."

"Anyway, Chief, there is a reason I had the officer guarding Vivian's hospital room contact you with such urgency. The victim is in great danger. I'd like us to meet privately with the doctors and administration connected to this case within the hour. Once we are all together, it will be clear why I have requested this emergency meeting."

"You can't lay out the information for me here and now?"

"No, everyone has to be there together."

"OK, I will take your word for it, but I can't hang around here forever. I've got a town to protect. I will do it due to our connection with Detective Cap. He wouldn't have had you as a friend unless you were a special person. But I won't give you such a special privilege again. Do you hear me clearly?"

"Understood."

"Can you help get the doctor in charge, the hospital administrator, and whoever else to meet somewhere privately in an hour? I'm begging you, Chief."

"Dr. O'Neal, getting everyone together so fast is highly unlikely, but I'll see what I can do. Please meet me back here in an hour."

Amanda looked slowly into his eyes and replied, "Thank you."

Once the chief turned around to go to the hospital administration office, she walked back swiftly to Ryan and grabbed ahold of his shoulder while catching her breath. "Thank God you are here."

Ryan lovingly rubbed the middle of her back and then cupped her face with both of his large hands. "Red, I have always thanked God for you. Now that we are together, I thank him even more, but this situation is getting entirely too serious. I just want you to know if we weren't in the hallway of this hospital, I'd probably throw you down to the floor right now and make wild, passionate love to your whole body."

Amanda rolled her eyes for a second with a smirk on her face. "There you go again. Wow!"

"Wow is right, Red, so let's do what we have to do in Vivian's room, get the meeting over with, and then sit by my fireplace tonight together with Ian hopping all over us until we have a few quiet moments alone. What do you say?"

"Yes, let's do this. I must be crazy tired or just feeling old because I feel kind of emotional."

"Everyone has a bad day, Amanda. I think you are due."

"OK, let's go. I sure don't want to become a sniffling baby."

Amanda and Ryan quietly entered Vivian's room and started taking photos like crazy. They took photos of everything, even though some perhaps were a bit embarrassing. Luckily, Vivian didn't seem to object, or maybe somewhere in her traumatized state, she realized they were doing this to help her. At least that was what Amanda was hoping for. She hoped they weren't causing more distress for the girl.

"Vivian, would you mind turning onto your stomach if you can and then getting on your knees? I'm sorry, but Professor McFarlan and I will get all your injuries recorded for evidence. We have carefully photographed every place else on your body. It won't take long. You don't have to if you can't due to pain or really don't want to, but it would be best if we got everything. I promise you they will only go to specialized law enforcement for court or to establish a profile of the individuals who did this, not the media."

With tears running down her face and an expression of combined confusion and anger, Vivian spoke out. "Dr. O'Neal, it may be hard for you to believe, but after everything that has been done to me these last few months, there is only one thing on my mind: getting those monsters! I haven't forgotten everything you've taught us in those criminal justice classes. Guess I was just a foolish young girl who was in the wrong place at the wrong time."

"That is right, Vivian. Stay strong. Ryan and I are here to help you do that, as well as a lot of other professionals. Honestly, it's going to take some time to get all the drugs out of your system and heal—physically and emotionally. I surmise right now you are in shock, but staying strong and a little mad is a lot better than being fearful or withdrawn. Hopefully, my plan for your protection will work, and you will get through this with God's love and strength. With help from a lot of trained individuals who care, keep telling yourself that everything is going to work out for good. Remember, God's circle of protection is around you. It is! Like a Bible verse my mother would often voice to me when I was discouraged: 'I can do all things through Christ which strengthens me' (Philippians 4:13 KJV). Now, get some rest, and after our meeting with the police chief and doctor, I'll come back to your room to let you know our next step. Vivian, you may not feel it now, but you are a very brave young woman. Don't let what they did to you dictate your future. A deputy is right outside your hospital room."

Vivian smiled briefly at Ryan and Amanda as her eyes slowly closed back to sleep. After gathering their things, they had just enough time to hurry to Amanda's vehicle, secure the photos, and get back to Chief Ward for the meeting.

Chapter 13

The Plan

The main door to the Huntington Hills Hospital conference room finally closed. Many people sat around the table, looking at each other, wondering what this secret meeting about a patient, Vivian Smith, was all about. Amanda looked toward Chief Ward, motioning to him to begin the introductions.

Chief Braxton Ward stood up in silence for a few seconds, shaking his head slowly with a soft smile on his face. "Well, ladies and gentlemen, Dr. Amanda O'Neal, sitting directly to my left, urged me with great conviction to call us all together for this urgent meeting. We truly thank you for taking a few moments out of your busy schedules to be present. Dr. O'Neal is presently teaching on a sabbatical at Huntington Hills College in the criminal justice department. Dr. O'Neal practices law in Tampa, Florida, as well as having a private investigator license. She has often worked with the Tampa Police Department to assist with difficult evidential criminal cases as needed. Vivian Smith, the patient, and victim is one of her students. At this time, Vivian has requested that Amanda be the only person able to see her besides assigned medical staff and law enforcement. Now, I'd like to make some quick introductions so we can proceed to the main point as swiftly as possible. Beside Amanda—if I may call you that?"

"Yes, of course, Chief, everyone simply addresses me as Amanda."

"As I was saying, beside Amanda is Professor Ryan McFarlan, who is also teaching at Huntington Hills College on a sabbatical from his nationally renowned photography career. He is working with Dr. O'Neal on somethings for the case."

"Just call me Ryan, please."

"Following him are Huntington General Hospital's administrator, Gena Jewel; the main physician in Vivian's case, Dr. Travis Marshall; and Maxwell Davis, the main FBI agent also involved in the legal investigation in relation to Vivian. Now that the formal introductions have been made, I hand over the meeting to Dr. O'Neal to explain why we are all here."

"Thank you, Chief. The reason for my request to call all of you here on behalf of the victim, Vivian Smith, is to confidentially inform you of what she has told me. I have a plan to protect her from this point forward, but I will need assistance from all of you to succeed. Vivian told me something very troubling in private as her friend, professor, and attorney. Usually, anything an attorney is told by a client is confidential, but since her statement indicates she is more than likely in imminent danger—along with everyone else on the campus and in the geographic area, for that matter—I made the decision to request this meeting."

Agent Davis's lean, well-toned body displayed that he couldn't take it another moment, and he blurted out, "For goodness' sake, Amanda! The suspense is killing us. Just spit it out!"

"OK, sorry. Vivian's exact words were 'I am in great danger. If you don't get me out of here soon, they will find a way to kill me to keep my mouth shut.'"

Rubbing his chin with his left hand as if he were thinking, Chief Ward looked into Amanda's eyes. "Well, Dr. O'Neal, what do you think that means? Something to do with a fraternity or sorority? A gang? A cult? What exactly?"

"Honesty, I'm not sure yet, but we do know that within the last three years or more, at least three or more female students have gone missing on or near the campus of Huntington Hills College. As far as I know, none of the other victims have been found yet. Vivian was the lucky one to escape, if what happened to her can be viewed as lucky."

"Well, it's the first time the FBI has heard anything about other missing females from the campus! Um, I can address that later with Chief Ward. Now our concern must be Vivian. She holds a lot more evidence in her memories that we'll hopefully be able to extract. After examining her, Dr. Marshall, what is your medical opinion?"

The young-looking, handsome doctor paused for a moment and slicked back his thick ash-brown hair as he opened his blue eyes before replying. "A physician often sees unusual things with patients entering the emergency, like Vivian did when the police secretly brought her in. Her injuries are certainly serious, both physically and mentally, but at least she is alive and has a chance if given the proper care as well as kept track of in the future. Someone will have to keep a close watch on her medically for sure. The Lord only knows the real trauma she has experienced. We will have to do more tests to determine if she will ever be able to have children or if she has permanent damage in various areas of her body. I'm truly worried about her emotionally too. With all that said, though, I don't believe this was a fraternity, sorority, or even satanic cult activity. I'm not a psychologist or profiler, but there is something about her torturous injuries to make me think one or more individuals did this for pure pleasure. Meaning they enjoyed what they were doing. It probably wouldn't have stopped but for Vivian getting away. It's going to take a long time for her to heal. Maybe even years. A lifetime for all we know."

Administrator Jewel fluffed her spiky blonde hair and glared at Dr. Marshall with her gray eyes, as if he were saying too much. "Travis—sorry. I mean Dr. Marshall. For the hospital's sake, we must be careful what we say or do regarding this patient. For the protection of this hospital and legal concerns, we sure don't want to give any absolutes regarding Vivian. Confidentiality is also a problem for Huntington General Hospital. If detailed information gets out about this patient and possibly similar cases that may have crossed our paths without proper reporting to authorizes, as required, we could be in a heap of trouble. Also, what if someone does come after her while she is in this hospital, and bullets start blazing everywhere?"

"Well, Gena, I know you are just doing your job, looking out for the best interest of the hospital, but I'm a physician, and my main concern is the well-being of my patient. Period!"

"All right now," Chief Ward said softly. "Let's not get all stirred up. Amanda, Vivian hasn't really given us much evidence to go on yet in relation to who did this. I mean, we all can see her horrible physical injuries. Besides that, what do we exactly have?"

"If I may, Chief," Ryan replied after clearing his throat with a quick cough.

"Go on."

"Well, I don't know if I should share all this with all these individuals in the room, but Amanda and I took a lovely, romantic stroll through the woods in back of the campus a few weeks ago and saw—"

Amanda calmly tightened her grip just above his left elbow and whispered, "Careful."

"Go on, Professor McFarlan. As you were saying."

"Yes, Chief. I should probably give you and Agent Davis all the details later. Basically, we saw some strange things out there. Right, Amanda?"

"For sure, but we were going to kind of check them out a bit more before presenting any theories or whatever to the authorities."

Chief Ward stood, took a deep breath, looked down while placing both hands flat on the table, and then rolled his eyes with frustration, as if he were thinking, *Doesn't anyone come to law enforcement anymore like they should? I'm the law around here, for God's sake!*

Agent Davis piped up. "Well, yeah, we'd like to hear all you have to say on that."

"This conversation is quite interesting, people, but I'm a busy physician around here, and my rounds to see my patients start in about ten minutes. Can we please move on and hear the reason for this meeting, along with Attorney O'Neal's alleged plan?"

Ryan looked at him for a few seconds, thinking, *OK, that chap is entirely too good looking to be a real medical doctor. I don't like the competition. Agent Davis isn't any loser either. That guy probably works out two to three hours a day.*

Amanda's eyes met Ryan's, and it was as if she could read his mind. *Oh good Lord. Men!* She then got ahold of herself and said, "There is one more thing I'd like to share before proceeding with the necessary plan to protect the patient and victim. When I asked Vivian whom she was talking about, she merely said, 'The bad people on campus.' Frankly, I'm hopeful she'll be able to tell us more later about that, but for now, I just want to thank Chief Ward for keeping a 24-7 guard at her hospital door and Huntington General Hospital for providing her the utmost medical care."

Administrator Gena Jewel smiled. "Of course."

Amanda let out a slow breath. "Like I said, I'm not sure my plan will work, but I was kind of hoping you'd all get on board to save Vivian's life. We'd sneak her out of the hospital and have her taken to my small farm on the outskirts of Tampa, Florida. I believe that would be much better than a closed-in safe house somewhere. It would be a great place for her to start the healing process. Far away from here. Plus, I trust the people keeping my little place going, as well as the great law enforcement there. Also, she'd be very close to Tampa General Hospital, which is superior medically on many levels. Her mother could go with her, with round-the-clock FBI security, as we start to put all the evidence together."

Agent Davis lifted his head. "Well, we'd have to assign FBI people to her due to the magnitude of this case and alleged others. Then Chief Ward could be investigating on this end and keeping us all abreast."

"Well, I don't know how Administrator Jewel and the hospital will feel about what I'm going to say, but as her physician, I'd suggest if you are going to transport her that far by helicopter or plane, then I should travel with her. Vivian is in too much of a delicate state medically just to be shifted to another location without a hands-on medical physician with her. She should go to Tampa General Hospital first for a while before being taken to your farm for the healing process."

Gena nodded. "I don't know, Dr. Marshall. I'll have to talk to the hospital board and those above me, you know."

Chief Ward jumped in. "It sounds a little hard, but we need her to be healthy and thinking straight when we catch these monsters and finally bring them to court for justice. It should be, but it's not all about Vivian. It's about the case too."

Amanda glanced over to the chief. "Well, I get that it would primarily be law enforcement, FBI, and the higher-ups to confirm such a plan. Agent Davis, I could have one of Tampa Bay's finest detectives, Brad Conner, fly here and assist with getting to Tampa General Hospital and the farm. If ever you could trust anyone, it's him! Chief Ward, he worked with Detective Cap Emerson on that case we solved there. They were very close."

"Well, that is good enough for me. OK, I will have to think about all of this and discuss everything with Agent Davis and the others. Once a decision has been made, we'll get back with everyone with 'It's a go' or 'It's a no.' Until then, though, Vivian must be taken care of security-wise and medically. There can be no mistakes. This girl and her case are too important. Thank you, everyone. You will be notified with the final decision ASAP. Now, you can all go back to your very important duties. Oh, and don't talk to anyone who shouldn't hear about this meeting and the proposed plan. Her life is in your hands. Take care."

As everyone was slowly leaving, Chief Ward came up beside Amanda. "Amanda, you and Ryan hold back for just a second. I just want to say a few words to you."

"No problem, Chief."

"I just wanted to warn both of you. No one has to tell you this, I'm sure, but I just have to express something."

"What, Chief?"

"If you weren't before, you—especially you, Amanda—will be blacklisted from this point forward by the criminal culprits, whoever they may be. If this plan goes forward, to them, you will have become persons under suspicion, untrustworthy, and enemies. You are potential targets. Do you understand that?"

"Chief, I believe Ryan and I understand that, but we both have been risk-takers our whole lives. We must trust our knowledge, good common sense, and faith. Without sounding like some kind of Bible-thumping nut, as many people of the world often say, I know there is something in trusting God. Braxton, I just keep verbalizing about a hundred times a day a Bible verse my parents always spoke to me during tough times: 'Trust in the Lord with all your heart and lean not on your own understanding; in all your ways acknowledge him, and he will make your paths straight' (Proverbs 3:5 NIV)."

"Detective Cap Emerson often spoke to me about your faith, Amanda, but that doesn't prevent me from being concerned about what this plan may direct your way."

"I understand, but I must trust that this plan came into my mind not by accident and that everything will work out for good. One way or another. Good night, Chief."

"Good night, you two. Get some rest."

Chapter 14

The Calm before the Storm

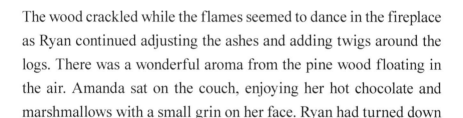

The wood crackled while the flames seemed to dance in the fireplace as Ryan continued adjusting the ashes and adding twigs around the logs. There was a wonderful aroma from the pine wood floating in the air. Amanda sat on the couch, enjoying her hot chocolate and marshmallows with a small grin on her face. Ryan had turned down the lights and put on some soft mood music.

"So, Red, what are you grinning about? You kind of look like the Cheshire Cat from *Alice in Wonderland*. I have been reading Ian that book."

"Oh, I don't know, Ryan McFarlan. Maybe it's because where I am right now this moment is as perfect as it gets."

"Well, if something as simple as this pleases you so much, I've got it made in the future!" Ryan laughed for a second. "You, Amanda, are a conundrum. You just got done with one of the most horrendous days and still have energy to enjoy a few simple moments afterward."

"You should be thankful for that, McFarlan." She glanced at Ryan for a moment and gave him a quick wink.

"Indeed. Point taken, Red."

Just then, Ian came storming into the room with footed red flannel pajamas on. He quickly jumped onto the couch and immediately onto Amanda's lap. Without a word, he placed his small hands on both sides of her face and kissed her while looking into her eyes. A soft giggle came afterward.

Ryan gave out a funny snort while looking back from the fire. "Ian, my lad, what was that all about?"

"Well, Da, I was thinking a little bit. If I kissed Amanda before you, then she would like me better and want to become part of our family. We'd be three instead of two. So I was thinking I should kiss her before you do, so you don't spoil it."

Amanda and Ryan giggled softly. "Pray tell, Son, whatever do you mean by it?"

"Oh, it is my wish."

"Your wish, you say. Pray tell, my little lad, inform us of your secret wish."

"Um, it's really a secret. I mean the whole thing. But I can tell you a piece of it."

"OK, we wait with bated breath."

"What does that mean, Da?"

"Like we are so excited for you to tell us a piece of your wish that we are holding our breath."

"Oh, I will keep it to myself, and you can both breathe now."

"OK, little man, if that is what you want."

"Yes, Da, for now."

Amanda turned Ian around so his back was leaning against her chest as she held him in a hug fashion. "Ian, I'm very proud of you. You speak quite well for a wee lad, as your da would say."

"Well, he speaks so good because I never spoke baby talk to him. From the moment we met, I have always spoken like he was an adult. Isn't that right, my Ian?"

"Yes, my da."

"I can tell you two are very close. Like we used to say, two bugs in a rug."

Ian started to giggle again. "That sounds kind of scratchy!" He dropped his little head into his small hands and continued with his deep giggles.

"Oh, lad, you are making your da laugh too much. My sides are hurting."

"Mine too, Da."

"Ian, did I ever tell you that I have a small farm in Florida?"

"No, Amanda. Da, we must go. Can we?"

"Yes, my Ian, I promise that someday we will visit."

"I have the best dog in the whole world, called Royal. He is a Labrador retriever and the smartest dog I've ever known. Royal is one of my best friends. A family member, really. I miss him very much. Sometimes I call the farm just so he can hear my voice over the phone. Then there is Jasper the cat. Jasper is kind of a stubborn old gal. She mostly lives in the barn because she loves to catch the mice and sleep up in the loft with the hay. She thinks she is queen of the barn."

Ian gave another soft giggle as Ryan looked at him lovingly in Amanda's arms. "Tell me more!"

"A boy I helped, José Emanuel, and his grandmother Soledad Emanuel now live on the farm, caring for it while I am gone. You would like José very much. He is around twelve years old. I'm sure he would love to show you around the place when you visit. Soledad is the best cook around, and all my friends love to visit when Soledad gets the urge to make her famous tacos. I love José and Soledad very much. They are like family to me. Don't tell anyone, but José calls me White Mama."

"I wouldn't do that. I'd call you just Ma, like I call Da just Da."

Amanda's heart warmed as she thought of Ian calling her Ma someday. How could her feelings for Ryan have changed so swiftly? Was God trying to tell her something? She looked over at Ryan briefly, with his soft smile and right eyebrow slightly lifted.

"Well, Ian, enough stories for tonight."

"But, Da, I like her stories. I want to hear more."

"Another time, lad. Us guys need to be getting you ready for bed now."

"Potty, washing hands, and brushing teeth. That is what Mrs. Beasley says!"

With that, Ian suddenly jumped down, and Ryan scooped him up, throwing the lad onto his back for a horseback ride to the bathroom.

"Giddy up, Da."

"OK! Giddy up I go!" Ryan made a horse sound as they playfully galloped away.

Amanda placed her head on the arm of the couch, closed her eyes, and lifted her legs, so her body was now completely laid out. With dinner and hot chocolate in her stomach, she suddenly realized how tired she was.

Without her noticing, Ryan quietly sneaked back into the room and rekindled the fire so the cozy feeling in the air remained. He lay over her body, holding his weight on his elbows and knees, and then placed his fingers underneath her head for support while softly touching his lips to hers, licking her lower lip and then entering her mouth. Their tongues united in a battle of longing. His kiss grew deeper, and this time, there was no hesitation by Amanda. She was as much in the moment as he.

Ryan kissed her forehead, eyelids, and neck and then traveled down to her chest and stroked the nipple of one of her breasts, placing his mouth upon the other to suckle. Amanda felt tingling all over. Their breathing became heavier as he quickly took her mouth again, as if he were going to ravish every inch of her. His hands moved to her bottom, pulling her closer to him. Her hands caringly moved to his chest, rubbing his chest in circular motions as one of her hands moved down to his stomach. His best friend, as he often referred to it, grew hard, ready for fantastic exploration. Amanda moaned, which only made Ryan crazier. That was when Ryan knew they were getting into a little bit of trouble there.

Breathing hard, he suddenly stopped and spoke quietly to Amanda. "Red, are you sure you are ready for all this emotionally?"

"No, not sure."

"Well, lass, I'm only asking because if we don't stop now, I will kind of be in a little bit of trouble. If you know what I mean."

"Sorry."

"No need to say sorry. I'd have no trouble proceeding to Glory Land, so to speak, but I know you might have some trouble with our actions later. I know how you were raised and how you loved Shawn."

"Yeah, we'd better stop. Ian is near too."

"Oh, I'm sure the lad is sound asleep by now. I'd have no trouble claiming that it felt so good that I just couldn't stop, but then I have to think about your feelings too."

"Thanks."

"No problem. At least in my mind, no problem. As for my body, it is kind of screaming for release right now."

"I know what you mean."

"OK then. You've got to tell me when the green light is on, because I can't keep having these sessions like we are teenagers, when we are both experienced adults. If you know what I mean."

"I know what you mean. It's just hard. No matter how old you get, the lessons of your parents and grandparents never seem to leave you. At least for me. We were raised not to engage full force until marriage. Sounds crazy, I know. Like God looking down, evaluating our actions."

"Well, for me, I sure hope the Good Lord thought I was doing a good job. I'm not no young stud anymore. Hurts to say that. I will say I'm pretty good with my skills in the loving area. Please say something, or my best friend down there is sure to deflate forever, I fear!"

"Indeed, Ryan McFarlan, you are a very good lover."

"Thank God! For a moment, I thought I'd lost my talents. I was hoping you would declare me 'best lover of the universe,' but I will accept 'good lover' for now."

Amanda chuckled for a moment as Ryan wiped his forehead and smiled back at her.

"Red, you do know I love you."

"I do."

"Do you truly believe that?"

"I do. You know, it is kind of hard to wrap my head around what Shawn would think of us together as a couple, but he is dead, I know."

"Well, he is probably up in heaven, giving God quite a conversation about it all. He was probably one of the best friends I ever had, and he knew how I felt about you. We used to discuss it to great lengths sometimes in our dorm room. You loved him first. I loved both of you. So I stayed away."

"Really?"

"Yes, really. Still, though, I truly believe he'd be happy that we found our way back to each other and that I'm here to take care of you. Who better than me? At least until we both go up to glory. God will just have to solve which soul you will be with for all eternity: Shawn or me."

"Maybe we will all be together. Like the Bible says."

"Great. It will be like a Mormon sort of thing, two men and one woman, up there with you, Shawn, and myself."

"I don't think so, Ryan. Heaven is sure to be something we humans can't completely fathom. Even Christians. I must come to peace about Shawn."

"Aye, indeed. How about if I just hold you for a while? I don't think Shawn or God will mind that too much."

"Sounds good."

"Don't wait too long, Red. I am longing to make wild, passionate love to you. For hours!"

"Can you last that long?"

"I sure hope so. Sleep now. Enough discussion for such a day."

"Enough."

Chapter 15

Making It Happen

Chief Ward called Amanda early that morning and informed her that last night someone had left a bouquet of dried wildflowers for Vivian that had a small card with a death threat attached. As soon as he had received that information from the officer stationed in front of her hospital room, the chief had met with FBI agent Maxwell Davis, and the decision to proceed with the plan had been approved.

Unbeknownst to Amanda, Agent Davis already knew detectives Brad Conner and Henry Brooks in Tampa. Both the hospital administrator, Gena Jewel, and Dr. Travis Marshall had given a thumbs-up as well. In fact, they already had arranged for the doctor to travel with Vivian, Detective Conner, and Agent Davis with half a dozen other FBI agents as a well-tuned group. She would be well protected and cared for during the trip straight to Tampa General Hospital for a few days and then to the farm. Of course, Henry Brooks, detective and senior crime investigative technician, was already working with others from the Tampa Police Department to prepare the farm for when Vivian was moved there.

Amanda trusted Brad Conner and Henry Brooks completely since they were experts at what they did as well as her dear friends. Ever since they had worked together to solve a horrible crime in Tampa, she'd considered them family, like José and Soledad.

Everyone was clued into what was going to take place and what each of them had to do. Confidentiality was the name of the game to save Vivian's life and solve the case.

As Amanda stood at the airport, waiting for Brad to step out of the plane, she was surprised to see Agent Davis walking toward her.

"Hey, Doc!"

"Hey, Mr. FBI Agent. How is it going? I'm surprised to see you here."

"Well, I forgot to tell you that I already know detectives Brad Conner and Henry Brooks. We have worked on a couple of cases together. Those two are something else."

"Tell me about it! Still, I love them all the same."

"I'm sure their feelings are mutual. It's always good to have great friends in this life."

"Yes indeed."

Just as Amanda glanced up, Brad broke out from the plane gate. *As always, Mr. GQ looks handsome as ever. Hm, let me see. Leather jacket, long-sleeved white dress shirt, tight blue jeans with a pressed seam showing, and black leather cowboy boots. Cowboy boots! What happened to his penny loafers?*

Brad dropped his bag and reached over to give Amanda a big hug. "Hey, White Mama. That hug is especially from José and Soledad." He then bent down and gave her a sweet kiss on her cheek. "Now, that kiss is from Lorri and me. Oh, the twins too."

By that time, Amanda had tears in her eyes and hugged him back while whispering in his ear, "It's so wonderful to see you, Detective Conner. I have missed you like a son."

Brad then reached over and gave Agent Davis a firm handshake. "It's great to see you, Running Horse. How are things going with this case?"

"Wait a minute. You just called Agent Davis Running Horse?"

"Oh yeah, Amanda, didn't he tell you? Maxwell is Cherokee. Running Horse is his Indian name."

She looked at Maxwell for a few seconds without blinking and then replied, "Well, I bet that has a real interesting story."

"Yes, ma'am, a real family story." Maxwell smiled as only he could do and then winked at Brad as if to say, "We got her! She'll never give up until she finds out everything about me now."

"OK for now. We'll save how you two know each other so well for another time. Anyway, glad you are here and safe. Um, Brad, what about those cowboy boots? I never saw you wear anything like that before."

He snickered. "Oh, you've missed a lot, Amanda. José, Henry, and I have gone a little bit country with having to watch after the farm for you. All of us boys went out to some fancy cowboy apparel store and went crazy with boots and everything else. You should have seen Soledad's, Lorri's, and Pearl's faces when we came back home all duded up."

"Oh, for crying out loud, wish I would have seen that!"

"Yeah, all José can talk about is getting all the horses back from Ben next door."

"Funny you say that because I've been thinking about doing that when I get back home. Don't tell him, though. I want to surprise him."

"All right, my lips are sealed."

"How are your precious twin boys?"

"The precious twins are monsters! Lorri and I are so tired we can hardly speak when we fall into bed at night. Henry and Pearl babysat them once for a few hours, and they thought they were going to die."

Detective Davis, a.k.a. Running Horse, and Amanda laughed.

"I've missed seeing your wavy black hair flopping about and those crystal-blue eyes."

Brad laughed. "I've missed your red hair flying about and those rust-colored eyes going brighter when you get angry."

"I think I've had enough of this love fest between you two. We really need to get our minds back on this crazy case and on Vivian's transport back to the Tampa Bay area."

Brad smiled. "For sure, Running Horse. Don't want you to run away from us or anything."

They all giggled for a few seconds.

The helicopter was almost ready to take off when Detective Conner and Agent Davis made it to Huntington General Hospital. They raced to the takeoff pad on top of the hospital. The roof door swung open, and Brad and Maxwell saw Dr. Travis Marshall holding Vivian's IV bottle beside where she lay all belted up and ready to go inside the helicopter. They glanced to their right as the wind swirled around from the helicopter propellers and saw Chief Ward motioning for them to hurry and jump in. Brad glanced back toward the chief, who signaled to Brad to give him a call on his cell. Once they were in, the door slammed, and the helicopter took off.

Unbeknownst to Brad and Maxwell, something else had occurred at the hospital that morning and caused the chief to escalate the moving of Vivian. Once they were up in the air, Maxwell was immediately brought up to date. The helicopter headed for the airport, where they'd then get on an unidentified FBI plane that would head straight to Tampa General Hospital.

Brad glanced at Maxwell, looking as if he were thinking, *Can you believe this? Evidently, something happened!*

"Wait until we are all safe and secure on the plane, and then both of us will call Chief Ward to get all the details. Apparently, they had no choice but to move Vivian now. Someone tried to get to her this morning after last night's flower incident."

Dr. Marshall leaned over to Agent Davis. "Don't worry about Vivian, Maxwell. I sedated her so the traveling wouldn't be so traumatic for her. Lord knows she sure doesn't need any more trauma. Her mom is supposedly already on the plane, waiting for our arrival."

"Did you get a chance to meet with her?"

"Yeah, Gena and I met with her briefly. She seems like a genuinely nice lady."

"Well, that's good to hear. Better than a hysterical parent on our hands."

"True."

Once everyone was secure on the plane and Vivian was resting, Brad and Maxwell went to a secret area in the plane and called Chief Ward.

"Hey, Chief Ward, this is Detective Brad Conner. Agent Davis is here with me as well."

"Nice to hear from you, Brad. Sorry we didn't get a chance to talk and catch up as well as go over the investigation of the case here in North Carolina."

"Well, Braxton—may I call you that when we are in private?"

"Sure."

"Anyway, don't worry about that. Once we get Vivian and her mother settled at Tampa General Hospital, I'll give you a call. I need to wait until she is physically and psychologically ready before we move them to the farm. After that, I plan on going back and forth from Florida to North Carolina to assist in the case. If that is all right with you, Chief?"

"Yes, Brad, that would be extremely appreciated. I know you have training and experience in similar complicated cases like this. Really, I was hoping you could work with our detectives here some, along with the FBI. I know it doesn't seem like it, but Vivian was extremely lucky to get away from whoever is doing all this brutality. Don't know if Running Horse has had time to clue you in that there were a few other gals missing from the campus prior to Vivian's incident, but we never solved them. The campus kind of inferred that the prior missing girls weren't doing well academically and left the campus unannounced. Now, my suspicion is that all these cases are somehow connected, and our victim you guys are protecting is the key to potentially solving them all."

"Well, as always, it's up to my bosses here on how much I can go back and forth to assist with these cases, but I will sure try to be there for you. Right now, we don't know how long Dr. Travis Marshall is going to stay here either. I guess until he feels he has the proper physicians in place to handle the victim's medical needs. He hasn't really said, but I believe he has kind of become attached to this specific medical case. His medical devotion is something to be thankful for. Vivian has been through so much."

"I know. I'm kind of wondering: Even if we do get these monsters and solid evidence for a conviction or two, will Vivian be able to solidly identify these horrid people and actually testify?"

"Hey, Chief. Agent Davis here. Let's not worry about that right now. Sounds like you are starting to put too much pressure on yourself and your police department already. I think you need to try to get some rest for a few days and then hit the case with refreshed diligence. We've got everything covered for now. So far so good."

"Thanks, Agent Davis, a.k.a. Running Horse."

"Man, I sure was happy you didn't use my Running Horse name in the hospital meeting. You know, it would have taken the focus from the plan."

"No problem."

"So, Chief, the other FBI agents were kind of updating me in the helicopter about what happened this morning, but can you go over it so Brad and I can both hear your take on things?"

"Well, guys, one of my officers was making some rounds around the halls of the hospital and found one of the nurses knocked out and his uniform gone. About that time, a nurse who didn't quite look like his Huntington General Hospital badge photo ID tried to force his way into Vivian's room, but the officer stationed by her room door prevented such."

"Did you guys get the culprit?"

"Hell no! Forgive my language. He struggled out of the officer's grip on him and ran out of there before hospital security could get there to help or close down the place. We had the officer meet with a sketch artist, so there is a small lead there."

"Sounds like you are on the right track, Chief. You did the correct thing in moving the victim immediately. She just wasn't safe there anymore. We are all trying our best. Don't worry; the Good Lord is on your side. I believe that."

"Thanks, Brad. You two try to get some rest also."

"Hey, we will try. At least we already had a plan in place should something happen."

"You guys, please give me a daily update. We'll call back and forth as needed. I want to handle this case. You know I'm actually hands-on with my detectives."

"No problem. Speak to you later."

Agent Davis and Detective Conner hung up and then put their heads back for a few moments of rest.

"This case is going to be something else, buddy."

"Don't worry, Brad; we are experts," Running Horse said as they simultaneously closed their eyes. They'd be at Tampa General soon and then off to the farm to double-check everything.

"Right. Experts. On a personal note, wait until Amanda finds out we went to college together."

"What a hoot! Don't tell her yet. Try to make her guess. It will drive her crazy."

"She's smart. She already thinks something is up between us."

"Whatever. Still, don't tell her yet."

"OK, partner. This is going to be fun. Whatever you say."

They both smiled and then went quiet for a while, putting their hands up under their heads simultaneously and leaning back for a few moments of rest.

After getting a quick phone call from Brad, Amanda scurried over to her office and unlocked the door. She was looking for something in her purse, so she didn't react to what the room looked like right off.

"Good God! What happened here?" Looking around, she could instantly see that someone had gone through everything in her office. Almost all her working papers and files from the desk were now on the floor, flung all over. Most of the books from the bookcases had been thrown all over as well. Her diplomas, certifications, and photos had been pulled off the walls, with a lot of broken glass from the frames scattered. She stood there for a few moments, trying to grasp the scene.

Just then, Dean Russet walked in. "What in the world happened? Man, this place looks terrible! What a mess."

"Oh, hello, Dean Russet. Can you believe this?"

"Well, I will have to call campus security right away. Are you all right?"

"I just got here. Never expected this mess."

"I'm truly very sorry, Amanda. Never expected something like this to happen at Huntington Hills College. I'm starting to wonder about this place. First the other two missing girls besides Vivian, and now this. We have really got to get ahold of all of this."

Amanda stood there dumbfounded and a little bit mad. "Well, yeah. I guess so, Dean."

"I was actually coming this way to find you to discuss a meeting I'm calling with all the campus security tonight. I was wondering what you can fill me in on regarding Vivian. I know that according to the hospital administration, most everything about the patient is presently confidential."

"Yes, that is correct, Dean. What I can share is that Vivian is in pretty bad shape medically. It's a miracle the girl even survived. Anyway, she is safe and being properly taken care of. As far as the other incidents with the previous girls, I wasn't here and really don't know anything about those. You probably don't need any advice from a sabbatical professor, but I would sure increase the security on campus and stress the importance of all the security officers being on high alert. We don't know whether we are dealing with one crazy lunatic or many. This is a serious thing for a campus, as you well know."

"Of course. My feelings exactly. I'm starting to get worried for the safety of everyone—administration, faculty, staff, and student body. All of this is a bit unsettling, to say the least. It is kind of driving me a little crazy. You should have seen Strongwell and his wife when I was speaking to them about everything last night. He has family connections with this campus dating back generations, and he isn't taking kindly to someone destroying the wonderful reputation Huntington Hills College has always had around the world."

"I'm sure. He is so proud of the architecture and everything about the campus in general. His heart must be broken right about now. I haven't seen him lately. Please give him and his wife my very best."

"Dr. O'Neal, do you think you might be able to attend the security meeting tonight?"

"Oh, Dean Russet, I just don't know. I had so much academic stuff to do today, and now this." Amanda pointed at the office mess.

"I can certainly understand, but please try to come if you can."

"Well, for now, I'm going to gather what papers and files I need and take them to my room to work by the fireplace, if you don't mind."

"No, not at all. Whatever you must do to get caught up. I can have security try to clean this mess up for you if you'd like."

"I appreciate the kind gesture, Dean, but for now, I believe I will just gather my things and lock the door behind me."

"Wonder how anyone got into this office. These old door locks wouldn't be easy to bypass."

"The door was locked when I got here just a few moments before you."

"Most individuals around here don't know this, but there is only one main key for each office and assigned room, and then there is a sealed box with master keys in a safe in my office. Just to let you know, I haven't been in that safe for at least a month. It's full of stuff that doesn't need to be utilized on a regular basis. Frankly, I'm a little shocked about this break-in myself!"

"Don't worry about this now, Dean. You've got enough to be concerned about. I'll be fine for now and let you know if something else occurs or if any help is needed with getting my office back to normal. Just leave everything as is. I'll address it later."

"That is fine, Amanda. If you don't mind, I am going to discuss this at the meeting with security. They need to start doing more rounds around these halls to make sure everyone and everything is safe and secure."

Unbeknownst to Amanda, when Dean Russet started to walk down the hall, the dean had a strange, smug smile on his face.

"That's fine. No problem," Amanda replied. She began taking photos like crazy on her cell phone, wanting them to compare to the office when she came back. That way, they'd be able to determine if the items were rearranged or tampered with. Also, she planned on studying the photos to see if anything unusual could be identified. *Man, oh man, what a mess.*

After gathering all she needed, Amanda locked the door. Suddenly, she realized how tired her body felt as she slowly moved down the hall. It seemed each step she took to her assigned faculty sleeping quarters felt heavier and heavier. When she reached her room, she placed the files on her desk by the window and sat down to enjoy the fire in the fireplace. Amanda placed her head on the back of the chair and looked slightly at Midnight from a distance. Midnight yawned as he looked up from his fuzzy bed the maid had placed near the fireplace. He glanced her way and stretched before running to her for some affection.

"Crazy little feline. How are you doing, boy? Sorry I haven't been around much. Hope the maid, Megan, has been taking good care of you. I've missed you, buddy."

Midnight gracefully jumped into her lap and began to purr as she scratched the top of his head. Amanda then quickly dozed off.

In her deep sleep, she thought she heard a pounding sound on her door. *Wait. That sounds like Ryan. No. It can't be. I've got to wake up. Wake up!* Suddenly, Amanda jumped up and staggered to the door.

"Ryan, is that you? It sounds like you are crying. Hold on. I fell asleep in the chair by the fireplace, and I'm trying to unlock the door. Ryan, what is going on?"

The door flew open, and Ryan stood there with tears running down his face. He was crying like a faucet, with his eyes showing a spooky kind of stare.

"Ryan, what is wrong? Tell me!"

"It's Ian. Amanda, he's gone! Oh, saints preserve. My sweet bairn has been taken. My laddie. He is gone! I can't take it, Red. I can't take it if anything bad has happened to him."

Ryan crumpled to his knees, sobbing like a baby. Her strong, masculine Ryan, destroyed in a second. Amanda sat down beside him in the hall. All she could think to do at that moment was hug him tightly.

"No! We won't accept this, Ryan. Do you hear me? We will get him back. God will protect him. God will lead us to him. God will put his circle of protection around Ian. I know this. When you speak in the name of Jesus Christ, there is great power. Sh, quiet your heart now. I am here. We will find our little Ian. We will prevail. He will be fine. We must believe this. Quiet now. I will call Chief Braxton Ward and tell him everything. You and I will then travel wherever we must go to claim our Ian. Your heart is broken, but I will not leave you. I will not! Neither will our heavenly Father."

Chapter 16

To Ireland

It was dinnertime in North Carolina, and the fall weather seemed to have kept the crowd at a minimum in the airport. No direct flight to Dublin International Airport could be presently found, but whatever it took, they would get there as soon as possible.

Ryan and Amanda sat to the left, past the middle of the plane, where it felt quieter. Their fingers and hands were interlocked as if they were one. They closed their eyes and leaned their heads back in rest.

Softly, Amanda spoke. "Rest now, my Ryan. I know in my heart that Ian is well. We will find him in time. We will! God is on our side." She then laid her head on his shoulder.

He opened his dark blue eyes for a few moments, looking out in a daze, as if he were in a trance or something. "I will not be able to go on in life without my Ian. I am sorry. I love you more than you will ever know, but Ian is part of my soul now and forever. I will not be able to go on, no matter how much I believe in God."

"Sh, my love. Until we know otherwise, we place Ian's life on this earth in God's protective care. I believe it is not Ian's time yet to cross over to our Savior. He has too much to accomplish, and we have too much love to give him. The guardian angels are with him. They will not fail us. Our spirits must remain strong and determined to find the lad and bring him home. We are educated, sensible individuals. God, his angels, and maybe also the Irish fairies will lead us to him. We must believe."

"Aye, I have no other choice. The laddie has a part of my soul."

"I believe you. If that is indeed true, then without a spoken word, he will think and pray to bring you to him. Ian, with our heavenly Father, will show us straight to his location. Ian is smart. Remember that! You taught him to be strong."

"I know what you say sounds good, but Ian is not even four years yet. Such a small bairn of mine he is. But I will try my best to be strong for all of us. I always told him that no matter what happens in this life, I will always love him and do my best to protect him. He knows that. I only pray he senses we are looking for him. He knows how to leave signs or messages if anyone takes him. Please, my Ian, lead Da to you. Please! Please, may there be no harm to my little lad."

"Once we land at Dublin International Airport, where is our destination? Do you know where to begin?"

"We will head for the place where I used to visit Ian before he became mine by law. We will let them know what has happened, so if Ian or anyone attempts to contact them, they will be on alert. I always showed Ian photos of the building where he was cared for and the wonderful people there. We would often speak of the orphanage. We'd go over their phone number and pertinent names there all the time, so he'd not forget. He knows. He also knows my contact information and a Father Bryan's, which I drilled into his little mind. He is smart about that for sure."

"OK, what if there are no clues there?"

"We'll head for County Meath, about thirty miles from Dublin. Mullaghmeen Forest in Meath is an isolated area of forest rising above the farmland of north Westmeath. We'll have to take a bus to reach where we need to go by the forest. I've already contacted Father Bryan there. He is an old friend of mine. He runs a tiny church and abbey there. Father Bryan will assist us with getting proper horses and needed supplies. I'm afraid we will have to travel to an area in the forest that can't be reached by a vehicle."

"That's OK. Shawn and I always rode on the farm. I've had much practice with horses."

"Thank God. You couldn't be as helpful if you didn't know a little bit about riding and the outside."

"Well, as you know, I've a little tomboy in me."

"For sure. I'm taking us to the area where I originally found Ian. I just have some feeling he may be near that area. I'm hoping at least. Don't really know why, though."

"We'll follow your instincts, unless we get some real evidence of another location right away. But why would anyone take him back into the forest where you originally found him?"

"Can't say I know an answer to that, but I have this strong feeling inside. When the weather was so bad on the day I found him, there was this strange feeling about the forest. Like I had just come upon a location where something awful had just occurred. Like a battle or fight. A sense of urgency came upon me, and I got us out of there. I always wondered if someone was watching us when we departed. Like I said, though, it was so cold, and Ian wasn't clothed properly."

"Maybe someone has been looking for him all this time."

"No one ever came to the orphanage and inquired about him, to my knowledge. Police always told me there was a lot going on at that time in the area. Unrest of some sort. Maybe between gangs or Irish Mafia. I don't know. They told me when I adopted him that he could be a child of someone like that. Their instructions brought warning that I'd have to be on high alert with the lad. At least until he was older."

"That is why you have been so careful in North Carolina then."

"Aye, apparently not careful enough."

Amanda didn't know how to respond to that comment, so she patted his arm and closed her eyes in prayer. She kept saying in her mind, *We have to succeed. We must succeed. Show us the way, Lord. Show us the way. Lord, make Ian know in his young mind and heart that we are on our way. Give the child inner peace. We are coming. Show us the way.*

After getting a connecting flight, they finally reached Dublin and found a hotel to rest and eat to regain their strength for what lay ahead of them. Ryan also contacted Father Bryan, who indicated he had the horses and proper supplies in place.

Once the bus dropped them off at the abbey on the outskirts of Mullaghmeen Forest, they'd sit around a table together to determine what course of action to take next. They had to decide whether they would involve local authorities. If so, how would they answer the endless questions? All that could waste valuable time. Another thought was that if someone was keeping a watch out, the person might see law enforcement and take Ian away before they got to him. Father Bryan had been instrumental in Ryan's adopting Ian, so he was just as upset about the events as they were.

The fall weather was getting colder by the moment, which made time of the essence to get to the thicker area of the forest where Ian had been originally found. The goal was to get there as soon as possible, locate Ian, and get out before winter started to show itself. Who would have thought Ryan's nice trip to the forest for photography would have been instrumental in his adopting wee Ian and now in the search for the lad to bring him home again. *Home* meaning back in the arms of Ryan McFarlan and Amanda O'Neal.

Father Bryan was as faithful as ever, meeting Ryan and Amanda at the place where the bus dropped them off. The men did a firm handshake and then hugged.

"Father Bryan, I want you to meet my love, Amanda O'Neal."

"Nice to meet you, my lady. Welcome to our tiny church and abbey near Mullaghmeen Forest. 'Tis called the Haven. People around these parts know to where you are referring when the words *the Haven* are spoken."

"Good to know, and nice to meet you also, Father Bryan. Um ..."

"What is it, Amanda?"

"Well, forgive me for being so bold, but Father Bryan speaks like he was born Irish or Scottish and is black. His eyes are as green as emeralds!"

Father Bryan slapped Ryan's back as they both laughed. "Aye, I am black, Irish, and Scottish. The family legend is that when my great-grandfather's eyes glanced upon my great-grandmother Jasmine for the first time, he never lusted for another woman from that point forward. Jasmine was so beautiful that her name was often mentioned in the same sentence as *black goddess*. There was much mystery and prejudice around her when she first came upon this land, but once the people tasted her glorious cooking, she was protected as well as revered by all who knew her. 'Tis said that many came just to taste her food. Jasmine O'Duinn stories cover this land for miles."

"That is something, Father. I don't know about Ryan, but I could sit down and eat one of her meals right about now. I'm famished!"

"Well then, we must head for the abbey first. There we will eat, drink, rest, and do some strategizing on your trip. The Good Lord has told me that Ian is safe and waiting for you. I am sure."

Ryan glanced over to Father Bryan O'Duinn for a few quiet seconds. "From your lips to God's ears, Father."

Amanda smiled softly and whispered, "For sure."

Chapter 17

At the Farm

There was a strange quietness around the farm. In Florida, the fall had brought a reduction in the heat. Mornings seemed to be cooler, with a few rainstorms in the afternoons. Quite beautiful the farm was. All the trees danced in the wind as if on guard should anything happen. The animals as well as the individuals sensed that there were important things to be accomplished there, especially the protection of Vivian.

There were FBI agents and police officers strategically assigned to the farm for Vivian's sake, all wearing regular plain clothes. No uniforms were visible. Some busied themselves with various farm tasks as they kept a keen eye out for any possible unusual activity. The help was appreciated by José and Soledad.

Others walked the grounds as if they were just going for a casual stroll to enjoy the property. Hopefully, no one would ever guess what was really going on, except, of course, those in charge. Everyone in town knew that Shawn, Amanda's deceased husband, and Amanda came from large families, so thus far, those in authority didn't feel that anyone was questioning why the farm had extra people around.

Vivian lay on the couch with Jasper, supposedly the barn cat, sitting beside her legs and purring, with Royal, Shawn and Amanda's beloved Labrador retriever, sitting on the floor nearby as Vivian scratched his head. Her mother, Lisa, was sitting in the lounge chair beside the couch, reading a book. The fire in the fireplace felt comforting, and for the first time in a long time, Vivian felt safe.

"Mom?"

"Yes?"

"This place is so comforting. Don't you agree?"

"Yes, dear. It was so nice of Dr. O'Neal to suggest this place for your recovery and protection. She must be a special lady."

"Oh yes, Mom. You will love her. I will never forget all she has done for me. She is like that with all her students. She says her students are her children. We always laugh to ourselves and remember that when she corrects us in the classroom. Man, we thought she was so mean on the first day of our classes."

Lisa snickered to herself while still looking at the pages of the book she'd found on Amanda's shelf. "That is lovely, dear."

"I wonder where she is now. Hope she is OK!"

"I'm sure she is fine, Vivian. Concentrate on yourself for now, and get well as soon as possible. A lot will be happening in the future with a possible trial. You need to be strong."

"Yes, Mother. I know I have a lot more healing to do. Inside and out. I wish Dr. Travis Marshall from Huntington Hospital was still here."

"Well, he is a busy man. I feel like he really cares about you as a patient, Vivian. Just remember that no matter what, you and I must stick together and remain positive."

"OK, sure. It's just that sometimes that's kind of hard, you know, under the circumstances. Oh, here are FBI agent Maxwell Davis and Detective Brad Cooper."

Her grayish eyes seemed to perk up a little as both guys walked in. Brad was fiddling with his hair, as the wind had given it a whirl. Maxwell removed his black cowboy hat, and they sat across from Vivian and Lisa, enjoying the fire for a few moments before speaking.

"Well, girls, how's it going?"

"Girls! I like that. Haven't heard that in reference to me for a long time," said Lisa.

Maxwell snorted in laughter. "Well, ma'am, we aim to please."

"Well, thanks anyway."

"Yeah," Brad replied. "How do you like Soledad's cooking? Man, that woman can cook up a storm."

"Really," Maxwell said. "Maybe I ought to hang around here more instead of the office."

"Soledad's cooking is fantastic! I feel like I've already gained ten pounds, and we've only been here a few weeks. Hope Vivian continues to gain like me. The only problem is that she is the one needing weight, not me. What are you guys doing back here?"

Brad paused for a moment before leaning in and speaking softly. "Vivian, Maxwell here informed me that when you first spoke to Amanda—you know, Dr. O'Neal—you told her you were in great danger. You also indicated that if she didn't get you out of Huntington General Hospital, they'd find a way to kill you to keep your mouth shut. Do you remember telling Dr. O'Neal that in your hospital room?"

"I remember. Yes, I told her that. I was medicated, but I knew what was going on. I knew she was there."

"Good. Now that you've had a few weeks at Tampa General Hospital and here, Maxwell, Detective Brooks, and I want to start to test your memory to see if you can provide us with clues to get whoever did this to you. We need to help Chief Ward and his law enforcement team up there in North Carolina. We'll start out slow and then work up to hopefully some information that will help everyone. Do you think you can do that for us, or do you need some extra time just to continue to heal? What do you think?"

"No, it's OK. I'll tell you if I can't take any more. Do you know when Dr. Marshall will be back to see me?"

Maxwell looked a little funny and replied, "Um, not sure, but I'm sure he'll be back soon to check on you."

"I sure hope so. I feel safer medically when he is with me."

"We can understand that. For sure," Brad quietly replied.

"So what is it about that statement I said to Dr. O'Neal? Remember, I'm a criminal justice student of hers. She has taught us well. I'm no dummy!"

Maxwell said, "Oh, we know that, Vivian. It is just that the injuries you're still healing from are so serious that we aren't sure if you've gotten back all your memory."

"Well, not all of it."

Brad proceeded. "Don't worry. I'm sure it all will slowly come back to you. What we are interested in tonight won't take that long. I promise. In the statement I referred to, we are most concerned about the word *they*. Do you know for sure if there was more than one individual who chained you up and tortured you? Carefully think, Vivian. Don't be afraid. When you think back, think of it as evidence, not bad events that happened to you. Think like a detective. Think how Dr. O'Neal taught you as a professional after the criminals."

"Maybe this is still too hard for her right now." Lisa voiced concern.

"No, Mom. I can do this. Wait a moment. I just need silence and to think."

Everyone remained quiet for a few moments. Maxwell got up and stirred the ashes in the fire to make sure it wouldn't go out. Brad got up and warmed Lisa's coffee. The three of them sat down, waiting in anticipation. Finally, Vivian spoke.

"There was more than one. I'm sure of it."

Brad looked at her and replied, "How is that?"

"Because I remember hearing someone giving orders to a few other people. When the main voice gave directions, the others responded to him. I'm sure they were all male. I don't remember a female voice. I think I heard at least three voices. I'm sure of it. One was the leader. Another was really mean, and another sounded like he was being forced into it. I don't know! I'm getting confused now. OK, I need to think some more. There was more than one. There was!"

Brad reached over and softly touched Vivian's arm. "It's OK, Vivian. It's OK. You did great. Rest now, and be at peace. Maxwell, Brooks, I, and all the special people here on the farm will not let you down. We won't. Know that. We are all here for you. We are here. Quiet yourself now, and have a restful evening with your mom. Besides, I see you have some personal admirers here with Jasper and Royal by your side. You must be special, because Jasper is usually very grumpy and almost never leaves the barn. She once saved Shawn from an intruder in the barn. Royal here usually sleeps with José. He knows you need him more than José does right now. Royal won't fail you. You won't, right, Royal?"

With that comment, Royal sat right up and lifted his paw for Brad to grab.

"OK, Royal. It's a deal. You are the assigned guard dog. Good boy!"

Maxwell and Brad stood and wished Vivian and Lisa a good night before leaving without another sound.

Lisa stood and locked the door after them. "It's been a long evening, Vivian. Let's get ready for bed. I'll let Royal out to do his job, and Jasper can wander back to the barn."

"No, Mom, let them stay a little bit longer. Please!"

"OK, just for a while. I'm going to get my pjs on and brush my teeth. Just sit here with them and rest. I will be back."

The fire in the fireplace continued to snap and crackle as Vivian slowly drifted off. Lisa let Jasper and Royal out and covered Vivian with a blanket. She clicked the last light out and headed for the bedroom. All seemed well.

"Rest, my sweet baby. Please rest in peace tonight."

A few hours later, Lisa heard Vivian frantically screaming. She jumped from her bed, ran to Vivian, and placed her arms around her in a hug.

"Sh, my baby, it's all right. Everything will be OK. Quiet now. Mother is here. I am with you. You are not alone."

Vivian, shaking and crying, said, "Oh, Mom, I had a dream. It was like I was still there in chains. It was horrible!"

"I know, Vivian. It must be horrible. All those terrible memories constantly circling in your mind. I'm so sorry you must go through all this. The doctors told you there would continue to be instances like this while you are trying to think back and remember details. So sorry, my dear."

"It's OK. I really do want to try to help everyone to catch those villains. They need to be stopped, Mom! They are just going to continue doing this with other girls if I don't get the evidence out of my head to stop them."

"I know. Don't put a lot of pressure on yourself, though. These things will come out naturally as time goes by. That is what I think anyway."

"Well, I don't know about that. Detective Brad said I should think back throughout the day and try to remember. After all, I am going into criminal justice as my profession. Maybe all these bad experiences will help me be better in my profession in the future. Guess I've just got to toughen up."

"No, sweetheart, you are quite tough enough. In fact, you are amazing!"

"Really?"

"Stronger than anyone I've ever known. But besides that, you must give yourself time to heal. Trust in yourself, and trust in God. He is there for you. He is there for all of us. He will help you remember, Vivian. Just give it some time. Now, be at peace. You are safe here. There are a lot of people putting their lives on the line for you, so have faith in everyone as well as yourself. Now, try to get some rest. Do you want me to sit here with you?"

"No, Mom. I'll be OK. Thanks. I think I'll stay here on the couch tonight rather than in the bedroom. It feels nice here by the fireplace. Night, Mom."

"Good night, sweetheart. My room is just next door if you need me again. In fact, if you get lonely, you can join me in my bed. You know, just like when you were a little girl." Lisa gave Vivian a great big hug, rubbed her back, and then slowly walked to the bedroom.

Vivian lay there watching the flames from the logs in the fireplace. She placed her mind on everyone working to protect her and on God being there for her. Finally, in the comfort of those thoughts, Vivian slowly drifted off.

Chapter 18

Campus Atmosphere

Another semester faculty dinner with Dean Russet in the great dining hall arrived. The room was, as always, beautiful and lovely to dine in, but it was obvious that both Professor Ryan McFarlan and Dr. Amanda O'Neal were absent.

Professor Timothy Norman leaned over to his wife, Professor Karen Norman, and whispered, "Oh God, another evening of having to sit here and listen to Dean Russet go on and on about everything. Well, my dear, at least the food is good, and you know how I absolutely love these huge fireplaces around us. It sure was cold out there today. Unbelievable!"

Professor Karen Norman moved closer to her husband and whispered a reply as she clinked her goblet full of Perrier water against her husband's goblet as if making a toast. "Yes, Tim, the food is delicious, but I must admit I am really missing the company of Amanda and Ryan. What an unusual couple they are. Always a joy to talk to. No boredom when those two are around. I bet how they originally met is quite a story."

"Oh yes, I agree. Quite a couple. It seems like it's been around two weeks now since I last spoke to Amanda near the library. She indicated she was going in there to do some research. Honestly, I really haven't seen either one of them since then. Wonder what is going on with those two. A little mysterious, if you ask me."

"Mysterious for sure. When you are a sabbatical professor, you just don't get up and disappear. Strange. Hope they are OK. Maybe Dean Russet knows something about that and will fill us all in on the details. I love gossip, you know."

Tim laughed. "Don't get your hopes up, baby doll. The dean is not necessarily someone you can trust. I know that sounds a little tough. Sorry! In fact, that is something Amanda and I briefly spoke about that day. About how bizarre Dean Russet is. Just someone you can't quite figure out. How in the world did he get to be the academic dean of this fine institution anyway?"

"Beats me. He probably has some family connection or pull by someone high up that got his foot in the door. Who knows? Forgive me for saying this, but sometimes when I look at the dean, I wonder if he is really a guy. Maybe he is a she. Don't tell anyone I said that. I will deny I ever said that."

That comment made Tim laugh, and he whispered in his wife's ear, "Really? You are unbelievable! We should make a bet between us on whether Dean Russet is a guy or a gal. Just between us."

"No way; that wouldn't be kind. Besides, the dean has always been genuinely nice and accommodating to me. Whatever supplies I needed for my art classes, he obliged those needs immediately."

"Really. Well, just so those are the only needs he is accommodating."

"Oh please. Don't be ridiculous. You are my only knight in shining armor."

Tim laughed again softly in her ear and then gave Karen a kiss.

Just then, they heard Dean Russet move his chair and stand at the end of the table like a king ready to speak to his subjects.

"Well, I see that love is in the air for some of our faculty." The dean's eyes focused on professors Tim and Karen Norman.

Looking at the dean, Tim replied, "Sorry, Dean Russet. Guess we don't get out much as a couple."

"Good answer, Professor Norman. That means both of you are working hard in your academic departments, as you should. You are assets to our engineering and art programs."

"Thank you, Dean. Your support is appreciated. After all, we are primarily here for the students. To help them. Our paychecks aren't bad either."

Everyone in the room snickered.

The dean continued. "OK, settle down now. As usual, tonight is one of our semester dinner meetings. I hope all of you enjoyed the food and comradeship. There are several subjects I'd like to discuss with all of you this evening. First is the security of the campus. After this incident with one of our criminal justice students, Vivian Smith, we are on high alert. Recently, Huntington's police chief, Braxton Ward, informed me that Vivian's incident was not the first. Apparently, there were at least two other student incidents prior to Miss Smith, in which prior campus administration originally believed the students had left the campus and their dorms due to poor academic achievement. Now police are investigating the disappearances of those students as well. All females from the same dorm areas. For these reasons, you will find that the campus's security force has been dramatically increased as well as stepped up. In other words, you may see campus security where you have never seen them before or just more frequently. Don't be alarmed by this. Chief Ward and I are working together with campus security and Huntington law enforcement to find those involved in committing these horrendous crimes."

A faculty member from the other end of the table shouted out, "You mean there are possibly multiple people committing these crimes?"

"We don't know that yet, but that is something the police department and security here on campus are looking at. We don't have enough information to confirm anything yet, but we are getting close to resolving this. So basically, about campus security, keep your eyes and ears open, and stay alert. The safety of campus students, faculty, and other college employees is paramount. Now, if anyone has any other questions or concerns about security, please feel free to contact me, and we can discuss. Are there any more questions at this time?"

Professor Timothy Norman shouted out, "We are missing the presence of Dr. Amanda O'Neal and Professor Ryan McFarlan. Do you know anything about their absence here today and if they are OK?"

There was an awkward quiet for a few seconds. Everyone could see a little frustration show on the dean's face before he spoke. "Yes, thank you for bringing that up. Many of you here may not have seen them around campus of late. Chief Ward has informed me that they have had a profoundly serious, unexpected family issue present itself, and both have had to go help that family member immediately. Besides that, I am afraid I haven't any additional information. I am not sure whether they will return to the campus or not. Since they are sabbatical instructors, we were able to obtain other teachers to take over the courses they were to continue to handle."

Another faculty member spoke out. "Besides increasing the security around the campus, which we are most appreciative for, do you know what is presently happening with the investigation regarding Vivian Smith?"

"Honestly, I don't know much. Chief Ward has a team of basic law enforcement, detectives, and FBI agents analyzing all evidence obtained related to her case and the others previously discussed. They will update the public, meaning us, as they feel necessary. What happened to Vivian Smith, and possibly these two other prior students, is horrendous, to say the least. We all must be careful for sure."

Someone sitting closer to the dean said, "Many of us had Vivian Smith as a student. She is a lovely girl. Are we able to go visit her in the hospital?"

"Unfortunately, I do not believe Vivian is still at Huntington General Hospital. As far as I know, she has been taken somewhere else for medical attention and safety. The FBI is also involved now. I have no knowledge as to where she is presently. I will inform Chief Ward of your request. Perhaps he will be able to pass on your good wishes. Are there any other questions in relation to security or the matter of Vivian?"

Once again, the room was eerily silent. Everyone was processing all the vague information. All the questions addressed only created more questions. Would everyone be safe on campus? Were there horrific criminals walking around the campus, looking for their next victims? It was beginning to feel as if the campus circumstances were more serious than the dean was letting on, or the law enforcement and FBI wouldn't have been lurking around, making everyone feel like a suspect. Besides that, where were Professor Ryan McFarlan and Dr. Amanda O'Neal really, and why? What was the real status of Vivian's health, and where had she been taken to? Those present left the faculty dinner with more concerns, frustration, and fear than they'd had prior to coming.

As Professor Tim Norman and his wife, Karen, were walking out, he suddenly looked to her and said, "I don't like this at all. You know, Amanda gave me her phone number, thinking we could all get together on a double date. I'm going to try to call her."

"If you don't get any additional information, then what?"

"I guess I will call Chief Braxton Ward or even pay him a visit. Something sounds not quite right about all this. I'm sure other faculty members have concerns also after tonight. Man, I feel like I should get my guns out at home and keep them loaded! Maybe come to the campus with one of my guns strapped to me. I have a license to carry, you know." Tim rubbed a hand over his face. "I don't know. Maybe I'm making too much of all this."

"You can say that again! Come on; let's go home. I'm tired of all this stuff. I'm going to get my pjs and fluffy slippers on, sit in front of the fireplace, and have some hot chocolate."

"Sounds good to me. Hope we can get all our minds off everything for a while."

They all slowly left the dining hall and disappeared into their vehicles. There was no telling what all the conversations would amount to that evening. An unusual faculty meeting had transpired. When all the dishes had been cleared from the dining table and the crystal chandeliers had been turned off, all that remained in the dark were the fading embers in the fireplaces at the ends of the large room. Once again, the mysteries of the old campus remained.

Chapter 19

Evidence Sharing

Detective Brad Conner walked swiftly into the North Carolina police department with an overnight bag over one shoulder and papers in the opposite hand. The wind was strong, causing his thick, wavy black hair to fly around his face. Walking right up to the front desk, he said, "Hello. I am Detective Brad Conner from the Tampa, Florida, Police Department. Chief Braxton Ward is waiting for me."

"Welcome, Detective Conner. The chief is in what we call the think-tank room, going over the Vivian Smith case with some of our best detectives. He will be pleased to see that you made it just in time to join the case review."

"Good."

The young front desk officer walked in front of Brad. "Follow me, sir. I will be happy to show you the way."

"Thank you very much."

They turned the first corner of the hall and entered a large office area just to the right. There were numerous desks for the detectives, with smaller rooms at the back for private meetings and evidence brainstorming.

Once they reached the back of the room, the young officer, known as Joey to everyone, slightly opened one of the doors. Joey did a soft knuckle tap before entering and respectfully addressed the chief.

"Sorry to interrupt, Chief Ward, but Detective Conner from Florida just arrived, so I brought him straight here."

"Good job, Officer Hanover. Thank you for walking Detective Conner to the room."

The young officer's pale face immediately turned red with embarrassment due to the chief's compliment and the smiles on the faces of the detectives sitting at the table. Chief Ward walked around the table to shake Brad's hand.

"Glad you made it, Detective Conner. All of us are thrilled you made it on time. Hope your trip was pleasant. Oh yeah, and don't worry about Officer Hanover. Joey is a good boy just getting started. Very eager, as you can see. That is how we like them. Willing and able to learn."

Brad smiled. "Well, Chief, I look at him and wonder if I looked that young when I first got started. Anyway, my trip here was good. Not to sound inappropriate, but anytime I can get additional rest away from my two little troublemaking twin toddlers, it's a blessing."

Everyone at the table laughed for a few moments.

"Well, we all remember when we had young children like that while trying to work serious cases. It's hell, to say the least!"

"You can say that again. My beautiful wife, Lorri, is about to kill me. I had to promise I'd do all kinds of stuff from her honey-do list around the house once I got home. She does understand the importance of this case, though. Believe me, that woman is a blessing and a saint all in one. I'm a lucky man, to say the least. Hope my little guys don't drive her crazy before I get home."

"What are their names?"

"Oh, my little monsters? Their names are Benjamin, after Lorri's father, and William, after my late father. We call them Bennie and Billy."

"That is really nice."

"Thanks, Chief. Yep, those little guys and Lorri are reasons for living. Anyway, I'm excited to get started to see what you guys and gals have come up with evidence-wise. We could have discussed this with a phone conference, but I really wanted to meet everyone working on this case. Comradeship never hurts an investigation. Also, I personally wanted to look at any additional photographs and pieces of evidence I may not have had knowledge of prior to now."

"Well, Brad—may we all go by our first names in here?"

"Sure, if it's OK with everyone around the table here."

All present nodded in agreement.

The chief walked back to his seat. "Let me do some quick introductions, and then we'll get started. Brad, I'd like you to meet one of our top detectives, Sara Johnson."

Brad took a quick glance at Sara and was impressed that such a young, beautiful, and petite black woman had made it to detective so fast. *She must be a tough cookie*, he thought.

The chief continued. "To her left is Jerald Mills."

Brad glanced at the white middle-aged man and could immediately tell he was seasoned in investigation. *No greenhorn here. Definitely from the Deep South.*

"Across from Jerald is Luther Cane. Luther and I solved many a case around here long before these others were even in the department. Believe it or not, for a while, Luther and I were it as far as detectives are concerned. Remember, Huntington is still a small town, but it certainly is growing."

Luther, an older black man, appeared to be a seasoned detective who projected great confidence in his own abilities. Brad thought, *Maybe Luther's been around so long he might retire soon. Once the investigation gets into their blood, it's very hard for detectives to move on. Still, we'll be able to use his talents in this case for sure.*

"Bet you two have some real case stories to share!"

"You better believe it," Luther replied with a smile. "This Vivian Smith case has so many facets to it. It would be a real icing on my retirement cake to help solve this one."

"For sure, Luther," the chief replied. "We have other fine detectives like these also in the department, but presently, the individuals in this room are the main detectives assigned to this case as well as the other similar campus cases. There is another seasoned detective familiar with these cases, Garcia Diego, but he is working on something else today, due to his Spanish-speaking ability. We'll catch him up to speed tomorrow."

"Yeah, he is a real pill," Sara Johnson added. Everyone else in the room seemed to smile and shake their heads.

"Garcia don't play when it comes to crimes like this in our own territory. Especially at Huntington Hills College since his middle daughter is going there now."

Brad looked up from his notes. "Nice to personally meet all of you. I know you've been working very hard to get the criminals who brutalized Vivian Smith as well as any similar campus victims from the past. Looks like the chief has a great team! Thank you so much for allowing me to be part of this evidence review."

The chief rubbed his hands together while looking at everyone. "Shall we get started?"

Sara immediately stood up. "Sure, Chief. Luther and I have visited Vivian's dorm room, where she was allegedly originally abducted.

We've been through everything there again with a fine-toothed comb. More than attempting to gather additional trace evidence, we were there to study the surroundings. To try to learn more about the victim and why someone might have selected her. We wanted to investigate her world a little bit more and then build a profile of what type of individuals would do such a thing to her."

Brad leaned over the table toward her. "Did you come up with any additional evidence or complete a profile?"

Luther broke into the conversation. "Yeah, we picked up a few additional trace-evidence items that were sent to the lab. We're still waiting for results to compare to what Dean Russet's security team gathered. The sad thing, though, is that her room appears to have been gone over by several others prior to us. Originally, our crime scene investigators told us there were so many prints in there it may be hard to pinpoint an alleged criminal from all the other students in the dorm hall. I mean, except for the mess caused by her struggle, on the night in question, the room appeared clean in comparison to other dorm rooms we've seen. Underneath the bed, way in the back, we found a capsule stuck in a wheel on the bed frame. Maybe the lab will get a fingerprint from that or at least be able to confirm that as the substance the culprit or culprits used on our victim, Vivian Smith. Hopefully, that will give us a lead."

"What else did you find?"

Sara jumped in. "A piece of chewed gum stuck on the front of the bed frame. As clean as Vivian appeared to be with the rest of the room, I highly doubt she would have left a piece of gum like that on her bed. Maybe we'll get some DNA from that and be able to compare it to other prior pieces of evidence already gathered for the case."

Brad smiled. "Well, it certainly will be helpful if we get some identifications with what you've found. OK, so now I have some information to share with you. Chief, I truly hope you won't explode with what I have to tell you."

The chief rolled his eyes and mumbled, "What now?"

"Guess it would probably be best if I came right out and told you instead of beating around the bush."

"OK, shoot."

"I don't know, Chief, if I should have clued you in privately instead of in front of everyone on what I'm about to share, but here goes! On the night Vivian Smith was kidnapped, Dean Russet was having one of his faculty dinners. He was sitting in front of everyone in the dining hall, when the butler came in and informed the dean that Vivian Smith was missing. Apparently, the dean also shared that information at that time."

"All right, all of us already pretty much are aware of that."

"Well, being the lawyer and investigator she is, Dr. Amanda O'Neal, with Professor Ryan McFarlan, raced out. Since Vivian Smith was one of her criminal justice students, Dr. O'Neal was immediately concerned about making sure nothing would be destroyed or missed in the investigation."

"You are scaring us now."

"Unbeknownst to everyone, Amanda and Ryan went directly to the crime scene to gather evidence, in fear that pertinent evidence and clues might be destroyed should the campus security get there first. Dean Russet doesn't even know this. Obviously, campus security hasn't had that much successful experience with such incidents since they pretty much blew off the prior missing-student cases. She was afraid that in approaching the dorm room, they might alter important evidence or even destroy it. Amanda always has a crime scene kit nearby, so anything she and Ryan located was properly packaged and sent to Detective Henry Brooks. Brooks has a history as our senior crime scene technician and a high-ranking detective in the Tampa Police Department. Since Brooks is so talented, the Tampa Police Department often rotates his investigative duties, utilizing all his experience, knowledge, and skills. We've solved many cases that otherwise would have remained cold without him. The guy is a genius when it comes to evidence. No doubt about it."

"What are you trying to tell us, Brad?"

There were a few moments of silence, and then Brad proceeded. "What I'm trying to share with you is that there is more evidence than what you presently have. There should not be a problem with a break in the chain of evidence, due to Dr. O'Neal's status. At least I believe a good prosecutor could get around any arguments about its admission during a trial or for the conviction process. Amanda told Brooks right out that she utilized the proper methods in not touching the items of alleged trace evidence. All the identifying pieces of information were placed in plastic envelopes or tubes and sent directly to the crime laboratory Brooks instructed them to forward it to. All of it is being analyzed as we speak. Professor Ryan McFarlan also took color photographs, which we have. If you don't already know, he is a nationally renowned photographer."

Luther Cane rubbed his face with his hands and then replied, "Why is all the alleged trace evidence just being analyzed now? It's been months since the victim was originally taken. Isn't that another problem?"

"That is the sticky part. All the evidence was immediately sent and received, but somehow, someone put the bag somewhere that wasn't immediately checked, so it wasn't found until a few days ago. They can prove it was in a safe place and that the seal on the evidence bag was never broken until they started analyzing it a few days ago. Brooks was so mad that the few hairs on his head stood straight up.

What a mess, right? Still, I think we will be able to use everything if an experienced prosecutor demonstrates his or her talents. Let's hope anyway."

Jerald Mills jumped in. "Do you know what kind of trace evidence we are talking about?"

"Well, if I remember correctly, I think there was listed such trace evidence as hair, fibers, drugs, soil, and blood. Oh yeah, Amanda indicated she had a tiny ultraviolet light in her bag, so she obtained samples of possible body fluids on the sheets, along with fingerprints around Vivian's bed. Tennis shoe prints on the floor as well. She and Ryan covered their feet and hands properly before entering the room. They followed the proper protocol that all expert crime scene technicians do. Brooks taught her well. Believe me!"

The chief rubbed his neck and looked up before speaking. "Man, this case has multiple layers for sure. I pray we don't have trouble getting all that evidence submitted into court. OK, let's make sure all this evidence doesn't get mixed up in any way. I'm talking about our evidence and the evidence you have. If we come up with anything that looks like it will direct us to a lead, then we will start comparing everything to see if we have a match. Fingers crossed, detectives, and please stay alert as you investigate the areas assigned to you today. Remember, we must keep in mind the requirements of proof required in court and attempt to locate related evidence. Also, don't trust anyone. When in doubt, question anyone who has a connection to this case or the previous cases. Let's stay focused, people. The clock is ticking on this. Stay positive and help each other."

Sara softly said, "Yeah, the corpus delicti evidence. You know, guys! Where each criminal offense contains a definite set of elements whose commission or omission must be demonstrated to have occurred in order to prove a case. The corpus delicti evidence substantiates the elements."

Jerald replied, "Sara, we get it. Thanks. The associative evidence should also help connect the perpetrators to this scene or victim."

Luther said, "Of course, or connect the scene or victim to our future suspects. With all this supposed evidence floating around, you'd think we'd get a hit on someone soon."

Brad nodded. "I agree with all of you. There must be more than just one perpetrator involved in Vivian Smith's case and the prior missing-person cases on campus. I kind of feel it in my bones that all these cases are somehow connected. We need to make a big fat miracle happen here and solve these crimes."

Chief shook his head. "Amen to that! This meeting is adjourned for now. Brad, you come with me."

"Yes, sir, coming."

Chapter 20

Beautiful Mullaghmeen Forest

The morning air was cool and getting colder by the minute. Father Bryan, Ryan, and Amanda stood by the abbey entrance to say their goodbyes for now. The horses were packed with all the supplies they would need. There was a nervous feeling around everyone as Father said a last prayer and words of encouragement. Even the horses could feel the underlying tension.

Amanda shook Father Bryan O'Duinn's hand one last time and mounted her horse. "If I do say, Father, these horses are beyond beautiful."

"Yes, Lady Amanda. Ireland is the best place to breed horses. We've been perfecting that for generations. We do love our horses! For sure, Ireland's grand environment and unique climate sure do help. Once you've been around for a while, you'll learn that our thoroughbreds come from the finest Irish steeds and mares. These beauties can race like no other, and they are extremely hardworking. Take, for example, these three horses. They will do you well on the trip to bring our little Ian back. The black steed you are riding,

Amanda, is Black Thunder. He can run like the wind. The gray-and-white steed that Ryan is riding is Spirit. He is the wisest of them all. Pay attention to what he is trying to tell you two. He can detect danger or locate someone like no other. In fact, Ryan, when you get close to the spot where you first found Ian, make sure you have Spirit, and the others smell a piece of garment belonging to Ian. Let them all smell the cloth every so often. They will lead you if they sense the area where he might be. Finally, the last one is Copper. Copper is loyal to a fault. That is why I loaded her with most of the supplies you'll need. She is a good mare, always working hard for her master. These horses are your best friends out there, so treat them well, and they'll help you like no other. Make sure they have plenty of feed, water, and shelter if possible. Get to know them. Sorry—I kind of get carried away when someone speaks anything about our beloved Irish horses. You'd better get along now."

Father Bryan paused and then hugged Ryan tightly and looked into his eyes one last time. "Keep the faith, my brother. Ian is nearby. He knows you are coming. You and Amanda will find him. Oh, and, Ryan, do you have all those special items for the trip that I gave you last night before retiring for some rest?"

"Aye, Father. I have them."

"Good."

"Thanks, Father. I shall never forget all you have done for my Ian and us. Never!"

"Go along now. You're going to make this humble father cry. Be safe. Come straight here once you have him. Don't delay."

Ryan and Spirit rode in front of the line, with Amanda in the middle and Copper following behind. The horses were acting as if they were loving the adventure. It was almost as if they knew they were on an important mission. Amanda and Ryan were glad Father

Bryan had made them put on several layers of clothing and warm jackets. The higher they climbed, the more the temperature dropped, but the fall air felt cleaner and fresher than any Amanda had ever experienced in her life. So much wondrous nature was around them. If she hadn't known better, she could almost have believed they'd crossed over to some other glorious realm. It was heavenly indeed.

"Hey, Amanda, my love?"

"Yes?"

"Don't get Father Bryan started on the subject of horses. He'll preach on that almost as much as our heavenly Father."

She giggled for a moment. "Yeah, I see that."

"He is a wondrous soul, my Father Bryan O'Duinn. I'd trust him with my life any day."

"Well, I guess he is our Father Bryan now."

"For sure."

"Oh, Ryan, look! We are coming upon a stream. The horses can take a small rest and drink."

"Aye, that will be good. This water must be somehow connected to the River Boyne. 'Tis lovely. Our horses will be able to eat as well and gain their strength. Us as well. The temperature is dropping fast as it grows dark. A mountainous, rocky area on one side of us and forest around the stream. We should be safe here. I think we should camp. I will build a fire for warmth and set up the sleeping tent nearby. We can start early in the morning. Maybe the temperature will rise in the morn, and all of us will feel fresh."

"Sounds good to me. A beautiful ride, but it seems like we've been riding for hours. I'm not as young as I used to be, and honestly, I haven't ridden for such a long stretch for quite some time. Come, Black Thunder, Spirit, and Copper. Let me take you closer to the stream and lighten your loads for the night."

136

Ryan did a laughing snort when Amanda mentioned her age. "Once they've drunk and eaten a bit, we can place them near the rocky area to shield them from the cold wind and possible rain for the night. A wondrous place."

"Breathtaking."

"And, Red?"

"Yes?"

"To me, you are still as beautiful as the day I first laid eyes upon you. Shawn and I were sitting under a tree on the campus grounds, watching the chicks, as he called them back then, as the lassies walked by to sign up for their semester courses. Shawn's eyes about bugged out of his head when he saw you walking by. Apparently, he hadn't seen you for quite some time, and you had matured into a beautiful lass from that little farm girl who'd trailed behind him and your brothers several years prior."

"Oh yeah, I remember when you both ran up to me, and he gave me a big bear hug. That was the first time you and I met. Wow, so long ago. My Shawn O'Neal was a handsome brute. Inside and out, he was grand. I will always miss and love him. He was a wonderful husband."

"Aye, and a wonderful friend as well."

"The horses seem happy."

"'Tis a good thing."

"Yes, good. The fire feels nice. Let's break out the food. Suddenly, I feel famished! What did you find in the satchel of food Father Bryan packed?"

Looking into the bag that had been attached to the saddle, he replied, "For tonight, I see biscuits and honey with some smoked jerky and cheese. Oh, a little ale I see in a bottle as well. That should fill our stomachs and help to warm us up as well. Nothing like Scottish and Irish ale for sure."

"Don't get drunk, Ryan McFarlan. I won't know what to do with you."

"Oh, I can think of a few things."

They looked into each other's eyes and laughed. Once the horses were finally settled, he held her by the fire with a plaid wrapped around them. They were each enjoying a cup of coffee.

Amanda had a smirk on her face. "Mr. McFarlan, look at the stars in the sky. I've never seen something so magnificent. The sky is so clear."

"Aye, clear."

"Ryan, are you all right?"

"I am. Just thinking of Ian. I hope he is warm and safe this evening."

"Of course. Me also. I thought about it as well and prayed for him all day. Trusting that God's circle of protection stays around him. What will we do if we search the areas of the forest you are focusing on, and there is no sign of our little Ian?"

"We'll go back to the abbey and regroup. Think of a new strategy. But for some reason, I am being drawn like a magnet to the original location in the middle of the forest. As you can see, this forest rises above the farmland of Westmeath. It's a bit isolated."

"We will follow that instinct for now. God may be directing you there for some reason. He has a plan."

"I wish my faith was as strong as yours."

"Faith is a funny thing. Sometimes you can feel it strongly deep inside you, while other times you must reach for it deep in your heart. Do you know what I mean?"

"I guess."

"Just remember, we are not alone on this search. Our heavenly Father and the guardian angels are with us. I feel it deep within me.

We are being watched over, and so is Ian. When do we call in any kind of law enforcement? The Irish Gardai or Rangers?"

"Father Bryan said if he hadn't heard a peep from us in a week, then he'd call them to head this way. I didn't want them originally involved because it might scare away whoever has Ian; thus, our precious laddie would be torn from us forever. I can't allow that to happen."

"I'm hoping that is a good plan for us."

"It's getting colder. Mayhap 'tis best to turn in and get some rest. It will be warmer for us if we wrap ourselves up together in those sleeping bags. We'll start early in the morning."

Ryan stood up and drank the last of his coffee, holding his other hand out for Amanda to grab and stand as well. After checking the horses one last time, they then walked toward the tent with their arms around each other and climbed in. It was so quiet all they could hear was the tent's zipper closing them in for the night.

After some time had passed, Amanda softly spoke. "Ryan, are you still awake?"

"Aye, I can't seem to sleep."

"Well, tell me a story or something. Maybe we'll both get tired and drift off."

"OK. Did you take a good look at the plaid I wrapped around us?"

"You mean the plaid blanket we were using by the fire this evening?"

"Aye. We call it the tartan or clan wrap. McFarlan is usually some combination of red, white, and blue. So you were wrapped by me in the McFarlan plaid."

"I'm afraid to ask, but what does it mean that you wrapped me in the tartan?"

He let out a soft, deep giggle. "When a lad wraps a lassie in his plaid, it means he has claimed her as his woman. In ancient times, it informed the other lads not to touch her. In other words, she was his property now."

"Great. So now I'm your property."

"Nay, Red. I do not think of you as my property. I think of you as my leannan."

"What in the world is that?"

"*Leannan*, in Gaelic, means 'sweetheart.'"

Amanda slowly turned herself around, and her rusty-gold eyes gazed into his deep blues. They stayed in that position for quite some time while holding each other close in the sleeping bag. She could smell the masculine, woody scent of Ryan, and he could feel the womanly softness of her. A flowery lavender scent hit his nostrils when she moved. It felt as if they were finally home together. Two spirits joined.

Amanda whispered, "Leannan. I like that. I can now acknowledge that I am your leannan."

She grabbed his head from the back, bringing him closer to her mouth. He licked her lower lip and then entered her soft, luscious lips and delved deeper, where their tongues dueled for a few moments.

"That is good to hear, my leannan. You know I'd love to continue this foreplay, but the sun is soon to come up, and we need rest. To be continued."

"To be continued."

Both hugged a little closer, and sleep came swiftly.

Chapter 21

Memories Unfold

FBI agent Maxwell Davis was walking the farm's property to see if anything suspicious could be viewed or sensed. It was his turn. Vivian tried to keep an equal pace beside him, taking two or three steps per his one. Maxwell took off his black cowboy hat for a few moments to slick his raven-black hair back before setting the Stetson back in place. He pulled it down low over his eyes to protect himself from the early morning Florida sun.

"Your hair is getting pretty long, Maxwell."

"Yeah, I'm trying to grow it out for a gal back home. You know the women like men with long hair. Sexy and all, I guess. Trying to impress them with my handsome Cherokee Indian looks." He glanced her way with a steamy, masculine smile.

"Well, I don't know about the hair, but your smile is sure appealing. I'm sure whoever she is will run straight into your arms."

"Sounds good to me," he said with a deep, sensuous tone.

They laughed together for a few seconds, and then Maxwell's look turned serious. "Sorry, Vivian. After everything you've been through, I probably shouldn't kid around like that. I know you are still emotionally and physically recovering from a horrible experience. When an agent spends a lot of time guarding someone, sometimes they kind of get close. You know that I'm here to protect you. Believe me, I take that responsibility very seriously."

"Please don't worry about it. It was nice having a few light moments back there. Almost made me feel like a real person again."

"You are a real person. Never doubt that, but I know what you mean. You'll get there, girl! Don't give up. Do you feel like the doctors are still helping you at Tampa General Hospital?"

"Oh yes. I still have a lot of pain, though. Especially the horrible headaches. Guess it's due to the beatings I endured during the kidnapping. Maybe some emotional stuff too. Like internal stress."

"You still feeling really stressed?"

"Well, I wouldn't really categorize it as stress. Maybe. I think it's more like fear. I'm always afraid someone is going to take me again. Scary."

"We're here for you. Just remember that. Hopefully, we'll catch these bad guys soon."

She whispered softly back, "Of course, everyone has been so helpful. I sure hope they will be caught."

"I can't promise you will always be safe, Vivian, but all of us sure are trying our best."

"I know that. Mom reminds me of that all the time. About you guys having my back, along with the Big Guy upstairs. God." She pointed upward while looking up into the beautiful blue sky.

Maxwell broke FBI protocol and reached over to give her a hug. "Just hang in there, OK?"

"I'm trying. Agent Davis, do you know if Dr. Travis Marshall is coming back to Florida to check on me?"

"Actually, that is one of the reasons I wanted to talk to you. Travis called me yesterday and said he was flying in today."

Suddenly, a great big smile came across Vivian's face. "I'm so happy." She did a little spin and then jumped up and down a few times.

"OK, I'm guessing you really liked him as your doctor in North Carolina, or there is something else going on in that mind of yours."

She glanced back at him with a sweet smile, saying, "Both." They both giggled for a few seconds.

"Well, darling, I'm going to leave that topic alone for a while. Sounds personal to me." He smiled back and suddenly realized Vivian was looking a little weak. Leaning down, she had her hands on the sides of her head, and she started to cough and then dropped to the ground. Maxwell immediately got on his phone and informed the other agents that Vivian needed an ambulance or a helicopter medical transporter to get her to the hospital sooner rather than later.

"Hey, guys, remember, it can't be just any ordinary ambulance transport. Several of you will have to go to Tampa General Hospital with her for guarding purposes. Oh yeah, one of you needs to get to Tampa International Airport to pick up Dr. Marshall. He is coming from North Carolina. The plane should be landing anytime. Bring him straight to the hospital for Vivian."

Agent Maxwell bent down to Vivian with a concerned look on his face. "Vivian, can you hear me? I'm here. It's Maxwell. You hang in there. You hear me, girl? Everything is going to be fine. We're taking you back to Tampa General Hospital. All of this is going to be OK. Remember, God is here."

There was no response, and she appeared lifeless, but he could still feel a faint pulse. There was breathing coming from her nose. It was slight but still there.

Just as he looked up, the EMTs and paramedics came swiftly toward them with a stretcher and with her mother, Lisa, right behind. Maxwell yelled, "Don't worry, Lisa! We'll at least have one FBI agent with her in the ambulance or helicopter to guard her. Several agents will meet the ambulance at the ER entrance or meet the helicopter on the pad on top of Tampa General. You and I will jump in my truck and be right behind them. It's going to be all right." He was trying to convince himself of that as well.

Lisa knelt by Vivian and spoke softly to her daughter. Maxwell saw that the ambulance guys needed more room, so he grabbed Lisa's arm, pulling her up. Maxwell could tell she was scared, so he stood holding her for a few moments.

He whispered softly into Lisa's ear, "It's going to be fine. Everything is under control. Vivian is a fighter. She'll make it. Don't worry. We are all here for her. She knows that. God's right here for her. The protecting ancient spirits too. They are praying for her. They are here for all of us. Come on; let's get your things and head to the hospital."

Maxwell appeared strong and larger than life as he stood there barking orders to all the agents around them, but deep inside, he was also scared. He thought, *This can't be happening. Come on, Vivian. You've got to make it. You must. You've got too much living to still do. Oh Lord, the case. We need you, Vivian. Stay strong.*

Vivian's mother, Lisa, and Agent Davis stood up from the hospital lounge chairs when they saw Dr. Travis Marshall running toward them with a couple other FBI agents following close behind.

Dr. Marshall gave Lisa a quick hug and then shook Maxwell's hand. "How is she? What happened?"

Lisa pointed to Maxwell. "He was with her when it happened."

Travis looked as if he almost had tears in his eyes. "Agent Davis, details, please?"

Maxwell took a deep breath. "Well, early this morning, Vivian and I were walking the farm grounds. She needed some fresh air, and it was my turn to check the grounds for anything suspicious."

"And?"

"I don't know—we were just walking along, and she dropped. She had just finished telling me she was still having these horrible headaches that just wouldn't go away. The next thing I knew, she was leaning over while holding her head between her hands and did a couple coughs before falling to the ground."

"Was there any response from her at all once she lay on the ground?"

"I'm sorry to say none. I bent down and felt a faint pulse as well as signs of breathing around her nose. That is basically it, Dr. Marshall."

"Man, I thought we were making progress." He paused for a moment, thinking. "OK, how long before you got her back to the hospital?"

"Well, we were going to transport her by ambulance, but when the EMTs and paramedics saw her condition, they immediately called for the helicopter. It landed on the farm property within fifteen minutes. I'd say they got her here within twenty-five minutes or less. Not any longer."

"Good, good. All right, I'm going to locate the doctors treating her presently and see what I can find out. Since I've stayed in touch with them professionally from the beginning, they've involved me in her care. Hopefully, I will be able to view her records and see her."

Lisa reached over to Dr. Marshall and gave him another hug, a little longer this time. "Thank you, Travis. Thank you for professionally caring about my daughter."

He slowly let go of her and then looked into her eyes while whispering, "Well, Lisa, I don't want to get myself into any kind of trouble—you know, lose my medical license or anything—but Vivian and I have stayed in touch personally quite a bit since her transport from North Carolina to Tampa. Confidentially, my caring is a little more than just professional. I'll say no more for now. Please keep what I just said under wraps for now. Please! We can talk later. For now, I just want to help her medically any way I can." Dr. Travis Marshall then headed for the nurses' desk to see what was going on with Vivian.

Lisa stood there in shock with her mouth open. "Um, I wasn't expecting that. Was he inferring what I think he was inferring?"

A smirk formed on Maxwell's face as he replied, "Well, he is kind of young. You know, Lisa, it wouldn't be the worst thing if Vivian ended up marrying a doctor."

Lisa raised her hands to her mouth and then started to laugh. "Miracles never cease to amaze me, Maxwell."

"You are telling me! I just got done talking to Vivian this morning about the guy. I kind of thought something was going on by the way she was acting. She was so excited that he was coming today that she jumped up and down in pure happiness."

"Do you think they are truly in love?"

"Only the Big Guy upstairs knows that. Sure sounds like it! For now, we must stay focused on getting her feeling better and staying safe."

"You are right. It's just kind of a shock. Yes, we've got to focus on her healing."

"Maybe the doc will help her do that faster."

"I sure hope so. All I can think of is to get all this mess over with as soon as possible so we can get some normalcy back in our lives."

"Yeah, I'd like to get this case solved and your lives back to normal as soon as possible. Whatever normal is. As an FBI agent, I'm not sure I know what that is."

"I'm sure. Come on, Maxwell; let's go get us some coffee and food. I'm thinking it's going to be a long night."

"Coffee sounds good," he replied as they walked together down the hospital hall to the elevator.

Lisa rubbed her eyes and removed Maxwell's large leather jacket, which had been kindly placed over her in the night. She stretched for a moment, hitting Maxwell accidentally on his shoulder. Just as his eyes peeked at her from the side, Dr. Travis Marshall walked swiftly toward them to give an update.

"Hey, guys. Well, Vivian has made it through surgery. Thank God. Due to all the blows she received on her head while she was kidnapped, Vivian had quite a concussion. Unbeknownst to doctors, her head started to bleed internally again since her last MRI. Man, that was a close one! No worries, though. Surgeons got the blood clot causing the trouble and cleaned up the bleeding. She must have felt the pressure on her skull like crazy."

Lisa rubbed her eyes with a Kleenex before asking, "Did she come to at all yet?"

"Believe it or not, she actually came to for a few seconds and then drifted back to sleep."

Agent Maxwell Davis rubbed his overgrown facial hair. "Um, did she say anything?"

A boyish smile came over Marshall's face before he replied, "It was a miracle. She briefly looked at me before saying, 'You're here.'

Then her mouth did a tiny smile before she went under again." Dr. Travis Marshall seemed pleased about that comment.

Lisa nervously responded, "What do you mean 'went under again'?"

"Well, the anesthesiologist said Vivian was the first he'd seen to wake suddenly like that after such a surgery. Most people stay unconscious. Basically, they've now put her in a semi comatose state for a while to give her brain some time to heal. We'll keep a watch on her. Everything looks good now. Only time will tell."

"When can I see my daughter, Travis?"

"Give us another forty-five minutes to get her completely settled in a room, and then you both can go in. We don't want to tire her body out too much."

Agent Davis let out a big breath and then looked up. He placed his hands together as if in prayer. "Thanks."

The three of them stood there for a few moments, and then Maxwell glanced toward Lisa. "I'm going to give detectives Brad Conner and Henry Brooks a call so everyone knows what is going on. Brad's been in North Carolina, working with Chief Braxton Ward and his detectives on Vivian's case and the previous cases where the female students were never found."

"Go ahead, Agent Davis. Dr. Marshall and I will be fine."

"Oh, Dr. Marshall, please keep me informed on everything. I know we are all first concerned about Vivian, but I must also be diligent to relay all details about her, due to the importance of her as a future criminal witness. Sorry to say that, Lisa."

"No problem."

With that, Dr. Marshall turned and headed back to check on Vivian again.

Agent Maxwell dialed Detective Brad Conner. "Brad, are you there?"

"Yeah, I'm here. What is up, Running Horse?"

Maxwell chuckled for a second. "A lot going on here in Tampa, Detective. Get your butt back here, man!"

"OK, settle down. Tell me what is happening. Have you called Brooks yet?"

"Hell no! Lisa and I've been at Tampa General Hospital the last twenty-four hours while Vivian had brain surgery."

"What in the world? She is all right?"

"She came through the surgery good. Dr. Travis Marshall says so. Apparently, they are in love. Confidential, that is. There was a new blood clot and bleeding on her brain, but Travis says they took care of it. They've got her in a semi coma for a few days to help her brain heal. Hopefully, we can talk to her in a few days."

"Man, remind me not to leave home very much. Between all the news you've given me and Lorri going crazy with our toddler twin boys, I'd better get back sooner rather than later."

"Sounds good to me, buddy."

"Don't forget to call Brooks to clue him in on all the details. We can't lose her. Please!"

"You can say that again. How has it been going in North Carolina?"

"Great, actually. Chief Ward has a fantastic investigative team here. It is an honor to work with them. I will tell you all about it later. Hopefully, I will be home in a couple of days."

"Good."

"Hey, call me again if any additional emergencies happen down there."

"Sure. See you."

"Later."

Maxwell hung up from the call and motioned to Vivian's mother. "Come on, Lisa. Let's go check on your daughter."

They walked to the nurses' front desk, and the head nurse led them toward the appropriate hall door. A couple of FBI agents followed directly behind them.

Everyone at the hospital involved with Vivian's case in one form or another felt a little numb as the days went by, waiting for her to wake up and assure all of them that she was going to make it. That day came, and she opened her eyes to find her mother, all her assigned physicians, Dr. Travis Marshall, FBI agent Maxwell Davis, and Detective Brad Conner.

Her main surgeon, Dr. Toni Russo, placed his face close to her face and spoke softly. "Vivian, hello. I'm your surgeon, Dr. Russo. You are at Tampa General Hospital after having emergency brain surgery. Vivian, you can wake up now. Are you there?"

Her eyes fluttered for a few seconds, and then they opened. Everyone gave her time to focus. Just as Dr. Russo was going to ask her a few questions to see if her thinking was in order, she opened her mouth, glanced straight at Detective Conner and Agent Davis, and said, "Randy."

"What did you say, Vivian?" Brad was so surprised that the question just popped out before anyone else had time to respond.

She kept looking directly at him. "Randy is the name of one of the guys who hurt me. Randy Kuznetsov. His nickname when he was taking courses at Huntington Hills College was Blacksmith. I remember more things now."

Everyone was so shocked that they stood silently for a few seconds, and then Brad turned to Maxwell and whispered, "Randy Kuznetsov. Alias Blacksmith."

"Wow," Vivian's mother said.

With that, Dr. Russo continued his examination, and Detective Brad Conner and Agent Maxwell Davis swiftly left. As soon as they were in the hospital lobby, Brad dialed Chief Ward.

"Braxton? Oh, sorry. Chief Ward?"

"Detective Conner. How are things going in Tampa? You kind of left in a rush the other day. Everything all right?"

"Chief, Vivian just woke up from her induced coma, and first thing right off, she gave us a suspect name."

"That is great news. What is the name?"

"Randy. Randy Kuznetsova. Alias Blacksmith. He is a former student of Huntington Hills College."

There were a few seconds of quiet that felt like forever, and then Chief Ward replied, "We are finally getting a break in this case. Praise God! Randy Kuznetsov. Wow! Don't worry, Detective Conner; the team will get right on it. Let's talk tomorrow afternoon. Give us a few hours to gather as much evidence as we can. Tell Agent Davis that I said to get some rest. Looks like we are all going to be racing against the clock once some evidence on this guy is obtained."

"Got you, Chief. Talk to you tomorrow."

Brad immediately hung up from the call as he and Maxwell headed for his truck. "You drive, Running Horse. Frankly, my adrenaline is going a mile a minute. I've got to calm down for a few moments before I get home to Lorri and the boys."

"No problem, Brad. Just sit there for a few moments and catch your breath. Running Horse has everything under control." They both smiled and drove off.

Chapter 22

Investigating

Detective Jerald Mills and Detective Luther Cane had spent most of the morning walking through the wooded area behind the campus dorms. Their goal had been to get to the garden area the college utilized for their botany, culinary, and horticulture departments. The talk of the town had always been that in those gardens, the ingredients of the campus's secret tea resided.

For now, the detectives were more interested in the small shack to the right of the field. Detective Brad Conner had mentioned it when they were all in the think tank. Dr. Amanda O'Neal and Professor Ryan McFarlan had apparently told him about seeing Dean Russet and the butler, Covington Strongwell III, allegedly pick some herbs, as well as finding some chains in the shack.

"Look, Luther. There is the shack we are looking for. Finally! Between you and me, I'm as cold as a frozen chicken in the freezer. Let's check things out and get back to the office as soon as possible."

Jerald and his southern twang and analogy set Luther off into another laughing jag. "You, Detective Mills, are too much. Southern through and through. Unbelievable. I know you are cold, but we are here to locate some evidence, so tighten your coat and britches, and come on. I'm not young, you know. The word *retirement* is already written in ink on the chief's desk for me. If my old bones can take the cold, so can you."

"OK, let's go in for a look. We need to be careful. Here—put on these shoe covers and rubber gloves. We don't want to destroy any evidence if any is around."

"Got it. Thanks, partner."

"Hey, Luther, look at all the herbs and stuff hanging around. Actually, it doesn't smell too bad in here."

"Yeah, well, it still feels kind of creepy, if you ask me. I'm going to walk toward the back of the shack, where it looks something like a horse stall. You keep looking around here in the front for anything that appears strange. You know what I mean."

"Sure, OK. No problem."

A few moments later, Luther called out, "Jerald, can you come down here, please?"

Jerald glanced at Luther's eyes and knew something was up. He looked bug-eyed and a little disturbed. Jerald glanced over Luther's shoulder and knew what all the fuss was about.

"Wow, maybe this is where Vivian was tortured or originally kept."

Luther shook his head. "Do you think? Look at the blood drops on the hay and dirt. Unless I'm just plain stupid, I don't know of any plant grown out there that bleeds."

"It looks like someone was trying to cover the blood and stuff up by placing fresh hay around it. I'm going to take a few photos and samples to show the rest of the team."

"Good idea. You'd better shoot some photos of the outside and inside of this shack. The surrounding area too. Take photos of everything, Jerald. Hey, wait a minute." Luther pushed some of the mound of hay away from the edge of the stall, where he thought he saw a metal object. "Now we are getting somewhere!" Luther yelled.

Jerald dropped what he was doing for a moment and returned to Luther's side. They just stood there for a few seconds, looking at the hooks, chains, and leather wrist and ankle straps. There were a few whips farther down in the hay.

Luther took a big breath. "Jerald, my partner, all I've got to say is, let's get these bastards! Call Chief Ward. He needs to see this firsthand."

"Man, Luther, right under our noses."

"Yep, we've got them now. There has got to be some trace evidence around this place."

"Sure thing. Hope we get some fingerprints."

"That would be great. Come on, God; show us the way. Help us stop this pure evil for good. Help us catch Randy Kuznetsov and the other monsters."

"For Vivian Smith and the other girls."

"Yes, Jerald, for everyone and for the glory of God."

"Amen to that, Luther."

"Amen indeed. In the mind of this old detective, I am God's warrior, and I'm not going to stop until we catch these wicked pieces of crap. Let's put an end to this evil madness for good."

"I'm with you. Dialing the chief as you speak."

Dean Russet and Chief Ward stood a few feet from the shack as officers yellow-taped the area off.

The dean looked up at Chief Ward with troubled eyes. "I know this investigation is extremely important, but taping the area off kind of leaves me in a pickle with the college. We need this area for the botany, culinary, and horticulture departments. There are research projects with grants attached to them as well as classroom assignments. What a mess!"

The chief softly placed one of his large hands on the dean's shoulder and looked down with a sympathetic smirk. "Don't worry, Dean Russet. This will only take two to three days, and then everything can be back to normal. For once, the students will have a valid reason for not getting their assignments in on time. Have the grant people informed also. We've lost two students, and one was seriously injured. This campus investigation is important. You know that."

"Yes, of course, Braxton. I hear you. I'd better get back and let everyone know what is going on. We'll make sure the students are informed not to travel this way. If a student comes near this area, please send him or her back to campus. Probably to my office, for that matter."

"Sure thing, Dean. Don't worry. We are going to get these culprits."

"Good to know. I'd like to keep Huntington Hills College's good reputation."

"I hear you."

As the dean started the walk back toward the campus with a couple of campus security and one of his assistants, Chief Ward strolled around the taped-off area, checking to see if he spotted anything helpful.

When he was finally alone, Chief Braxton Ward's thoughts continued to turn like wheels in a clock. *Finding the chains and stuff in the shack almost feels too easy. What are we missing, Lord? Maybe the individuals got sloppy because no one was checking this area. Maybe they are trying to lead us away from another location. I've got to really think this through. Help us, heavenly Father, and we will give you all the praise. Help us.* As fast as his pleading prayer ended, a certain Bible verse instantly came to his mind: "No one will be able to stand up against you all the days of your life. As I was with Moses, so I will be with you; I will never leave you nor forsake you. Be strong and courageous, because you will lead these people" (Joshua 1:5–6 NIV).

The chief shook his head for a moment in amazement and then walked to the end of the field, to the left, where he spotted the beginning of a stomped-out path almost hidden by foliage, going away from the garden, deep into the woods. Another second looking another way, and he would have missed it. He immediately waved his arms toward detectives Luther and Jerald to join him.

"Hey, look, guys. There is a path over there. I almost missed it, but I bet that will lead us to another significant location. Maybe where the girls were possibly kept. Get a team of officers to follow the path to see if they find anything. You may need some supplies— you know, water, food, emergency kit. Jerald, you'd better go with them. You start in front of the grid search, and take any necessary photographs. The crime scene technicians are too busy here. Luther, you stay with me for now."

Detective Jerald Mills immediately sprang into action. Down the path he went with a few officers and necessary backpacks.

Luther looked deep into the chief's eyes. The two seasoned law enforcement experts could almost read each other's mind.

The chief rubbed the top of his head and then said, "I know what you are thinking, partner."

"No, you don't. OK, what am I thinking then?"

"You are hoping that maybe we will find the other girls alive."

Luther glanced up to the sky for a split second. "Well, that sure would be a miracle."

"Yes, a miracle. Reality tells me it has been much too long. I'm going to give detectives Henry Brooks and Brad Conner in Tampa a call to keep them in the loop on what is happening here. We all need to meet here within twenty-four to forty-eight hours. No later."

"Sure thing, Chief. Oh, I forgot to tell you that the FBI just arrived. Guess FBI agent Maxwell Davis wants to talk to you. They've got a helicopter on standby to check the surrounding areas where Jerald and the officers are heading. What do you want me to tell them.?"

"Time is of the essence now that the news of us being at this location might have already begun to spread throughout the campus. We can't take any chances. Have the helicopter go now, as we speak, while there still are a few hours of light today. Please send Agent Davis directly to me."

"OK, Chief. I'm going to call Detective Sara Johnson back at the office to see if she has found any leads on Randy Kuznetsova."

"Luther, once you get back to the office, set up the largest think-tank area we have. We need to go over all the information and evidence we have. Time to get the wheels of justice moving faster. I want everyone involved in these cases to be there as soon as possible."

"Done, Chief. We're hot on their tracks now. Victory will be ours!"

The chief remained standing there. *God, I sure hope so.*

Agent Davis held up his phone as he swiftly walked toward the chief. "I've got one of my agents on the helicopter on the phone. I think they've spotted something about three miles down that path. Looks like Detective Jerald and your other officers are about a half mile from where they saw something suspicious."

Chief Ward got on his phone. "Detective Mills! This is Chief Ward. Can you hear me?" Finally, after a few seconds, Chief heard Jerald's voice.

"Hey, Chief. I can hardly hear you. What's up?"

"Can you hear the FBI helicopter hovering around you?"

"Yeah, we wondered who that was at first but then saw the FBI seal on its side with our binoculars. What is happening? Have they seen anything?"

"Yes, Agent Maxwell Davis is here with me, and one of the agents in the helicopter said they saw something suspicious about half a mile from where you are. Keep walking straight another half mile. Let me know when you reach that destination."

"OK, Chief. Will do."

Chapter 23

Deep in the Forest

Amanda and Ryan's traveling seemed slower than in the beginning. The wind had grown a bit colder and sharper as they rose a little higher in their climb. They decided to stop one last evening before, hopefully, finding the correct destination.

The horses appeared to be glad to finally rest for the evening. They seemed to be having a good time together, chomping on some hay Copper had carried and drinking water from a nearby stream. Since the air was much colder, Ryan made sure the horses had their warm bulletproof and waterproof coverings on for the night. For extra comfort, he and Amanda had tied some extra canvas they had brought to make a horse shelter. For now at least, their horse companions looked content.

"We're coming upon the fifth day, Amanda."

"I know. Don't worry. Tomorrow we'll locate Ian, or if nothing else, the Irish Gardai or Rangers will reach us."

There was silence for a moment as Ryan continued to build the fire, poking the embers to help the flames rise to engulf the logs sitting above them.

"The warmth from the fire feels cozy."

"Aye, lass, cozy. We'll sit here for a while and enjoy before retiring to the tent."

Amanda giggled to herself for a few seconds, until Ryan couldn't stand it any longer. With a big smile, Ryan glanced her way and said, "Pray tell, Red. What in the world are you giggling about?"

"Oh, I don't know. When you said we'd sit by the fire before retiring, the phrase made me feel like we were sitting in a huge, wealthy mansion or somewhere all prim and proper instead of sitting by a fire in the deep forest in Ireland. You know, with our butts freezing from the cold fall winds."

She heard his deep, masculine laugh. "Well, what can I say? We're in nature. The best home I know a person can be in. It's wondrous up here in so many ways. So enchanting, with an isolated feeling."

"You're right. Breathtaking beauty everywhere."

"Finish your coffee and food, woman! I don't know about you, but I want to get my butt warm."

Amanda smiled at him with an impish grin and yelled, "To the tent!"

"Yes indeed. To the tent!"

In the tent, they lay quietly holding each other for a while.

"You know, Red, I'm an Ulster boy."

"Um, OK, what does that exactly mean?"

"That, my dear leannan, means I was raised in the province of Ulster in the north of Ireland. The McFarlans of Ireland are mostly found in Tyrone and Armagh, counties of the province. My last name can, of course, be spelled many different ways. It's an anglicized form of the Irish and Scottish surname Mac Pharthalain from long ago. We are a very proud people. When I was a wee one, my seanmhair—grandmother—used to tell me Gaelic mythology stories. Parthalan was a native of Grecian Sicily and the first king to take possession of ancient Ireland. So she used to say our McFarlan name was derived from the Gaelic meaning 'waves of the sea.'"

"I like your bedtime stories, Mr. McFarlan. Are you getting warm?"

"Aye."

"Good," Amanda responded while cuddling closer to him with a soft smile upon her face.

"Anyway, there is a reason for my tale. I want you to know what you are getting yourself into with me. My history. Upon this eve, I want to handfast with you. Just you and me."

"What exactly does that mean, my Ryan?"

"They used to do it in ancient times. It was a medieval practice abolished around 1939 by Scotland. It means just the two of us, without witnesses, make a promise of marriage that is to be done in the future. Like you are married even though you haven't done the legal ceremony yet. In the past, the handfasting without witnesses would last one year and one day, and then they had to have a wedding ceremony before that time ended in front of a priest or clan laird. You know, where the marriage would be recorded by the priest or laird for proof. A long time after that came betrothal, where a man and woman pledged their troth to each other in the presence of only themselves or witnesses. Their love was seen as a gift of God. They'd hold hands and then wrap the man's plaid—Irish or Scottish clan colors—around their hands, signifying they were now one. Their hands bound together were the evidence of the binding of their spirits."

A tear slowly moved down Amanda's cheek as she looked deep into his eyes. Her reply was a soft whisper: "We can have a traditional marriage ceremony once all of us return to the abbey at the Haven."

"Yes, Father Bryan will be ecstatic to perform the ceremony."

"Ian will be ecstatic also. We would finally have a complete family."

"Aye, 'tis what this excursion is all about. Ian is forever in my heart as my little laddie, but soon he will be ours."

Amanda replied with an "Aye," and Ryan snickered quietly while he continued to hold her tightly with his deep blue eyes sparkling.

"Amanda Lynn Livingston O'Neal, I, Ryan Michael Christopher McFarlan, choose to handfast with you this night. I don't remember the Gaelic words right now, so I will do the best I can, lass. We need this in case God's plan isn't as we expect, and one of us doesn't come through this."

Looking seriously into Amanda's beautiful rust-colored eyes that carried flecks of yellow and green, Ryan held her face close to his. His low, masculine voice was soft and shaking with emotion as he attempted to earnestly begin speaking. There were a few seconds of silence between them, almost as if time had stopped, and then he began.

> "I, Ryan Michael Christopher McFarlan, do take thee, Amanda Lynn Livingston O'Neal, and bind us together through handfasting forever more from this day forward, for better or worse, for richer or poorer, in sickness and in health, to love, cherish, and obey each other, till death do us part, according to God's holy ordinance, and thereto, Amanda, I plight thee my troth."

Amanda's mind and body felt almost numb as she gazed deep into Ryan's blue eyes. It was like looking into two pools of water. For a few seconds, she thought there was soft fairy music around them. Overcome with emotion, she paused and then replied,

> "I, Amanda Lynn Livingston O'Neal, do agree to handfast with you, Ryan Michael Christopher McFarlan, this very night with all my heart and all that this sacred pledge

holds, according to God's holy ordinance, and thereto, Ryan, I plight thee my troth."

They were one, standing upon their knees, continuing to embrace, kissing as they had never done before.

He finally lay over her and artfully began removing, one by one, all her articles of clothing. Amanda started to undo his belt and jeans zipper, and Ryan immediately responded by grabbing both her hands and swiftly raising them above her head. He got up and removed all his clothing. She looked at him for a few seconds, and with a devilish smile, he shook his right index finger back and forth as if saying, "No deal. I'm in charge this evening."

"Do you trust me, leannan?"

"Yes."

He slowly moved his thumb across her full lower rosebud lip back and forth.

Starting around one of her ears, Ryan nibbled for a while. He then traveled down her neck to her shoulders with butterfly kisses, until he reached her breasts. She felt his eyelashes sweep across her skin at times and his breathing as his lips traveled down her body. Amanda's body felt electric at that point—so much so that she almost forgot to breathe.

Without warning, he grabbed one breast and began to suck ever so slightly at first as he held the nipple of the other breast between his fingers, moving it back and forth. As he rotated from one breast to the other with his mouth, Amanda's breathing became more rapid. Down below, between her legs, the heat was getting hotter and hotter, with moisture starting to come from her vaginal flower. She grabbed his shaft, feeling how hard it had gotten, rubbing back and forth for a few seconds.

"Ryan, now. OK?"

"No, leannan. Not OK. Be patient like me."

Playfully slapping her hand away from his manhood and raising it again above her head, Ryan continued to kiss down to her stomach and thighs, toward her magical bud. Her desire was climbing to madness as the pressure below intensified. He could hardly contain himself.

"You're going to kill me for sure!"

He let out a deep giggle and then tenderly raised her legs over his shoulders to be able to suck and devour around her clitoris. Heat began moving swiftly up her legs as everything seemed to go multicolored with the explosion from her body—just what he was hoping for. Her body shook for a while as he lovingly stretched her out under him.

Her tiny whimpers and then a scream drove him crazy, and he wondered how much longer he could take it.

"Red, sorry, but I can't hold it any longer."

Ryan opened her thighs with one knee and positioned himself, entering her slowly at first and then increasing the motion, thinking to himself, *Lord, help me. I'm not a young man here. Not wishing to use God's name in vain, but I might need a bit of help here for my lassie.*

With that, they both came together. Their first fireworks were much better than both could have imagined—so much so that they made love another time before reaching total exhaustion.

Before Amanda drifted off to sleep in Ryan's arms inside the cozy sleeping bag, she heard his voice softly speak.

"Not bad, my friend," he said as he looked down to his privates. "I guess God does answer prayers in time of immediate need. I finally made love to my leannan. My Amanda. Thank you for her. Glad I didn't have a heart attack. Believe me, I give you all the praise! Oh, heavenly Father, I know I've asked for a lot on this eve, but could you not forget to lead us straight to Ian tomorrow? My precious little laddie. I love him so. Please, Father! Good night."

Amanda woke in the morning to the smell of coffee and warmth from the fire outside the tent. She felt surprisingly refreshed. She sat up and stretched out her arms while yawning. Just as she popped out of the sleeping bag to get her clothes on, the tent flap flew open, and there was Ryan with an impish smile on his face and a fresh cup of coffee.

"Did you have a good night, wife?"

"Hubba-hubba. Oh yes! How about you, husband?"

With that comment, he gave her a kiss.

They broke camp swiftly once both had gotten up, dressed, and eaten. The horses were getting restless, as if saying, "Hurry up! Let's go!"

Once on their way, they galloped at a faster speed. Black Thunder raced past Spirit and Copper, taking the lead for a while, as if to say, "Time is of the essence."

Finally, all the horses came together again at a normal pace, leading Ryan and Amanda deeper into the forest.

"Ryan?"

"Aye?"

"What was Father Bryan talking about as we were leaving? He asked you if you'd remembered the special items he gave you."

"I have them. A cross around my neck. A Bible with my other belongings. Finally, a gun in a place where I can swiftly reach it if necessary. Do you have your gun near, Amanda?"

"Locked and loaded. It's ready should we need it."

"We're getting close to where I originally found Ian. I can feel it, and Spirit does too. We've risen above all the farmland of north Westmeath. About as high as it goes in Mullaghmeen Forest. It's said this is the lowest forest in Ireland."

"Really? Great. Now I really feel tired, like I'm a baby. Seems like we've ridden through all of County Meath, County Westmeath, and Mullaghmeen Forest."

"We probably have. Sorry. If it makes you feel any better, Mullaghmeen Forest is the largest planted beech tree forest in Europe. As you can also see, there are other types of trees, like Sitka spruce, Scots pine, noble fir, and more. Nothing like the woods at Huntington Hills College, though."

"I see. How did you get permission for us to ride horses in the forest and camp?"

"Don't ask. The public paths were closed to the public this week."

"Another miracle."

"You could say that. Father Bryan O'Duinn knows how to do that for sure."

Ryan slowly climbed down from the horse and reached into a leather pouch carrying one of Ian's small sweatshirts. He bent down low to allow Spirit to smell the shirt, since the steed had been nibbling on some grass nearby. Ryan then went to Black Thunder and Copper, repeating the process. All the horses became a little restless. Spirit suddenly raised his head and made a soft sound while breathing out.

Amanda, on Black Thunder, had been following along while drifting a bit as the movement of the horse relaxed her. "Ryan, what is going on?"

"We're getting closer to where we should be, Red. I just stopped to let the horses smell Ian's sweatshirt. I believe they can feel Ian's presence in the forest. Amazing!"

"Well, praise God for that! See? I told you we'd prevail in our search. God and his warriors are with us. The angels are here. I know it! It's like I can feel them around us like a circle of protection. Like we could almost touch them if they were in our sight. Besides, Ian knows we will be there for him soon."

Ryan stood there for a few seconds as his hope grew stronger. "How do you know that?"

"I don't know how I'm aware of that. It's just there in my heart and mind. Father Bryan must be deep in prayer for all of us as we speak."

Ryan got back onto Spirit and then turned the horse so the horse was in the lead once again. Next came Black Thunder in the middle and, finally, Copper at the end, as it should have been.

"OK, Spirit, show us the way. You, Black Thunder, and Copper will lead from this point on. Father Bryan told us to let them guide us when we got close to the exact location. Do your magic, you two steeds and lovely mare."

Chapter 24

Campus Revelations

While the remaining officers spread out through the Huntington Hills College woods, Detective Jerald Mills, with two other officers, rounded the corner toward what looked like a cave entrance, which was almost hidden by shrubbery around it. The officers had already begun to check around the bushes and rocks. They could still hear the FBI helicopter above them as its light shone down brightly to assist in their search. Jerald waved his flashlight back and forth to let them know they'd found something, and then he heard the helicopter turn to land in a clearing not far from where he stood. Footsteps and yelling from FBI agents and other officers could be heard coming from all directions as Detective Mills stood at the opening of the cave, shining his flashlight toward the ground, where two different shoe prints could be detected. He carefully stepped around them and had the area blocked off.

They were losing evening light, but some fresh footprints had also been detected along the path, which was already being handled appropriately by a crime technician. Time certainly was of the essence, as the temperature continued to drop, and the sun began to set.

One of the officers approached Jerald, smiling with pride while holding a tiny object with a pair of tweezers in one hand and a small evidence bag in his other hand. "Hey, Detective Mills, I found this piece of cloth in the bushes. Looks to be from a woman's torn blouse or dress."

"Great work. Bag it."

Just as Detective Jerald Mills was bending down near the cave entrance, Chief Ward and Agent Maxwell Davis reached him.

The chief worked to catch his breath. "OK, Detective, what'd you find?"

"Well, thus far, we've found fresh footprints back around the path and two different shoe patterns near the cave's entrance, with some scraping marks. Not sure what that is all about. Officer Elmer here also just found a piece of cloth appearing to be a piece of a woman's clothing. Not sure yet. Anyway, look down here, guys."

By that time, everyone was standing nearby in a half circle. FBI agent Maxwell Davis bent down and took a closer look where Detective Mills was pointing with his flashlight.

He took off his cowboy hat and brushed back his long jet-black hair with his right hand. Finally, pointing, Maxwell looked back at the group.

"Well, guys, there is some barely visible dried blood with some lose hairs caught on this specific rocky location. Wow, Jerald, how in the world did you see that?"

"It seemed to be directly in my sight path, I guess."

The chief rubbed his chin. "A miracle. These criminals are either sloppy or plain stupid, leaving that there. I'm no rocket scientist, but it looks mighty suspicious if you ask me! Considering, of course, I do have almost forty years of law enforcement experience."

The group stood there for a few seconds and snickered to themselves. Maxwell rose from his knees and then turned toward the group standing behind them.

"Don't take this wrong, Chief, but I think my FBI agents should take it from here. We need to get down that cave as soon as possible. I know night is upon us, but what if there is another victim down there alive and suffering? We just don't know."

"All right, Agent Davis. I know your team has more experience than we do at this point, so take the lead, and get down there."

"OK, assigned agents, please gather the necessary equipment we'll need. Make sure someone is setting up a station over there with a tent overhang, so we have a proper communication station. Tape off this area for now. The chief and Detective Mills can wait at that station while we agents enter the cave and check everything out as much as possible for tonight. Tomorrow we'll reenter and gather any pertinent remaining evidence. Tonight we're more interested in locating any suffering victims if they exist. The rest can wait until the morning. I'm sorry, Chief, but some of my agents and your officers will have to stay the night to protect the alleged crime scene."

"No problem. I'm not leaving myself until I'm assured there isn't anyone down there in need of medical attention. After all, the whole campus, including these woods, of Huntington Hills College is my jurisdiction and responsibility."

"Understood. Our responsibility too, Chief. Let's go, people!"

Detective Jerald Mills took Agent Maxwell Davis to the side and whispered, "I know you are in charge at this point, Maxwell, but please let me enter the cave once your agents are down there if anyone or anything is found. Please?"

"Look, Jerald, I know you are thinking about your career and all the work you've done on this case. If we find victims tonight, they're our immediate priority. If there are victims, we won't do much else tonight, but I'll make a deal with you, Detective. First thing in the morning, you and I will go back down there together before anyone else enters. You've earned that. Deal?"

"Deal. Thanks."

"Sure thing."

Agent Davis and several other trained FBI agents entered the cave that evening. All the crevasses and openings were thoroughly searched, as well as around the small waterfalls and pond in the middle of the cave. Being of Cherokee heritage, Agent Davis viewed the inside of the cave as sacred. He almost felt as if they were disturbing some of the old spirits.

It was difficult, as no light was coming from the cave opening at that hour, but at least they knew what they were dealing with. They could hear the bats above them; most likely, the animals were not happy about being disturbed. Almost done for the evening, Maxwell turned to head back, and then he heard one of his agents.

"Running Horse! I mean sir. Agent Davis, I think you'd better come over here."

Agent Spencer glared his flashlight over a flat ledge above them for Maxwell to be able to see everything. A ladder made of rope and leather hung upon the left end of the ledge, which led to the ledge's large, flat surface—enough room for numerous people to reside or hide. Another opening in the middle of the ledge was visible.

Agent Davis stood there in amazement and then glanced at Agent Spencer. "Let's go."

Before they started their climb, Maxwell called the other agents to wait below them and assist with additional light and supplies when needed. Maxwell glanced at the iron chains attached on each side of the cave and pondered what those had been utilized for.

"Oh my God! What in the world have we come across?"

"A torture chamber, sir. Take a glance in the small entrance here."

There the agents found the remains of two dead females. Agent Spencer grabbed his mouth so as not to throw up on the evidence. Whips and other instruments to inflict severe pain lay around the bodies. There were also candles, blankets, and other supplies.

"Sorry, Agent Davis."

"No problem."

Without another word, Agent Maxwell Davis fell to his knees and bowed his head. Softly speaking with tears running down his cheeks, he prayed, "Heavenly Father, please forgive them. They know not what they do. Have mercy on these suffering souls. May God the Father, his Son, the Holy Spirit, and all the spirits from above surround this space of horror and fill it with God's grace. Release any sign of evil that remains to the depths of hell. And, Lord, usher any lingering anguished soul who has long carried the effects of pain home to heaven. Help us, heavenly Father, to solve this case, so no others will ever endure the torture that these two girls and Vivian experienced. We ask you in the name of Jesus Christ and give you all the praise. Amen."

Agent Spencer helped Maxwell up, and the two macho FBI agents patted each other's back.

"That was quite a prayer, boss."

"Well, thanks. We had better wipe the tears from our faces before the rest of the team see us. Don't want to look like a couple of FBI wimps. I just got a little overcome by what they went through here—that's all."

"Nothing wrong with having faith, Maxwell. After all, let's face it. You've got it as a Christian and as a Native American Indian. Pretty awesome if you ask me!"

"That is what gets me through everything we agents experience without going a little crazy. Faith is the answer. Come on, Spencer. We'll update the team waiting below, get out of here, and return in the morning."

Both carefully hurried down the ladder, filled the team in on what they'd found, and headed for the entrance of the cave. Suddenly, everyone was feeling the adrenaline-rush exhaustion from the day. It was time to get a few hours of shut-eye if possible.

True to his word, early the next morning, Detective Jerald Mills and FBI agent Maxwell Davis entered the cave first before anyone else. This time, Maxwell knew exactly where to direct everyone to go. They had described the cave crime scene beforehand, but once they got a firsthand view, everyone was sickened. Experts from the coroner's office bagged the victims' remains, while crime scene technicians scurried around, gathering all the evidence they could. Chief Braxton Ward, Detective Luther Cane, and Detective Sara Johnson were also there.

The techie girl, Detective Johnson, glanced over the whole scene while feverishly tapping on the iPad in her hands and then made eye contact with Chief Ward. "Man, I sure hope we get some fingerprints, DNA evidence from blood spatters, or something."

Deep in thought, the chief turned. "That sure would help us, Sara."

She kind of shivered for a few seconds since the chief had never voiced her name before without uttering the word *detective* in front of it. She guessed he and Luther were too astonished as they looked around. Her quiet response was "Yes, of course."

Luther slowly turned to the chief. "Braxton, doesn't it make you super angry to think that while we've been shuffling papers and supposed evidence back at the office, these cruel and wicked nutballs have been doing this kind of stuff? Right on campus property, no less. Frankly, it makes me mad as hell!"

"You better believe it, partner. You better believe it."

Detective Johnson suddenly let out a deep breath. "Come on, you two. I'm going to assist in getting all this evidence properly packaged and taken to the crime lab as soon as possible. Maybe Detective Henry Brooks, the great crime scene expert from Tampa, Florida, will have some ideas on how to speed up this evidence analysis process. I think I've seen enough of this place."

Chief Ward and Detective Cane turned to go as well. "Good idea, Detective Johnson. You can personally transport the bagged evidence we have thus far, so there is no breaking of the chain of evidence for legal purposes. Make sure one of the crime scene technicians goes with you. Remember, no mistakes, people! I'll meet you back at my office. Someone must control the media, along with the nerves of the campus and community in general. See all of you later. Are you coming, Detective Cane?"

"Yeah, Chief. I'm right behind you."

Just as they were leaving, one of the FBI crime scene technicians and Agent Davis swiftly moved forward to complete the assigned duties.

"Hey, Chief and Detective Cane, before you leave, we want to show you what one of the guys just found."

"What?"

"You are not going to believe this. Three sets of prints, and one print absolutely belongs to the suspect Vivian identified to Detective Brad Cooper and me in the hospital."

Chief tilted his head. "Randy Kuznetsov."

Detective Luther Cane stood there with a growing smile on his face, speaking in a pitch one octave from a whisper. "We've got them,

Chief! If those other prints are the two monsters who worked with Randy in doing all this evil, then we've got them! Glory be!"

Unbeknownst to everyone, Chief Ward had placed eager young officer Joey Hanover undercover on the Huntington Hills campus as a student named Joey Solomon. Officer Joey was there to see what he might learn about suspect Randy Kuznetsov and anyone else connected to him. Chief knew that Officer Joey was as loyal as anyone in the Huntington Hills Police Department and would keep him informed of any new information as well as observe the campus atmosphere. Waiting for solid information on the other two sets of fingerprints found was stressful for everyone involved in the investigation.

Meanwhile, back at the office, Chief was sitting at his desk with his feet up, while Luther continued to rummage through some files nearby. "You know what, Detective Luther? That Joey is going to make a great detective someday. I never have seen a guy more eager to please than that young officer. Good for him."

"Yeah, that kid is something else. What? Did you send him on an errand or wild goose chase?"

"Yes, you can say that."

The two seasoned law enforcement experts looked at each other as if saying, "Remember when we were young and just starting out together?" Both laughed while looking at each other.

"Hey, Chief, remember when we were both summoned by old Chief Clamps to come into his office on our first day of work?"

"I sure do! Both you and I were sweating like crazy when he lectured us for over an hour. Man, I thought we'd never get out of his office. I had to pee so bad after his speech that I started to question my decision to enter the Huntington Hills Police Department."

They snickered together for a few moments.

"I know what you mean. I felt like throwing up after everything old Chief Clamps said to us. Man! Anyway, Chief, I forgot to tell you that there is a Professor Tim Norman from the college here, waiting to speak to you."

"Do you know what he wants?"

"No, not really."

"OK, Luther, my friend. Show him in. Give me a few moments, though."

"Will do, Chief."

Professor Tim Norman walked in at a confident pace and smiled. "Good morning, Chief Ward. Thank you for speaking to me without an appointment or anything."

"No problem, Professor Norman. Please have a seat. What is on your mind this fine morning?"

"Well, my wife, Professor Karen Norman, and I have gotten pretty close to Dr. Amanda O'Neal and Professor Ryan McFarlan. We wondered what was going on with those two. We've kind of been worried about them. Can you share anything confidentially with us to ease both of our minds?"

"Um, I'm not sure. Wait a minute." The chief slowly got up from behind his desk, walked over to his office door, and quietly closed it before moving back to his desk chair. "If a word of what I'm going to share with you ever gets out, it could mean the possible deaths of some people and the end of my career. Understood?"

"Now you are kind of scaring me, Chief Ward."

"Well, the situation is pretty serious, but all any of us can do at this point is to keep our mouths shut about their situation and pray for them."

Professor Norman sat there silently for a few moments, rubbing his face in thought. "You have our word. I mean it, Chief. My wife almost cried about them the other evening, just contemplating that maybe Amanda and Ryan have been killed or something. Frankly, the whole faculty and student body have been a little stressed about their sudden departure, hearing no word from them or even about them. You know, due to the matter of Vivian Smith and the criminal investigation going on."

The chief moved into his desktop, closer to Professor Norman, and said, "I don't know why, but I believe you for some reason that you and your wife will stay quiet. Being quiet is imperative. I can't stress that enough. You must never say anything to anyone until they return and their issues are resolved. Never tell anyone you received information from me. Agreed?"

"Agreed."

"For Amanda and Ryan, it is a family matter. A life-and-death matter for a little boy connected to them. The small child was recently kidnapped, and they're in a desperate search for him. Time is of the essence to save the child's life. That is all the information I can share with you now, but remember the serious promises you've made today. Don't say a word to anyone about this. Don't speak to your wife about this on campus or in any place where someone might overhear your conversation with her. For everyone's sake, please pray like you have never prayed before."

Standing to leave, Professor Tim Norman held out his right hand to shake the chief's firmly. "Thank you for your honesty, Chief Ward. The information is very much appreciated. I think there will be some heavy prayers for them this evening. Prayers for you and your department as well. You can be assured that these secrets will be kept safe. May God give you the personal strength you need to lead and handle everything."

"Your prayers and confidentiality will truly be appreciated. Take care until we meet again."

"Goodbye."

Professor Karen Norman from the art department walked slowly down the hall toward Dean Russet's office. She had to speak to the dean about how they were going to set up the student art gallery at the end of the semester. The students had worked hard and were excited about the public showing and publicity. Finally, they had something else to think about besides what had happened to criminal justice student Vivian Smith and the other missing girls from the past.

She turned the corner and suddenly bumped into one of the new transfer students, Joey Solomon from Michigan.

"Hey, Joey."

"Hey, Professor Norman."

"How are you liking it at Huntington Hills College?"

"I like it just fine, Professor. It's your watercolor painting class I am enjoying the most. Very informative and relaxing. Maybe someday I'll be able to actually paint something that looks better than a five-year-old's artwork."

"Oh, Joey, you really aren't that bad. I loved the landscape scene you did last week. With practice, you have real promise."

"Thank you, ma'am."

"Anyway, you heading to Dean Russet's office?"

"Yeah, he wanted to talk to me about something to do with my transfer transcripts. We had an appointment."

"Oh, I see. I'm heading that way myself. I just have to talk to him for a few moments about this year's student art gallery."

"I'll walk with you if you don't mind."

"Of course. No problem."

Joey and Professor Karen Norman were just outside the dean's office door. They paused for a moment and then did a slight tap and made a quick entrance. Both of their mouths flew open as they viewed a couple on Dean Russet's enormous desk, doing the wild thing.

Professor Dubois was lying on his back on the desk, with all the stuff from the desk thrown on the floor, including their clothes. He was of slender frame and bald on the top of his head, with the hair around his scalp sticking straight out. He had only his shoes and socks still on, which was quite a sight as his legs flailed everywhere. His boxer shorts had been tossed into the air and landed on the large globe nearby. The boxers were white, with large red hearts on them, and were moving around and around as the globe spun.

The woman on top of him was naked expect for a bra and a cowboy hat. She was moving up and down with her right arm up in the air as if she were riding a bucking bronco. Teacups and saucers sat on the table by the fire with a teapot that carried the aroma of the famous campus tea.

Professor Norman finally said to Joey, "Oh my, it's Professor Dubois from the science department and some lady on top of him. Um, wait a moment. Is that Dean Russet? What? OK, I'm a little confused. Dean Russet?"

Alleged student Joey Solomon, known as Officer Joey Hanover only to Dean Russet, just stood there quietly for a few seconds with his arms crossed. He softly snickered and then replied, "Ride 'em, cowboy."

179

The woman suddenly turned as she realized Professor Norman and Joey were standing there. "Oh, Pierre, you forgot to lock the office door. Oh my word! Wait. I can explain. Please close the door and lock it."

Joey kindly obliged Dean Russet by immediately closing and locking the door. Then he and Professor Norman quietly stood there as instructed until the woman, Dean Russet, and Professor Dubois fumbled to get off the desk, grabbing whatever nearby clothes they could reach to swiftly put something on.

Professor Norman got enough nerve to finally gather herself and speak. "But, Dean Russet, I'm quite confused. You were a man, and now you are a woman? You and Professor Dubois? This is highly irregular, I think."

Dean Russet started to cry. "But Pierre and I are in love!"

Professor Pierre Dubois stood there half dressed beside the dean while slowly placing his arm around her as the dean continued to cry with her face in the palms of her hands. "I would like to introduce you to my lovely fiancée, Dean Susan Russet."

Professor Karen Norman continued to shake her head. She stood there for a few seconds in silence as she glanced at Joey, and then she finally said, "Nice to meet you."

Dean Susan Russet, not Dean Jonathan Russet, wiped the tears from her face. "I'd like to explain. The butler, Covington Strongwell III, and the head maid here, Grace, are my uncle and my maternal aunt. They were all I had in the world family-wise until I met Professor Pierre Dubois, my true love. My parents were tragically killed in an auto accident when I was but a tiny child. Anyway, as I obtained my education and administrative academic experience, Uncle Covington decided to have me disguise myself as male instead of female, so I would allegedly have a better chance of being hired as the academic dean at Huntington Hills College. You must understand it was a different time then!"

Professor Norman spoke. "Why didn't you just be yourself, Susan? We would have accepted you! Anyone who didn't accept you we wouldn't have wanted working on the campus anyway."

"I don't know. I was young when I first took this position. I just did what Uncle Covington and Aunt Grace told me to do."

"Well, I think it's time for you to come out and be yourself, for God's sake!"

"Yes, I feel like a great burden has been lifted from me. I promise I will call a meeting soon with faculty and the student body and reveal my secret with a huge apology. It won't be easy, but I owe everyone that. Truly, I love this campus and want to remain as academic dean if the majority approve."

"Your gender shouldn't have anything to do with your position here. To my knowledge, at least until this present incident, you've been a good dean and leader," Professor Norman replied while rolling her eyes.

"Thank you, Professor Norman, for voicing that. Any assistance in being accepted as myself will be extremely appreciated. I'm so tired of those wigs and JCPenney suits."

Joey rubbed his nose and then pointed to the teapot. "But what about the mysterious campus tea?"

Professor Dubois entered the conversation. "All the generations of mystification about the tea have been to merely promote the uniqueness of the campus. It brought individuals from all around the world to taste its special flavor and experience its symptoms."

Dean Russet added, "I don't know everything in it. Only Aunt Grace and Uncle Covington guard the secrets of all the ingredients. Basically, I believe it consists of a passionflower that supposedly comes from an old farm village somewhere in northern Italy. The plant is said to cause the feeling of relaxation. Thus, the wondrous flowers, leaves, and vines, blended with other herbs we grow on the campus property, create this special campus tea heritage. That is my guess anyway. As a child, I would sometimes hear my uncle and aunt whispering about it."

Professor Pierre Dubois nodded in agreement. "Yes indeed. A flower called the *Passiflora incarata*, with perhaps young green tea leaves, hops, linden flowers, chamomile, and possibly a tiny drop of liquidized marijuana added to each teapot. That is what my dear Susan and I think anyway."

Joey rubbed the top of his head for a moment. "Wait—is the tea even legal?"

The dean turned to the young man with a soft smirk on her face. After all, she knew that Chief Braxton Ward had placed Officer Joey Hanover, a.k.a. student Joey Solomon, on the campus to do some undercover investigating. "Joey, who is going to really argue against a tea that has been around longer than we have? To my knowledge, no one has ever been hurt by it. The tea makes you relax and is possibly an aphrodisiac."

"What do you mean by that, Dean?"

"Oh, Joey! You are in your early twenties, aren't you? A love drug that possibly increases the romantic and sexual desires of those who partake in sipping its wonderful blend."

"Well, if that's true, there has to be something other than what you've described in it."

Professor Dubois looked into Joey's eyes. "We'll never know, will we?"

Professor Norman finally chimed into the conversation. "All of this is almost too much to take, but if the tea does all that, I'm going straight to the campus gift shop to buy myself a box. Frankly, my husband and I could use a little rest, relaxation, and romance. Unbelievable!"

Dean Susan Russet suddenly got a worried look on her face. "Oh, Professor Norman and Joey, you aren't going to reveal how you found Professor Dubois and me this afternoon, are you? Please don't compromise our lives and positions here on campus. I beg you!"

Professor Norman grabbed Joey's arm as she headed out of the office. "No, Dean Russet. I assure you that except for speaking to my husband in confidence, I do not plan on saying a single word to anyone else. Your careers and love relationships are safe for now if we are assured that Dean Russet will soon announce who she really is. A female as our academic dean instead of a male."

Joey seconded the comment. "Ditto on that, Dean Russet and Professor Dubois." He thought, *I'll have to share confidentially all of this with Chief Ward. The chief might have a good laugh privately in his office, but we are more interested in getting the other two culprits who tortured those girls from the campus than we are in all of this.*

Dean Susan Russet, not Dean Jonathan Russet, and her paramour, Professor Pierre Dubois, blew out large breaths at the same time in relief and then said simultaneously, "Thank you." They hugged each other.

"Oh, Professor Norman, you can have any arrangement you want regarding this semester's student art gallery. Just write up your requests and email them to me as soon as you can. Joey, we'll discuss your transcripts another time."

The door to the dean's office suddenly closed behind them. Joey looked at Professor Norman as they casually walked down the long hall, trying not to laugh.

Professor Norman finally held out a hand. "Well, Joey, it has been my pleasure spending this time with you. Remember, mum's the word."

"Yes, Professor Norman, confidentiality is my second name. My lips are sealed."

They glanced into each other's eyes for a few split seconds and then darted off in opposite directions.

Chapter 25

The Faith of Ian

The small canvas tent had been covered with foliage to camouflage it. Toward the end of the tent, a large dog cage sat with little Ian inside. The child lay there in the fetal position, dirty and exhausted, but somehow, Ian wasn't concerned so much about that.

His muddy face showed marks where tears had traveled down his cheeks. His thick, wavy hair was now filthy and matted. He hadn't eaten in who knew how long, but Ian just hugged himself tightly while whispering over and over to himself, "Da is coming. I can feel it. Da is coming."

Suddenly, the flap of the tent opened, and a hideous-looking old woman screamed, "Shut your trap, filthy brat! You'll get no sympathy from me. 'Tis told your real ma died having you, while my dimwit son, your real mafia da, just buried her in these forests' dirt. Your real da only wants you as a pawn for money from that stupid photographer, Ryan McFarlan. He'll pay for sure." She let out a wicked laugh and then yelled, "Stop whimpering, or I'll bury you just like your ma! She was nothing but a tramp. Just like your real da, my no-good son. 'Tis the money I do this for.'"

The old crazy lady left the tent. Ian could hear her scuffing footsteps walk beside the tent, until there was silence. The temperature was dropping fast. For some reason, he knew to rub himself all over and stretch his legs as much as he could, as if someone or something were subconsciously telling him to do so.

Ian was confused; he couldn't remember when he'd had a drink of water or a bite to eat. His young mind kept going back to Ryan saying bedtime prayers with him. He got on his little knees and prayed, "God, this is Ian. Please bring Da to me. I know you can. Bring Da. Da said to always stay strong. Like Superman. Da is coming. We are buddies forever. Love you too. Amen."

Ian drifted to sleep for a while. His dreams were surprisingly good ones of himself and Ryan. He dreamed about his beloved babysitter, Mrs. Beasley, and even Amanda O'Neal. He thought about his cozy little bed and his teddy bear. Just before he was startled back awake, his dream gave his mind a vision of Jesus holding him in a warm, protective hug.

He could hear several male voices arguing with the wicked old lady. At least that was how he thought of her, like in the story of Hansel and Gretel, which Mrs. Beasley had read to him one evening. There were sounds like the rustling of leaves on the ground, and then it sounded as if someone were hit hard with a rock or something. It sounded as if a body hit the ground with a thud, which scared Ian for a few seconds. A few moments of quiet went by, and then came the sound of several footsteps seemingly moving in his direction.

One of the men yelled out, "Someone is nearby! Take your places, you bloody fools!"

The men began arguing again. Ian closed his tearful hazel eyes while holding himself as tightly as possible. Once again, he whispered, "Da is coming. I can feel it. Da is coming."

It was as if Spirit, Black Thunder, and Copper were working as a team. The horses pressed forward. Ryan and Amanda had been around horses enough in the past that they could tell the horses were getting anxious.

"Wow."

"Wow what, Ryan?"

"Well, you are going to think I'm a little crazy, but it almost feels like someone is walking in front of Spirit, controlling the reins. Not pulling, but it's as if the reins are floating and leading Spirit."

"Wow indeed."

"Yeah. OK, this feels kind of strange. Not bad strange but good strange."

"Remember, Ryan, God knows what he is doing. We must trust him. After all, you are the one who taught Ian to always have faith. It might be a guardian angel. Animals are very sensitive to the spirit world, you know."

"Aye. Father Bryan has always told me that. Especially horses."

Spirit suddenly stopped, raised his head, shook it for a few seconds, and then stomped on the ground. Surprisingly, Black Thunder did the same thing, while Copper remained still beside them.

Ryan whispered to Amanda, "I think they are trying to tell us something."

"Feels like it. Doesn't it?"

Still whispering, Ryan slid off the horse, rubbing Spirit's neck for a moment. "Good boy, Spirit. Thank you for helping us. You horses are something else. Hey, Red, I think we should quietly get down and find a safe place to hide the horses where they will be safe. After we've done that, you and I can look around for a bit. What do you think?"

"Sounds good."

Once they handled the needs of the horses, Amanda and Ryan tried to be as quiet as possible as they looked around.

"Do you hear something?"

"I believe so. Like angry talking. They're too far for us to really get what is being said."

Both crouched behind a large bush beside a tree. Suddenly, they saw several men standing close to an area with a lot of foliage.

"Ryan, is that a body on the ground over there?"

"Looks like it, but don't worry. It is much too large to be Ian."

"Well, thank God for that!"

"What do you think we should do, Red? After all, you are more the expert when it comes to criminals and such."

"Let's not get crazy here. These guys could just be hunting or something. We've got to be sure we have a solid plan before taking any action."

"Amanda, with a human body lying over there, I think we are safe to conclude they're not just out on a camping trip. Besides, that is not how the rules of Mullaghmeen Forest work. Normally, no one would be around here now. The forest is for the people to enjoy, with trails and such. Somehow, Father Bryan had it closed to the public for us to search. Don't ask me how he accomplished that! The man is a saint. That is all I have to say."

"For now, let's quietly walk around in a circle and get a better glance at what is actually lying on the ground—a human body or something else. We also need to find out why they keep looking at that wooded area to the left where they are standing. Maybe something is there. Maybe Ian."

"I sure hope so. Be strong, Ian. Da is coming."

"Ryan, this way. We need to get closer before this gang disperses in all different directions and sees the two of us. I know you want to get to Ian as soon as possible, but we've got to keep our wits about us. We can't afford to do anything stupid."

She whispered to herself, "Please help us, heavenly Father! You are all we have at this point. Oh, and our intelligence, training, and good old common sense that you gave both of us."

"Don't forget the guardian angels and possibly Irish fairies."

"At this point, we can use all the help we can get."

"This is it, Amanda. I know it! Ian must be around here somewhere. I can feel it."

"Come on. We'll find him."

Ryan and Amanda quietly moved some more around the perimeters of the campsite until they were closer to the back of the camouflaged tent. There they whispered for a few moments, devising their plan.

"I think we are running out of time. Soon this group of men will disperse. We need to move quickly. I'm going to cover you, Ryan, by riding Black Thunder like the wind across the center of the camp as you cut the back or side of the tent and get Ian free. Once you have him, swiftly run to Spirit and Copper. Black Thunder and I will meet you there. Ryan, I am an excellent shot. Remember?"

"Aye, that I do, but I still worry for you, Red."

"No time for worry, my husband. We must totally trust God. Ian needs us."

"Aye. Do you have your classic Glock 17 unlocked and loaded, my dearest?"

"That I do. It will take both hands for me to shoot and aim properly, but I guess I've trained my whole life for this moment. For our Ian. Is the Glock 19 that Father Bryan slipped you ready?"

"Yes. I see, my wife, that your Glock has a longer barrel than mine. Not a good thing for a man to see."

Amanda softly giggled. "Ryan, no worries. I've been using guns on the farm since I was a child and have done much training as a lawyer and licensed investigator. I am very accurate. Believe me!"

He blew out a lot of air as if he'd been holding his breath. "Well, if you say so, Amanda. Glad to have a wife who knows how to use a semiautomatic pistol. Especially at a time like this! Just don't ever pull that out when you're mad at me."

"I will be sure to remember that request. You know, humor can be good sometimes when you are nervous and under stress. Anyway, let's pause and say a short prayer. 'God, as always, we lean on you for strength and guidance. As parents of our precious Ian, it is our duty to protect him at all costs. We ask you to once again circle us with your protection as we fight to recover Ian from the clutches of evil. Let no harm come to us, Holy Father. In these next moments, as we act as your warriors, fill our minds with wisdom and our bodies with supernatural strength that only you can give. If it be your will, God, let us succeed. We give you all the praise forever. Amen.'"

Ryan placed her face in both his hands as they looked deep into each other's eyes. "Red, I sure don't know what I've done in my life to deserve you, but I sure am thankful for you."

"I know. I feel the same way."

He wiped a tear from her cheek and gave her one final hug. She motioned for Ryan to start toward the back of the tent as she climbed onto Black Thunder. Amanda spoke softly into the horse's ear, placed her handgun firmly in both hands, and readied herself for the battle ahead.

Ian heard a cutting sound from the side of the tent. He glanced over to see Ryan holding a finger to his mouth to inform Ian to stay quiet.

Ian whispered emotionally, "Da, you are here."

"Yes, my laddie. I am here. Just like I've promised."

"Yes, Da. I knew you were coming soon. Jesus told me. The angels are here, Da! They are around us."

"I know, my beloved Ian. I know. Praise be to God. Now, laddie, we must move swiftly. I know you are very weak and tired, but I need you to put your arms around my neck and your legs around my waist. Hold on tight, Ian. Da must get us to the horses quickly and meet Amanda there."

"Horses? Amanda?"

"Aye. Here we go. Hold tight, and remain quiet, no matter what."

"I am ready, Da. We are Supermen," his brave little four-year-old said.

"Yes, my Ian, Supermen." With that, Ryan slipped out of the tent and ran like hell into the forest toward Spirit and Copper. In the background, he could hear bullets flying and the huffs of Black Thunder pounding into the ground as Amanda covered the area to protect him and Ian. *Please, Father, protect them also. Thank you.*

Amanda had secured the reins to the saddle, so Black Thunder was in control of himself. It was up to the horse for now, and he knew it. Suddenly, Black Thunder took off, racing like the wind through the center of the campsite from one end to the other. As he confidently moved like the best of any Irish racehorse, Amanda turned her waist to make sure her bullets were covering the areas needed to protect Ryan at the tent.

Strands of her hair had escaped her braid, looking like red fire carried by the movement of the horse and nature. She felt as if everything were in slow motion. In the background, she could hear screaming and bullets, but she and Black Thunder kept going until they reached the other side of the camp.

Without delay, Black Thunder entered the forest and circled completely around the perimeter of the campsite as Amanda continued to let bullets fly. She kept up until met by several members of the Irish law enforcement, the Gardai, and some Irish Rangers began moving in from the depths of the forest.

The Ranger leader came close to her as she slowed down. "Dr. O'Neal, we have them surrounded. Meet Ryan McFarlan where you have arranged. He has Ian. Once you are all together, ride to the nearest trail to the west. There are some official vehicles to take you all to the hospital. We will make sure Black Thunder, Spirit, and Copper are returned to Father Bryan O'Duinn unharmed. He contacted us just in time. Go now, and don't turn back!"

Another Ranger caught up with the leader after Amanda departed. "God, what a woman. Did you see how she and the horse covered the location to protect McFarlan and the child?"

"Aye. She was shooting like one of us. Unbelievable!"

"I'd never have believed it if I hadn't seen it with my own eyes."

"Glad my wife can't shoot like that."

"You're telling me. Come on; we've got business to attend to."

"Aye. Let's move in." He raised his arm to have the others move in swiftly toward the campsite. They were finally getting some members of an Irish gang who had been playing havoc throughout Ireland for some time.

Ryan reached Spirit and Copper safely. They could hear all the movement and gunshots around them but stayed at their safe location, as directed. Both horses let out a few breaths of air in excitement when they saw Ryan break through the nearby foliage and trees of the forest as he ran to them. As soon as he came to Spirit, he grabbed his water jug and proceeded to lift it to Ian's lips. The child hesitated at first due to weakness but then started to drink in gulps, almost choking himself.

"Slow your drinking down, Ian. You'll make yourself sick if you haven't had any water or food for some time. Da is here. No worries now."

Ryan jumped upon Spirit, and he tied a large McFarlan plaid blanket, his brat, around the child to secure him to himself. He had originally brought it to wrap around himself or Amanda to keep warm, but such was now perfect for his beloved son. Ian laid his head back almost instantly once he was safely in the arms of his da.

Ryan thought, *At least I'll be able to feel the beat of the lad's heart to know he is still alive, as he will also feel mine.*

It seemed that just as they were settled, Amanda and Black Thunder came whipping around the corner.

"Praise be to God; you're here, Red. Were you or Black Thunder harmed in any way?"

Almost out of breath, she rode to him, placed a firm kiss on his lips, and then softly rubbed the small shoulder of Ian. "Ryan, we are both fine. The Irish Gardai and some government Rangers are here in force. I spoke with one. They've been watching us from afar. Father

Bryan O'Duinn was successful in sending them. Anyway, we must move fast. To the west we are to go. At the first Mullaghmeen Forest trail, some vehicles are waiting for us. Ian needs to be transported to the hospital immediately."

"Aye."

"Hand me Copper's rein. She'll follow Black Thunder just fine. You place all your attention on Ian. Spirit knows he is carrying precious cargo."

"Off we go then."

They could hear screaming and gunshots but continued to move swiftly westward. Soon the forest cleared, and the trail with the Gardai waiting was in view. Once up close to the vehicles and truck trailer to transport the horses, Ryan paused for a moment with Ian in his arms as he placed his forehead on Spirit's neck.

Amanda glanced over. "Ryan, it's all right. The horses will be well cared for. The Ranger promised me they'll take them directly back to Father Bryan. Please don't worry. We must go now!"

She rubbed Black Thunder and Copper one last time before quickly running to the ambulance, where Ryan had already entered with Ian. Some of the Gardai were caring for the horses and loading them up as they drove by.

Chapter 26

Healing at the Haven

The hospital transport van stopped in front of the Haven's gate, and Father Bryan O'Duinn was the first to step out. Several within the abbey stood within the inside borders, waiting for them. He gave them all a friendly wave.

Fall was upon them, and the crisp, cold temperatures had arrived. The nearby trees whipped around as the wind made their leaves do a dance. Father Bryan reached for his wool scarf around his neck and wrapped it a little higher to protect himself from the cold wind as he reached to hold the passenger door for Amanda.

During their return trip, Ryan had been sitting in the back of the van, with them on the opposite side, with Ian in his arms. Once the van stopped, he sat there for a moment and then swiftly carried the lad toward Father O'Duinn's cabin. Amanda and Father Bryan glanced at each other with soft smiles as they watched Ryan's back as he walked toward the front door. Once in the designated room prepared for the three of them, Ryan softly laid sleeping Ian down in a small bed that sat beside the larger one for Amanda and him.

After almost ten days at the hospital, the child was feeling much better but had fallen asleep in Ryan's arms on the trip back to the Haven. Both guys had stayed as tight as glue to each other since the reunion. Ian would often call out in the night at the hospital, "Da, are you here with me?" Ryan would always go to him, giving the child assurance he was safe, loved, and not alone.

Prior to Ian giving in to exhaustion in the van, he asked a million questions about Father Bryan's life. His special interest was in the horses, which he couldn't wait to see. To make the rescue circumstances less dramatic, everyone had made out that the horses were the complete heroes in finding him, rescuing him, and getting him away from the bad guys. That wasn't too far from the truth, but no one wanted to discuss with him too much about all the other details involved.

The doctors had informed Amanda and Ryan it would take a while for Ian to feel completely safe again. With some counseling and tactful police questions, the information would come out. Ian was young but very intelligent. Ryan had taught him well to be observant, so everyone was confident Ian would have no trouble in spilling the beans, as Ian said, about everything that had happened during his capture.

Amanda and Father Bryan were glad to enter his warm and cozy cabin. After taking their coats off, the father immediately walked toward his small kitchen to put on a kettle for tea.

"Amanda, would ye be wanting a spot of hot tea with me? I'm sure Ryan will be wanting some once our Ian is settled and fast asleep."

"Yes, Father Bryan, some tea would be lovely right about now."

They settled themselves on the couch near the fireplace to get warm while waiting patiently for Ryan. He finally quietly came out, carefully closed the bedroom door, and walked their way.

Ryan rolled his eyes for a second. "The wee lad continued to sleep when I tucked him in. I think he wore himself out asking all those questions about Father Bryan."

They all softly giggled for a few seconds together.

Father Bryan looked his way. "Well, that lad certainly has a very inquisitive mind for his age. For a moment or two, when I visited the hospital, I felt as if one of the Gardai officers were giving me the roundabout, with all those questions he had for me!" Amanda and Ryan chuckled a bit while enjoying their tea.

"Such a blessing to see Ian now in the protection of the Haven. I think he has grown quite fond of you, Father."

"Aye, 'tis a good thing indeed. For I have grown quite fond of the lad myself. Like he is one of my own. You know, I will always be there for him and both of you."

"Aye. We know, Father. We feel the same about you. We, in return, will always be there for you as well. Don't forget that."

Father Bryan O'Duinn took another sip of tea, leaned back to rest, and replied, "Aye. I shall not forget."

They talked on for a bit until they were all too tired to think. Suddenly, the tension was lifting, while exhaustion took its place. Ryan especially felt as if he hadn't rested for a month or two.

"Red, I think I will be heading to bed. I can hardly keep my eyes open. I think I'm much too tired for a late dinner. Will you come?"

"Yes, of course. Thank you, Father, for your hospitality. I think we will be turning in. See you in the morning."

"Aye. God willing," Father Bryan responded as he also shuffled to his room.

Everyone within the abbey grounds had been generous. Upon Father Bryan's directions, they had placed a queen-size bed and a twin in the same bedroom so the McFarlan family could be all together.

A bowl and pitcher of water were in the room as well, should anyone needed the use of such. Close by, on a small side table, was a plate of fresh bread, cheese, and fruit. A small bottle of wine, with two Waterford goblets, stood near the food.

Amanda and Ryan removed their clothes quietly. Ryan grabbed a swig of wine or two with a bit of bread and cheese and then crawled into the covers beside her. Without delay, all of them relinquished themselves to peaceful sleep.

Both Amanda and Ryan were usually early risers in the morning, at least at Huntington Hills College in North Carolina. There was much to get done regarding their students and classes. Ryan, like any parent of a small child, had to think about Ian's needs as well as extra security precautions, never really knowing who might try to cause harm or when or where.

Back in North Carolina, Ian would pop himself out of bed to greet Mrs. Beasley, who often prepared a wondrous breakfast for him and Da, not to mention Ian's homeschooling. Ryan had always tried his best to make sure Ian was protected, but now maybe everything would change regarding the constant fear of something in the child's past that they had no knowledge of.

Anyway, on this morning, everyone slept in. *No harm done*, Father Bryan thought when he got up and the other bedroom was still quiet. He glanced out the front window. "It looks to be a fine fall day. I think I'll go to the barn while I wait for the McFarlans to stir. Spirit, Black Thunder, and Copper will be happy to see their favored Father Bryan O'Duinn."

Ryan was startled awake by a loud whisper from Ian. The lad had climbed onto his father's stomach and was sitting up with Ryan's body between the child's legs. Ian had his little hands on Ryan's face, with their noses almost touching. His sweet little breath hit his father's face.

"Da, it's Ian. Are you awake?"

Ryan grumbled, "I think I pretty much am now!"

"Da, why is Amanda sleeping in our bedroom? Why is she in your bed? Is she afraid too?"

Ryan slowly opened his eyes, trying to focus. "Ian, on second thought, I'm not fully awake yet, and that is quite a story. Do we have to discuss it right this moment?"

"Yes, Da. I think it is important. Don't you?"

Amanda's back was toward them on the other side of the bed, and suddenly, Ryan felt her body shake a little with a soft giggle coming from the other side.

"Well, OK," Ryan said, trying not to laugh. "You see, there is this tradition. This Irish thing called handfasting. It's kind of like two people marrying each other with no other witnesses than God. They promise each other to be husband and wife. When Amanda and I were in the woods all alone, before we found you, we did that. So you could say we are a married couple now. At least that is how we see it. It's an Irish thing, Ian."

Ian sat there quietly for a moment, glancing into his father's eyes. Ryan could tell the lad's little mind was in deep thought.

"So, Da, we are a family?" Ian then pointed to Ryan, himself, and Amanda and counted out, "One. Two. Three."

"Yes, my boy. You are correct. The three of us are now family."

"So I have a ma?"

"Yes, Ian. You are correct again. Amanda is now your ma."

Amanda slowly turned her body around and softly rubbed his little back as he turned to glance into her face. She gave him a smile and a wink to confirm his thinking. Ian then turned his view back to Ryan and gave his father a kiss on his lips and a big hug.

"You picked good, Da."

A deep chuckle came from Ryan. "Well, thank you very much, Son. I'm glad you approve."

"Da, I'm going to find Father Bryan before we eat, because you and Amanda must be very tired since handfasting. I think you should sleep some more."

Amanda and Ryan laughed as Ian slipped out of the room and down the hall. Ryan told Ian to check the barn if Father Bryan wasn't in his bedroom or the kitchen, and then he locked their bedroom door and climbed back into bed with his wife.

Ryan mumbled, "Boy, I bet he is going to have some conversation with Father Bryan this morning."

Amanda moved closer to Ryan, placing her hands in his rather long, wavy hair. He leaned over, and their lips met. Soon they were caught up in each other's arms. A little necking began, with one of his hands squeezing one of her nipples and the other rubbing her firm bottom.

Amanda caught her breath for a moment and whispered, "Ryan, wait. Um, we have a four-year-old and priest just outside that door. Don't you think we should be somewhat careful? Ian could run in at any moment."

"My leannan, quiet now. The door is locked. Father Bryan and Ian are probably out to the barn, visiting the horses. Let's just enjoy the few moments we have. If it's OK with you, we'll do a quickie here before breakfast. Calm yourself down, and relax. I was just getting to the good stuff."

Amanda smiled and relinquished as she looked into Ryan's deep blue eyes. She thought, *How have I become so comforted and relaxed in his arms so fast?*

Ryan popped his head under the covers again after smiling one of his devilish white smiles at her and then began kissing her soft stomach while holding on to her bottom with both hands. He said to himself, *Paradise! If I was going to die right at this moment, this is surely where I'd want to be.* He kissed her wondrous clitoris and sucked for a few moments while feeling her wetness around her flower, as he called it. *She smells and tastes like honey and mint down here to me. Yum, 'tis a fine thing for a husband to believe. I can't get enough of my wife.*

Panting as she felt his hardness rubbing against her, Amanda softly spoke. "Ryan, you are driving me crazy. Is this really a quickie? I need you to be part of me. Now, please!"

Ryan did his deep giggle, entered her slowly, and gradually increased the speed until he was lunging back and forth, bringing her body to a total culmination of joyous explosion. She let herself go while trying not to scream out as he let go into complete release and satisfaction. Sweet perfection.

Both lay back on the bed, looking at the ceiling, before Ryan spoke. "Excuse me, Red, but that was glorious indeed. I mean flashing lights. Explosions. Like a volcano eruption. A pretty good quickie if you ask me!"

Imitating his Irish talk as her rusty-gold eyes glanced into his deep-sea blues, she replied, "Aye, Ryan McFarlan. A grand ride it was." She did her romantic giggle and smile.

He smiled back at her while thinking, *Wow, if that quickie felt that good, I can't wait to feel what the rest of our union is going to bring. Something miraculous for sure. Saints preserve!*

"Come on, lover boy. Let's take a quick shower together and then meet the guys for breakfast."

"OK, you are killing me now. A quick shower together. Is that even possible?"

She smacked his awesomely firm-looking bottom with the towel she held as she moved to the bedroom door. "Come along, Mr. McFarlan. Time is a-wasting, and a shower and food are a-calling to me."

"Yes, ma'am," he responded as they hurried to the shower together.

Ryan and Amanda finally met Father Bryan and Ian at the kitchen table. Ian, sitting at the table, was devouring a bowl of porridge. Father was pouring himself another cup of tea at the sink.

Ian glanced up. "How come you two look funny? Did you tell a joke? I want to hear it."

Father Bryan started to choke for a second and then smiled at them. "No, Ian, I think they are just happy to have you back safe and at home."

"Is this our home? We're going to live here now?"

Father Bryan sat across from Ian and placed one of his tiny hands in his. "Laddie, you, your da, and Amanda will probably be living somewhere else together. Wherever you live, though, this place will always be home to you. I will always be your Father Bryan O'Duinn forever."

Ian stopped eating, walked over to Father Bryan, and replied, "Aye, Father, you will always be my Father Bryan, and I will be coming home often. Besides, someone must be checking on Spirit, Black Thunder, and Copper."

Father Bryan hugged the child tightly and then gave him a loving, soft smack on his bottom to go to Ryan. Both Ryan and Amanda gave him kisses and hugs and then sent him back to finish his breakfast.

It seemed the days passed swiftly as the little family worked to get closer. Ian met with a psychologist a few times at the hospital as well as the Irish police, the Gardai. Bits and pieces of his abduction and everything that had happened to him slowly came out as the child described the events in his own time.

They went on horseback rides often and helped in the garden and chapel. A few days after arriving, Ryan and Amanda were truly wed by Father Bryan O'Duinn in the quaint chapel, with Ian, of course, being the best man. It was a simple ceremony but a blessed event. The happiest was little Ian, who stopped calling Amanda by her name in no time at all and now referred to her as his ma. Amanda cherished that since she hadn't had children of her own. Ian started sitting on her lap often as she read him stories at bedtime or in the afternoon before naps.

The evening before their departure back to North Carolina and then to the farm in Florida, Ian was trying to play chess with Father Bryan by the fireplace and fell fast asleep. Ryan calmly picked Ian up; kissed the top of his soft, curly head; and walked him to the bedroom to tuck the child in. As he was walking back to the sitting room, he heard Father Bryan speaking to Amanda.

"Well, I guess I'm not a very good teacher when it comes to Ian."

"No, Father, I'm sure that isn't it at all. Ian is young, and he has had some pretty exciting days around here. He finally has given in to exhaustion. That is all it is."

"Well, very nice for you to say, Amanda, but I think the lad was a bit bored."

Ryan walked up to them and laughed as he plopped himself beside Amanda on the couch.

"So I guess you two will be going back in the morning."

"Aye, Father. In the morning. Our flight is booked for North Carolina. Amanda and I want to thank you for everything. You are our family. You know that."

"Thanks much."

Amanda glanced over at Father Bryan. "In fact, I was hoping you'd fly to the farm in Florida before we arrive there, so all my special people can have a special Thanksgiving dinner together in the barn. We always do something special each year. This year, instead of the whole neighborhood and church members, I just want us and my extended family. I will be happy to notify you of the details and dates."

"A very nice offer indeed. I will be considering and praying on that."

Ryan rubbed his head. "Don't think too much, Father. I know how your mind works. It would be good for you to get out of Ireland for a few weeks, seeing that we've probably stirred up the Irish gangs and mafia to get Ian back."

"Aye. I didn't think of it that way."

Amanda looked at her husband. "Well, here we go again. Blacklisted again, I suppose."

Father Bryan paused and then asked, "What do you mean by that?"

"Well, the chief of police in North Carolina, Chief Braxton Ward of the Huntington Hills Police Department, told Amanda and me in a meeting to watch out for being blacklisted by some criminals in the area. Before everything concerning Ian, we were assisting in an investigation into several linked cases. Amanda is very good at solving things like that. She has a good professional reputation in the United States. Anyway, the chief thought both our names could possibly be blacklisted, meaning the bad guys in North Carolina would come after us. These incidents don't have anything to do with what happened to Ian, though. They are just cases in connection to our teaching at the campus."

Amanda added, "Yes. We are sure these cases are totally unrelated. This is one reason why we must go to North Carolina first."

"I see. Well, please be careful."

"We will. God will protect us. We hold firmly to that," Ryan said.

Father Bryan paused for a moment and then said, "I was wondering if Ian has said anything to the child psychologist or Gardai about one of the gang members being his real father."

A worried expression fell on Ryan's face. "Nothing as far as I know. All I know is the Gardai and Irish Rangers got him. He's dead. Guess he was going to use Ian to squeeze some money out of me. He supposedly killed Ian's mother some time ago and didn't care at all about the lad. We no longer have to worry about him, I've been told."

"What was the man's name?"

Amanda leaned over and whispered, "I think they said it was Vincent Coll IV. A nasty brute who cared only for himself. I looked his name up on the internet. He has quite a criminal past and told everyone that allegedly, his great-great-grandfather was Vincent 'Mad Dog' Coll, an Irish American hit man in the 1920s and 1930s. I hope that isn't true. Maybe the crazy nut legally changed his name and was lying to get prestige in his gang. Anyway, it's over now. They're all dead, Ian has no knowledge, and he is ours. I'm going to go through the legal adoption of him, like Ryan did."

Father looked into the fire and said firmly, "I hope all will be well for all of you. You deserve it. Especially our Ian. Both of you have proven your love for the child. No doubt about that."

Ryan firmly replied, "Ian is mine, and that is all there is to it. Forever! That is the last word about it. I am his da."

Father Bryan, Amanda, and Ryan took their last swigs of hot tea, clanked their mugs together like a toast, and then headed off to bed.

Early morning was there before all of them knew it. It was time to say goodbye. The airport transport vehicle was already there and waiting for everyone to load up. Ryan and Amanda finished placing their luggage in, while Father Bryan O'Duinn held tight to Ian.

Father Bryan softly spoke. "I will miss our morning time with the horses."

"Yes, Father. Be sure to give them an extra carrot from me. Oh, and don't forget to let them breathe into my shirt I left, so they won't forget me. Hug their necks for me too."

"I'll be sure to do that, lad. Don't worry; they won't forget you. Never."

"Are you sure?"

"Aye, I am sure. You are special to them. They won't forget."

"Good. I was a wondering about that."

"Spirit, Black Thunder, and Copper are very smart."

"Yes, I know."

Ryan smiled at Ian as they walked up. "Are you ready, lad?"

A tear fell down Ian's cheek, and he hugged Father O'Duinn tightly. "I love you."

"Oh, lad, I love you too. Remember, you are my best friend. I will be calling you all the time. Da can connect us on the computer so we'll see each other and talk."

"Is that true, Da?"

"Aye, Ian. 'Tis true. We will be sure to do that at least twice a week. Don't worry. Father Bryan will be able to keep you informed about the horses, and you'll be able to tell him all the adventures we'll be having. You'll see him soon. I promise."

Looking a little melancholy, Ian went into Amanda's arms as Ryan and Father Bryan shook hands and hugged. Delaying for a few moments, they looked into each other's eyes.

"How can I ever repay you, Father Bryan, for helping us get our beloved Ian back?"

"No thanks will be needed, Ryan. I only do what God leads me to do. We are all a great big family in this world. I will miss all of you. Time to get back to tending to the needs of my community. There is always someone to help or something to do."

As they turned to get into the vehicle, Father Bryan spoke out. "Before you depart, I want to be wishing you a safe trip the Irish way."

Amanda looked into his eyes. "What do you mean, Father Bryan?"

"I want to say the *Old Traditional Irish Blessing* that everyone knows around here. 'May the road rise to meet you. May the wind be always at your back. May the sun shine warm upon your face; The rains fall soft upon your fields and until we meet again, May God hold you in the palm of his hand.'"

Ryan, Amanda, and Ian waved a final goodbye as they got into the vehicle, which slowly drove away. Father O'Duinn stood at the gate until they could be seen no longer.

Chapter 27

Victimizing Ends

Surprisingly, when Academic Dean Susan Russet, not Dean Jonathan Russet, called a campus meeting for all the student body, faculty, and administration to announce her true gender and explanation and declare her eternal love for Professor Pierre Dubois from the science department, the confessions were accepted with rave reviews. In fact, instead of being fired from her position, the dean was met by liberating reviews throughout the Huntington Hills campus. It seemed that all over campus, individuals were apparently now getting up the courage to announce their love to those they secretly admired from afar.

Just shortly before, the atmosphere around campus had been grim due to the unsolved criminal acts perpetrated against Vivian Smith and two other former students from years past. Yet everyone was longing to create a new mood, despite still being careful, until news of the culprits' capture could be announced.

The mysteries of the infamous tea grew more fanatical around the campus and town as the days went by, especially after Professor

Dubois professed his love for Dean Russet in a flamboyant, theatrical manner at the dean's meeting, which pretty much everyone attended. He professed that their love had developed over the sharing of the wondrous campus tea, which, to his declaration, had relaxed them and been an aphrodisiac, releasing their inner most feelings for each other.

Needless to say, the purchase of tea at the campus bookstores and restaurants increased dramatically. So it appeared the tea legends would continue. Dean Russet's aunt Grace and uncle Covington were ecstatic since generations of their family had guarded the secrets of the tea and campus for generations. They hoped the historical campus ambiance never ended.

Oddly, with all the happenings, the campus finances continued to rise instead of decreasing. To campus administrators' surprise, more student applications for entrance into the campus flooded in than ever before, even despite the publicity of Vivian Smith's ordeal and the criminals still on the loose. The events seemed to add to the unique nuances of Huntington Hills, North Carolina, instead of scaring people off.

Things were not as perfect as they seemed, though. Chief Braxton Ward and his detectives were as concerned as ever about catching Randy Kuznetsova and the others involved in the horrendous crimes. The long hours all of them were working were beginning to take a toll on everyone's nerves. Even Officer Joey Hanover, the undercover student known as Joey Solomon, was getting a bit worn out.

Just when Chief Braxton Ward thought they were getting nowhere in locating the suspects, Joey and some campus security guards came upon some suspicious activity one evening. Three guys were hovering around the back door of one of the female student dorms while laughing and fumbling with the lock.

"Hey, guys, those characters look like they've had a few too many to drink or something. Best we go check them out." Officer Joey Hanover's training kicked in—maybe because there were three of them, and he knew there were at least three involved in the abduction of Vivian Smith.

"Probably just some students trying to wake their girlfriends up for a good time," one of the security guards replied with a smile. "Besides, aren't you supposed to be incognito on campus, acting like a student?"

"Yeah, but I don't know. They look kind of rough to be students."

"You never know. Especially on weekends. A lot of these students go crazy."

"Well, let's just walk over there casually. I'll stay in the background like I'm another student you caught snooping around."

The three security guards liked Joey's plan, so they sauntered over to the giggling trio.

One of the guards yelled out, "Hey, guys, what's going on here? You need to move along now, since it's getting late. Most of the gals are sleeping or have already left for the weekend. Move along now!"

The drugged hooligans laughed, and one said, "Oh no, Mr. Security, we can't do that. We've got to get our homework papers from my girlfriend, Sarah Carmicle."

"OK," said the guard. "Then show me your student campus IDs, and one of us will go get the material from her."

The drugged-out loons began to laugh again as they fumbled in their pockets to locate their campus identifications.

"Look," another security guard yelled out, "we just caught this loser lurking around the girls' dorms, and now you guys. Stop screwing around, and hand us your IDs."

Finally, all three of them handed over their campus IDs.

"OK, guys. You think we are stupid or something! These IDs look to be three or four years out of date. Especially yours, Mr. Randy Kuznetsov."

Joey's eyes suddenly bugged out, and he grabbed Randy, who struggled with him like a wildcat on the ground.

"What the hell are you doing? You're not even a security guard! Get your stinking arms away from my body!"

Joey looked at Randy's bloodshot eyes and said, "I don't think so. We've been looking for all of you for quite some time. Shut your mouth, and stop squirming! Get into gear, security people; these are the culprits the police department has been looking for. For God's sake, don't let them go!"

"Oh crap," said one of the guards as they all lunged in to handcuff the three alleged criminals' hands behind their backs.

Joey got up while yelling, "Whatever you do, don't let these guys go free!" He scrambled to check all their pockets and ankle areas to see if they were carrying any guns or other weapons. Some slip ties were found in one of the guys' coats, so Joey quickly began tying their ankles as well as their arms.

Grabbing his phone, he dialed Chief Ward's private phone number. "Chief, get some additional officers and detectives here right away. We got them! They slipped up. We got them. Hurry!"

The chief was standing in the lounge, getting some coffee, talking to Detective Luther Cane. Detectives Sara Johnson and Jerald Mills sat at a table not far from them.

"We'll be right there. Hold them. For God's sake, don't let them go!" Chief screamed on the phone before hanging up.

Everyone nearby glanced at him.

"Come on, everyone; let's roll! Officer Joey Hanover has Randy Kuznetsov and the other two perpetrators we are after. They've got them at the back entrance of one of the female dorms on campus. This is it. Don't screw it up, guys! Get there as soon as possible. Let's go, Luther; you can drive."

The parking lot of the police department looked like a tornado as they ran to their vehicles and raced out. Sirens blared as, one by one, they sped out. The FBI was immediately contacted, and Agent Maxwell Davis wasted no time in getting their helicopter up and moving toward the scene.

Agent Davis rode in the helicopter and viewed where Officer Hanover and campus security had the suspects down on the ground. "Hey, Chief."

The chief had his cell phone in his ear, listening, as Detective Cane drove like a race car driver toward the dorms. "Yeah, Agent Davis, I can hear you. What do you guys see?"

"They are at the back entrance of dorm C. I can see Hanover and the guards have them down on the ground. We are going to find a clearing to land in and then meet you there as soon as possible. What a great job!"

"I can't believe it! Our own Officer Joey Hanover. That kid is turning into something else. What a catch. Glad I set him up undercover around the campus. No telling what would have happened without him being there when security came upon those culprits."

Maxwell replied over the noise from the helicopter, "For sure, Chief. OK, we'll see you in just a few moments."

"OK. Thanks."

To the whole police department's surprise, Officer Hanover had indeed captured the monsters they'd been looking for all that time. The whole campus around the scene was covered with law enforcement and FBI. Students came out of their dorms like bees from their hives. No doubt this would be top news in the morning in Huntington Hills College's campus newspaper, on the radio, and on TV stations. It would be news all over town. People once again would be able to breathe a little bit easier instead of always worrying about who was lurking around the campus grounds and community, causing mayhem.

Chief Ward left no stone unturned, despite catching the three drugged-out most wanted. He had all the dorm rooms double-checked, as well as the main buildings and surrounding woods. As everything was in motion, detectives Mills and Johnson transported Randy Kuznetsov and the two others to the police station. One was so stoned that he completely passed out, while another was vomiting his guts up into a bag provided to him in the backseat of the police vehicle. Randy, who seemed to be coming out of his drug-induced stupor, was fighting and screaming like a wild animal in the back of Detective Jerald Mills's car. Things got so crazy with him that Mills had a couple of regular armed officers ride along while transporting Kuznetsov. Talk about an adrenaline rush for everyone. Wild!

By morning, the other two former students had been identified and booked along with Randy Kuznetsov. Thanks to all the trace evidence from the various scenes, campus data, and endless previous investigation work from North Carolina to Tampa, Florida, the rope of justice around the three suspects' necks seemed to be tight. Everyone deserved his or her due process in court, but the evidence looked to be pretty stacked up against them.

Time would tell at the trial why the other two former students had followed Randy Kuznetsov's crazy criminal rampage. Unfortunately, Randy Kuznetsov had experienced a troubling life since childhood. Yet both Dimitry Volkov and Yegor Romanoff had come from good Russian American families and been above-average students prior to linking up with Randy. For whatever sinister reasons, the once promising young men had been led astray, causing death and violence that many would not soon forget.

The McFarlan family returned to Ryan and Ian's beloved North Carolina cabin in the middle of the night. They were exhausted and wasted no time in heading for bed.

Mrs. Beasley, thankfully, had recovered well from her head injury suffered during Ian's abduction. While Ryan and Amanda had been in Ireland to get Ian back, both Mr. and Mrs. Beasley had seen to the cabin repairs and yard work. Ryan made sure they were well compensated financially. Besides, Ian saw them both as grandparents. He loved them.

Mrs. Beasley, after seeing the lights on when they arrived from the airport, sneaked over and started breakfast. The wonderful aroma of fresh coffee could be smelled all over the cabin. Ryan rubbed his eyes and glanced over to Amanda, who was just waking up.

They looked into each other's eyes and softly said simultaneously with a smile, "Mrs. Beasley is here."

They shuffled into the kitchen, and there sat Ian talking a mile a minute with pancakes stuffed in his mouth as Mrs. Beasley was starting another pan of bacon, eggs, and pancakes.

"Good morning, Da. Mrs. Beasley is here!"

"I see. Ian, please chew your food good before talking. It isn't very polite to speak with your mouth so full."

"Yes, Da."

"Hello, Mr. McFarlan. Don't be too hard on our little laddie here. After all, he is just excited to tell me all the adventures all of you experienced. And you can call me Mrs. B., as always. Fern isn't necessary."

"Thanks, Mrs. B. Oh, and thanks to you and Glen for caring for the cabin and property while we were gone."

"No problem. With Mr. Beasley being retired now, you've given him a whole new reason to keep busy. He loves caring for both our places. Makes him feel like an important caretaker. Good morning, Mrs. McFarlan. I guess congratulations are in order."

"Yes, Mrs. Beasley. Thank you."

"Will all of you be staying here at the cabin for a while?"

Amanda sat down at the table as Ryan handed her a cup of fresh coffee. "Well, actually, I have a small farm in the Tampa Bay area of Florida, and we thought we'd head that way in a week or so. I'm really missing my home and all my important people there."

"I see," Mrs. Beasley said a little worriedly.

Ryan sat down at the breakfast table across from Amanda. "So, Mrs. B., I was wondering if you and Glen could continue to watch over the property here until we decide what to do. I will, of course, continue to pay you for the labor and expenses. Besides, I'd really hate to sell this place, since this is the first home Ian ever knew, and he views you two kind of like surrogate grandparents."

With that comment, Mrs. B. had tears in the corners of her eyes as she looked back at him. "Well, I guess we can do that. No trouble at all."

Ian looked up and added, "Yeah, and I can come stay with Mrs. and Mr. B. when you and Ma have to go on another mission."

Ryan and Amanda laughed. Ryan looked at Ian with a smirk. "On another mission? What in the world would that be, lad?"

"You know, Da. To save another child like me or something."

"Oh, I see. Of course, Ian, you can come stay with Mr. and Mrs. B. anytime you want to."

"Yeah, just like I can go see Father Bryan."

"Yes, just like going to see Father Bran in Ireland."

"Man, I have a lot of big people who love me now. Not just you and me anymore. Right, Da?"

"Right, my son."

Amanda grabbed Ian and placed him on her lap while giving him a big morning hug. "Ian, Da and I must go over to the campus for a while today to start to pack up our personal stuff from our offices. We'll mail most of our stuff back to the farm. Do you think you will be all right with Mrs. B. while we are gone? We'll be back for dinner."

"Yes, I'm a big boy."

Ryan rubbed the top of Ian's head. "That's a good laddie."

Mrs. Beasley started to clean up the breakfast table. "Oh, he'll be fine while you both are gone. Besides, Ian, I haven't had time to tell you about Mr. Beasley getting a new border collie puppy. He named him Trigger. I'm sure he'd love to play with you today."

Ian's eyes got as big as saucers. "Wow, Trigger. Can we go get him now?"

"No, not now. He is most likely helping Mr. Beasley with the chores. Once you are dressed and I've finished cleaning up the kitchen, we can go find them. How's that?"

"Oh boy! I'm going to hurry up and get dressed. A dog. Trigger!"

Ryan softly patted Ian's butt as he ran from the table toward his bedroom. "Ian, don't forget to wash up some, brush your teeth, and comb your hair."

"Oh, Da, OK."

Mrs. Beasley, Ryan, and Amanda smiled at each other.

Amanda stopped at her sleeping quarters to check on Midnight, the feline she had rescued. He had grown and appeared to be content, looking out one of the large windows, as she entered her room.

The maid, Megan, came around the bathroom corner as Amanda entered. "Oh, Dr. O'Neal, you are finally back. Midnight has missed you."

"Thank you for taking care of him."

"Aye, well, he is a good cat, even if he is black."

They both laughed, knowing about Irish and Scottish superstitions regarding black cats. Amanda reached for Midnight and rubbed the top of his head before she grabbed him and placed him down on her lap as she took a moment to sit by the fire. Midnight began to purr as he snuggled in her arms.

"Anyway, Megan, Professor McFarlan and I will be leaving in a few days to go back to Florida. You might as well know that we had to go to Ireland for important family business and were married there."

"How exciting, Dr. O'Neal. Oh, I mean O'Neal-McFarlan."

"Oh, don't worry. You can still call me Dr. O'Neal or Amanda or whatever."

They laughed together.

"Anyway, I only have a few days to pack up this room and my office before leaving. I would appreciate it if you could help me. I will pay you for all your extra work. Do you want me to say something to the butler and his wife, Covington Strongwell III and Grace Strongwell?"

"That would be good. Aye, thank ye. What will you be doing about Midnight?"

"Oh, he'll be going home with us to my farm in Florida. I have another cat, Jasper, and a Labrador retriever named Royal. I've really missed them. Hopefully, all of them will become fast friends. There are many farm animals and people on the property as well."

"Sounds lovely."

"Yes, it is to me. It's really my home. Well, if you don't mind, I'm going to get cleaned up and then go to my office."

"No problem, Amanda. If you give me some ideas of where to begin with the boxes and luggage before you leave, I can start packing for you."

"Believe me, that will be much appreciated."

Amanda turned the key to her office, expecting the prior horrible mess of everything scattered about. She thought to herself, *Wow, my whole office is put back together. You'd never know it was destroyed before I left. Wonder who cleaned it up.* Walking to her desk, she saw that all her academic files were in order, and the broken wall frames had been replaced with new ones like the originals. To the best of her ability, she could find nothing significant missing. She even did a quick scan to see if any bugging devices or cameras were still around. All evidence of anything like that was now gone.

"Unbelievable," she softly said out loud to herself.

"Oh, Dr. O'Neal, I see that you are finally back. I was just going to shoot you and Professor McFarlan another email, requesting the date you both would return, but I see that won't be necessary."

"Hello, Dean Russet. I see by your appearance and all the news around campus that you had quite a few changes in your life while we were gone."

"Yes, Professor Pierre Dubois and I are deeply in love and plan to wed soon. Oh, of course, I'm sure you've heard by now about my true gender, which I've covered up all these years for professional reasons."

Amanda had her back to Dean Russet still, so she smirked to herself as she turned around to reply, "Yes, we heard." She paused for a few seconds. "Dean, I was very surprised when I just opened my office door and saw my office was all back in order. Did you find who messed it up in the first place?"

"Well, that is why I wanted to speak to you as soon as you arrived back. I'm afraid while I've been confessing of late, I have something else I must confess to you. Something I'm certainly not very proud of."

Amanda felt deep in her heart that she knew what Dean Russet was going to confess. "OK, what is it?"

"Um, sorry to say this, but I came into your office one evening with the campus security and messed everything up. I had them do it to scare you, hoping you'd leave in fear, but I know now that something as stupid as that would not have frightened you off. All the bugs and cameras have been removed also. Believe me, I've learned my lesson. I'll never do something that stupid again."

"Good to hear, Dean Russet. Ryan and I thought it might have been you but didn't really know why. Besides, you know there are a whole list of things I could possibly charge you and the campus with."

"I know. I'm truly sorry. Can you please forgive me, Dr. O'Neal?"

"Yes, I can forgive you. There won't be any legal charges brought against you and the college. I've found that life is too short and hard enough as it is to hold grudges. Especially for the small things. I'm still going to hold you accountable for anything significant destroyed or missing, though. I'll let you know about that when I've gone through everything of mine."

Dean Russet swiftly moved to Amanda and grabbed her in a hug. "Oh, thank you. I've been so worried. Seems like I haven't been able to sleep for months, thinking about what a fool I was and what you might do about it."

"No more worrying about that, but please tell me—why in the world did you do it in the first place?"

"Truthfully, I was jealous. I saw how the students loved your classes and you. I was afraid that you were aiming for my job. I was scared, due to my not telling the truth about so many things in my life."

Amanda instinctively moved her left hand to her mouth as she started to laugh. "Believe me, Dean Russet, your position was the last thing on my mind. I came here on a sabbatical from my full-time job as an attorney in Tampa because my colleagues and I had just completed the solving of a horrible satanic case in Tampa Bay. We'd just lost one of our dearest friends, Detective Captain Emerson, who was shot dead. Besides that was the sudden death of my beloved husband, Shawn O'Neal, of a massive heart attack. Honestly, if I hadn't surprisingly hooked up with our old family friend Ryan McFarlan, I'd probably have gone a little crazy."

"Oh dear, I don't know what to say. I'm so very sorry. Truly, Amanda."

"So you see, Dean Russet, taking over your position as academic dean was never a thought in my mind."

"Amanda, really, what can I do for you?"

"What you can do for me, Dean Susan Russet, is be a true friend for me from this point forward. I'm serious. Please, let us just forget everything from this point forward and start fresh."

Surprised, Dean Russet, whose eyes became teary, softly replied, "I can do that."

"Good. Can you tell me who took all the time to put my office files and broken items back together?"

"Yes, with you and Ryan gone, I had a faculty meeting where we discussed what happened to your office. I didn't tell them it was security under my direction. That is, hopefully, between you and me.

Anyway, professors Timothy and Karen Norman volunteered to get your office back in order. They've been very worried about you."

"Well, I'm glad they did that for me. Thank you for letting them help. Frankly, I'm tired after all Ryan and I've been through. I don't know if I would have had the energy to clean everything up, plus pack."

"Pack?"

"Yes, Dean Russet, pack. Confidentially for now, Ryan and I had to go to Ireland to get his small son, Ian, back from being kidnapped. Thank God, we got him. Ryan and I also, confidentially for now, got married while we were there. I guess like yours, all our news will become public news soon."

"I'm glad you told me, Amanda. Really, what can I do for all of you?"

"Well, Ryan and I have decided to go back to Florida. Shawn and I had a family farm there outside Tampa, and I miss it very much. Since you were so kind to have other people take over our classes, we just want to get our offices packed up by the end of this week and go home."

"I understand. Dr. O'Neal, no worries. I will personally, with security and whoever wants to help, assist in getting both your offices packed up. I promise no destruction will take place again. I want to help."

"That would be much appreciated. I don't know why, but I'm kind of feeling exhausted. If you don't mind, I'm going to leave for the day and come back tomorrow for all this."

"That will be fine. Please let me see you out. No worries for now. Go get some rest."

"Thank you."

Amanda picked up her purse, feeling suddenly quite exhausted, and quietly walked out of her office as Dean Russet locked the door behind her. No words were exchanged between them as they walked side by side to Amanda's vehicle. The dean waved to her as Amanda drove off.

True to the dean's word, by Wednesday afternoon, both Ryan's and Amanda's offices and Amanda's faculty sleeping quarters were packed. All boxes were Federal Expressed off to her beloved little farm. Many goodbyes were exchanged through that week as another adventure in their lives ended. They'd leave North Carolina for now and determine what to do about Ryan and Ian's sentimental cabin in the woods later. It was time to go.

Chapter 28

Back to the Farm

On the flight home from Huntington Hills, North Carolina, to the Tampa Bay area in Florida, Ryan and Amanda sat together, holding hands. Ian was on his father's lap, fast asleep, with his little arms around Ryan's neck and his head lying on his father's left shoulder.

Ryan squeezed Amanda's hand and looked over. "Saints preserve, Red. The little lad is dead weight. He is sleeping dead to the world! My neck and shoulder are getting numb."

Amanda let out a soft giggle. "What are you going to do?"

"I really don't know. Should we wake him up and place him in the empty chair near you?"

"Well, he probably won't want to lie there away from you. Let's slowly move him down across both our laps, and I'll cover him with this blanket. I bet he won't even stir awake."

"OK, careful. I don't want him to be startled and start crying or something. Oh Lord! If that happens, all of us will probably be kicked off the plane."

Amanda giggled again. "Ryan, don't be ridiculous. We are almost home. The plane is going to land in a few minutes."

Ian moved without waking, so they had a few moments before the plane descended for landing.

"OK, I can breathe a little bit easier," Ryan said. They looked at each other and smiled as Amanda wiped a strand of hair from Ian's face. He looked sweet.

"I guess Trigger, Mr. Beasley's new pup, ran him ragged before we left."

"Aye, maybe I should get him a new pup."

"Well, we'll see. He will probably take to Royal, Shawn's and my Labrador retriever. Poor Royal. He lost Shawn, his best friend, and then I took off! Thank God José and his precious grandmother Soledad have been there to care for him and all the animals. Really, we are all family. You will see."

Ryan kind of snorted with a smirk on his face. "It seems like I haven't been on the O'Neal farm in ages. I think Shawn and I were just ready to graduate with our bachelor's degrees the last time I was there. His father always looked at me as his wild rebel friend."

"Oh, don't be silly."

"No, I'm not kidding. Mr. O'Neal always seemed to be glancing at me like I was going to lead Shawn into doing something wild or out of character. Now, his mother loved me to death! Every time we went to the farm during break, she'd go on about my beautiful, wavy dark hair and put her hands through it."

"What?"

"I just stood there, kind of laughing, like any young man would do. Really, I was afraid Mr. O'Neal was going to punch me in the face or something. Shawn just shook his head. Anyway, she'd go on about my deep blue eyes. How someday I'd break some girl's heart."

"Little did she know you'd already done that several times."

"Please."

"It's true. Shawn and I would often watch you flash that McFarlan smile as the girls swarmed around you like bees going for the honey."

"Oh no. That is too funny. So not true."

"Oh yes, Ryan McFarlan. You were something else!"

"And now?"

"Now I am praying you are settled down with your loving wife and wondrous son."

"Aye. I am settled for sure. You are my family forever. Until death do us part. You and Ian can't get rid of this guy!"

"Good to hear. I'm happy, you know. Truly. I mean, I miss Shawn terribly, but maybe it has all ended like it was supposed to be. I think he would approve."

"Aye, there is a hole in my heart about Shawn being gone too soon also. He was my best friend. You and he both were my true friends. We were brothers, he and I. What great times together the two of us had. I guess it will take a lifetime to tell you about all our adventures. We were crazy! His father would have died if he knew about everything. Soon after graduation, you and Shawn got married and took over the family farm. I always knew you'd be together. Sometimes that made me sad."

"Why was that?"

"Well, because it became all about you and Shawn. I kind of felt like the third wheel."

"Is that why you took that photography assignment to go to Africa for *National Geographic* right after we graduated?"

"Aye, that was the true reason. I told Shawn it was a great opportunity I couldn't pass up, but really, I was a little brokenhearted."

"I'm sorry. Deep inside, I always sort of knew you had a thing for me."

"True. Well, Red, we are together now, and for that I feel like God has given me a second chance. No greater blessing could he have bestowed upon my life than giving me you as my wife. And my lad, Ian. I'm more blessed than words can say."

With misty eyes, Amanda whispered in his ear, "Thank you, Ryan Michael Christopher McFarlan. Both of us are blessed also to have you." They kissed.

The Tampa International Airport transport van finally came to a stop close to the front door of the farmhouse. It was around four thirty in the afternoon, so Amanda was surprised when she looked out the van window and saw everyone waiting for them. When she opened the passenger door, Royal was the first to greet her with doggy licks. He tried to get into her lap before she succeeded in getting out of the vehicle. Once her feet were solidly on the ground, Amanda crouched down and gave him kisses and the biggest hug, all while whispering sweet words to her beloved Labrador retriever.

By that time, Ryan was standing by her side with Ian in his arms. "Well, Red, I guess you weren't kidding when you said Royal was probably really missing you."

With tears in her eyes, Amanda said, "I told you!"

Ryan reached down and rubbed one of her shoulders to give her some comfort. She glanced at the barn door and saw Jasper the cat peeking out to see what all the commotion was about. Suddenly, the female calico feline realized what was happening and came running up to her also.

Amanda picked up Jasper while rubbing the feline's head. "Oh, Jasper, I've been missing you too. Jasper, I've brought you a big surprise." The driver of the van placed the carrying case with

Midnight down on the ground beside them. "Jasper, this is Midnight. He is going to be a wonderful companion for you and Royal. You guys need to get acquainted."

Ian looked as if he were in a trance. "Da, do you see? We have two cats now and a dog."

"Aye, Ian, my lad. We are lucky indeed."

"Yeah, lucky."

Amanda placed Jasper by Midnight's carrying case so they could start to get used to each other, while Royal walked up again to get more rubs and pats from his greatly missed master. Ryan leaned over and gave Amanda a small kiss while handing Ian over to Amanda to hold.

While Ryan was shaking hands with Detective Brad Conner and Detective Henry Brooks, Amanda was emotional, hugging Soledad and José Emanuel. She and Shawn had saved them from a life of poverty and suffering. José and his grandmother Soledad now lived on the farm, in their own private cabin a short distance from the barn and main house. Amanda had been José's assigned attorney in juvenile court. She had gotten him out of juvenile detention when his little sister, Dulcinea Emanuel, was killed by a horrible satanic cult near Hyde Park. Everyone on the farm had become an instant family, just as it was always supposed to be.

Speaking to the guys, Ryan said, "Nice to see you gentlemen again. For a while, I didn't know whether that was going to happen for Amanda and me."

Brad replied, "Well, that is what we heard from FBI agent Maxwell Davis and Chief Braxton Ward. You will have to fill us in on all the details that happened in Ireland. I mean about getting Ian back. Wow!"

Brooks broke into the conversation. "We've already heard about you two handfasting in the woods and then being married at the Haven abbey by Father Bryan O'Duinn. Congratulations, you two."

Ryan looked shocked. "What? Is Father Bryan here?"

Brooks smiled while tapping him on the shoulder. "Oh yes, you could say that. He and retired Chief Ward are in the barn with the horses just returned from Sheriff Ben's farm next door. Ben is introducing them to Flame and Champagne right now."

Suddenly, José spoke out. "We call Champagne just Champ for short. She is a sweet mare. Flame is our stallion. He is the feisty one. Shawn and Ben were always the ones best at handling him, but I'm going to learn now that they are back home."

Amanda hugged José tightly. "My, how you have grown since I've been gone. I know you visited our horses often at Ben's place after Shawn died and after I left for the sabbatical in North Carolina. I'm so sorry for all you've lost at such a young age. You lost your parents to drugs and gang violence; then your baby sister, Dulcinea; and then my late husband, Shawn. Then the horses had to be removed for a while. Please forgive me for leaving you, José and Soledad, but I was a little messed up after Shawn's death. Don't you worry, José; I've decided that if your grandmother allows, I'm going to adopt you while I adopt Ian. You think about it."

"That means I will be José Emanuel O'Neal McFarlan?"

"Yes," Amanda replied. "If that is what you want, that would be fine. I know how you loved Shawn. He would have loved that you wish to keep the O'Neal name. After all, the name of O'Neal will always be part of this farm's history."

Detective Brad gave Amanda a big hug and then started to lead her and Ryan toward the main house. "Lorri, my wife, and Pearl, Brooks's wife, are still in the kitchen with the chief's wife, Annabelle, cooking up a storm. We aren't allowed to go in there. My twin toddler boys, Billy and Bennie, thank God, are taking a nap."

Soledad clapped her hands and then started to walk fast. With her Spanish accent, she blurted out, "Oh yes, I must get back to cook and instruct the girls."

Ryan let out a deep laugh. "Well, Soledad, I've already been told by everyone that you are the best cook around these parts. I can't wait until dinner."

Brooks added, "Yeah, Agent Maxwell Davis, whom we respectfully call Running Horse, almost cried like a baby when he had to remain in North Carolina for work rather than be here as part of the welcoming committee. He loves Soledad and her awesome food."

Ian pulled on Ryan's pantleg while jumping excitedly. "Da, José is going to take me down to the barn so I can see all the animals. Is that OK?"

"Fine, Ian. You can go. Have a good time. Stay with Father Bryan when you're done. Da and Ma need a bit of a nap before dinner. Oh, take Midnight's carrying case with you, and release him in the barn so he and Jasper can be together."

"OK, Da. We will."

José picked up Midnight's case with one hand and held Ian's small hand on the other side. Ian was thrilled about the prospect of having an older brother. Without even being told, Jasper and Royal followed behind them. They were all happy.

Brad leaned into Amanda, giving her a kiss on the top of her head, just as they reached the front porch. "Oh yes, we almost forgot to tell you that Ilene, deceased Captain Lukas Emerson's widow, is bringing Cap Jr., Cliff, and Perah for dinner tonight."

Brooks piped up again. "Don't forget Vivian Smith is to arrive soon with Dr. Travis Marshall. Her mother, Lisa Smith, said she couldn't make it. Oh yes, we also will have a couple of surprise guests get here just before dinner."

Ryan tiredly glanced at Amanda as they went up the porch stairs and into the house. "Frankly, I'm getting exhausted just thinking about all the people who will be here for dinner. Where is everyone going to sit?"

Amanda lovingly whispered in his ear, "It will be all right. You'll see." She then put her arms around him and led him to her bedroom door. "OK, everyone, Ryan and I are going to lie down for a little bit. We are bushed. We'll see all of you later."

Brooks replied, "Sounds good to me. Come on, Brad. Let's go to the living room and watch the football game. Maybe Pearl will make us some popcorn before dinner."

"Sounds good to me," Brad replied as they both headed that way.

Amanda quickly pushed Ryan through the bedroom, slammed and locked the door, pushed him against the wall, and kissed him deeply.

Ryan gasped for a moment to breathe. "This nap of ours is sounding better with every second that goes by." They giggled softly together while quickly undressing and climbing onto the bed.

"Ryan, this bed feels so heavenly. I feel like I truly haven't slept for hours."

"I know what you mean." Ryan then got on top of her while giving her a frisky glance.

"Oh, Ryan, I'm so tired, though."

"I know, leannan, but it will relax both of us. Make us feel happy."

"OK, but just a fast session. Everyone is here, and I'm exhausted."

"A fast session? How in the blazes? OK, my love, I guess I'm destined to do a fast session, so to speak, until everyone is finally gone and we are honestly alone. Saints preserve!"

Amanda giggled again as he came forward for a kiss. They necked for a while, and then Ryan started at her forehead. He kissed her eyelids and then nibbled on one of her ears. He let out a deep, masculine giggle. "I'm coming to get you."

"Oh God," Amanda said as she started to moan.

"Uh, Red, I don't think the Good Lord is going to help you on this right now. My thinking is that he is leaving it up to me."

She moaned a little more. Ryan kissed between her breasts and then sucked on one nipple while pinching the other. Her breathing was increasing, and tingling and heat began to rise between her legs.

Suddenly, they heard Ian at the door. "Da, are you taking a nap? Can I come sleep between you and Ma for a while?"

Ryan popped up his head and looked at Amanda, who softly laughed. "Dear Lord, I guess I do need some help here."

Father Bryan's voice could be heard outside the door. "Come along, Ian. I think they have fallen asleep. You come along now and lie down with good old Father Bryan. We'll steal some of Brad and Brooks's popcorn and then have a bit of a snooze together."

The tiny voice sounded a little disappointed. "OK, Father."

Amanda looked into Ryan's eyes. "I guess your prayer was answered."

"Well, yes, but Ian kind of broke the mood. If you know what I mean."

"Nonsense. I can feel your hardness beside my leg. Carry on, my husband."

They both started to giggle, and then Ryan kissed her stomach while rubbing her clitoris at the same time.

He moved up and whispered in her ear, "I still feel like I'm on a time clock here."

She smiled, turned sideways, raised one of her legs over him, grabbed his shaft, and began rubbing it seductively up and down with her closed hand while placing its head near her moist opening. He gasped with pleasure.

Softly, she whispered, "You're trying too hard. I think you're a big boy. Just go for it."

He was so surprised at first that he didn't know quite what to say. So he said nothing. Entering her slowly, he thought, *Oh, praise be, I'm finally home.* He moved in and out of her tightness slowly at first and then started to speed up. Just when he felt her on the edge of coming, he abruptly stopped.

Panting with desire, Amanda opened her eyes and blurted out, "Oh no, you beast. What are you doing? Ryan, I'm going to go crazy here!"

He smiled and then entered her swiftly and deeply and continued moving in and out as he felt her inside wall tighten down around him firmly, until they both exploded in ecstasy at the same time.

Both lay on their backs, while catching their breath. Ryan turned to her and said, "Wife, I'm thinking I'm kind of getting the hang of this quickie-session thing. Wow! Our little romping about there just may have been the closest thing to heaven on earth a man can get."

Amanda smiled at him while wiping his wavy, thick bangs from his eyes. "It was grand, my handsome husband, like going into space together. Aye?"

Ryan returned her smile as she snuggled closer to him, placing her head on his chest.

As they held each other tightly, their breathing grew shallower as they both relaxed and drifted off to sleep. Rest had finally come for them.

The sun was setting in Tampa Bay. The twinkling lights from the barn and the huge dinner table that had been set up could be seen from the house. It was November, just before Thanksgiving, so oddly, there was a cool feeling to the tropical air.

Vivian and Dr. Travis had arrived while many were taking naps. Travis was glad to be able to view some of the football game, while Vivian was helping the gals with carrying the food out to the barn. Brooks had decided he'd be the one to greet the last-minute arrivals.

Detective Captain Lukas Emerson had been Detective Henry Brooks's best friend for years, so when Cap's widow, Ilene, arrived with her youngest son, Cliff, Brooks was overjoyed. Detective Cap Emerson had been tragically murdered during a satanic crime investigation they had all worked on and solved several years ago. His death had created a huge void in many people's lives. Soon after Ilene and Cliff arrived, Amanda's legal secretary, Beatrice, with an unexpected date, arrived as well.

The house started to suddenly sound quiet as one by one, people headed for the barn. As during every Thanksgiving and Christmas season, the barn had been designated as the place for the celebration dinner. That was a wonderful surprise for all the barn animals. Once again, they sensed that something special was going to occur. Brad, Brooks, and Ben hoped the barn animals would be extra good, meaning not suddenly smell the barn up, during the dinner. José giggled when he overheard their discussion.

Amanda pulled on a thin sweater as she grabbed Ryan's hand while running down the front porch stairs toward the barn. Tears formed in her eyes as she saw the huge table—more like a train of picnic tables placed together in the center of the barn. Twinkling lights had been strung all over the barn's ceiling. It was a breathtaking view. She couldn't believe all the work everyone had done to celebrate her return home, Ryan's and her marriage, and Ian's safe return from his dreaded kidnapping. There were black-and-white-checked tablecloths all the way down the long line of tables, with pumpkins, candles, and other decorations. She could smell cinnamon and other spices in the air. *Beautiful!*

Ryan looked at the barn and said to Amanda, "Red, you are a very lucky woman!"

With a little soft cry, she replied, "I know."

Just then, all there could hear a motorcycle in the near distance. Royal gave out a few barks, while Jasper and Midnight retreated to the hayloft. The horses stomped on the ground, while the cows mooed, and the goats sounded out. Everyone was anxious to find out who was coming.

Soon a Harley-Davidson pulled up. Professor Timothy Norman and his wife, Professor Karen Norman, waved as they got off the motorcycle and headed their way.

"Hope we haven't arrived late," Tim said as he and Karen reached the table.

"Nope, just in time!" Brooks yelled out.

Amanda and Ryan ran to welcome them to the feast. Once everyone was greeted and seated, Amanda, who was sitting at the end of the table, with Ryan and Ian on her sides, requested Chief Braxton Ward give a prayer of thanks.

"Our dear heavenly Father, all of us have much to be thankful for this evening. Thank you for bringing us all together to celebrate and share this evening. Thank you for these wonderful family and friends. I also want to slip in much thanks for your helping all involved in solving the horrible crime spree in my beloved home in Huntington Hills, North Carolina. But this event is about joy! We give you thanks for each other and the wondrous food we are about to partake in.

Turkey and ham, mashed potatoes and gravy, yams with cooked marshmallows on top, corn on the cob, fresh green beans—"

Braxton's wife, Annabelle, touched his arm and said loudly enough so others could hear, "Braxton, dear, you don't have to list every food item on the table."

The others couldn't help but laugh out loud while keeping their heads down in prayer.

"Oh yeah, I just want to end the prayer by saying thanks for having my wife, Annabelle, bake her great pies for dessert. Pumpkin pie, apple pie, and pecan pie. Amen."

Everyone said, "Amen," except for Ian, who yelled out, "Yummy to my tummy!"

Father Bryan said, "The chief's prayer of thanks is ended. Praise be to God!"

That brought laughter across the table as the food started to be passed down the line.

Amanda sat there silently for a moment, taking in all the wondrous sounds and conversations around her, thinking, *I am blessed. Blessed so much.* She then reached down and gave the top of Royal's head a nice rub.

Everyone seemed to be busy passing the plates and deep in conversation. Vivian was telling Detective Brad and Lorri Conner about the status of her medical recovery and mentioned that Dr. Travis Marshall had finally proposed to her. She was thinking about being married on Amanda's farm and couldn't wait to ask her when they were alone together. Dr. Marshall just held her hand firmly and smiled.

Detective Brooks and his wife, Pearl, were sharing with Ilene, Detective Emerson's widow, the story of Ian's dramatic rescue. Cliff, Ilene's youngest son, mentioned his law enforcement goal and said that Cap Jr. had been unable to come, due to his college final exams. He was getting a degree as a forensic profiler. Brooks smiled when Cliff proudly talked about his oldest brother that way. As for Cliff's sister, Perah, she was studying for middle school finals but hoping to eventually go to New York for college. Her goal was to have a career in fashion. No surprise there! Detective Cap would have been proud of all three of their children. Ilene feared for her boys especially, due to the murder of her much-loved husband, Detective Captain Lukas Emerson, but despite those uncertainties, she also knew from much experience to allow the children to follow God's will for their lives.

Sitting nearby, Ryan was laughing with Tim and Karen Norman about the surprising campus announcements at Huntington Hills College of Dean Russet's true gender as well as her torrid love for Professor Pierre Dubois. Life was always full of surprises!

Just down the table, Father Bryan was discussing Irish and Spanish recipes with Soledad, Chief Braxton Ward, and Annabelle Ward. When it came to food, Chief Ward was up for anything that tasted good.

The children finished eating before the adults, so José kept Brad and Lorri's twin toddlers, Billy and Bennie, along with Ian, occupied by the horses, Flame and Champ. José tried to demonstrate to Billy and Bennie how to properly feed them. Ian, of course, was acting like a professional, since he'd spent so much time with Father Bryan's horses in Ireland. It was a cute sight.

Beatrice, Amanda's loyal legal secretary, chatted with Pearl Brooks, glad that Amanda was back home. A lot of casework had piled up. She was also proud to introduce her new boyfriend, Lenard Bernard. They looked like a lovely older couple. They had met because he was a senior clerk at the courthouse, and Beatrice had kept calling him on the phone about various pending cases when

Amanda was gone. He said with a twinkle in his eyes that she yelled at him all the time.

As Amanda observed all the activity from the head of the table, it seemed everyone's stress had been released at the barn door, and all were enjoying the fantastic food and company. It was a special dinner. *So good to be home.*

She picked up her spoon and tapped it on her water glass to get everyone's attention. Once everyone quieted down and looked her way, Amanda smiled sweetly before speaking.

"This gathering is truly lovely. No person could ask for any greater gift than that of true faith in God in his or her heart, family around him or her, and the dearest of friends always nearby. Thank you so much. Really. When I pause for a moment and think of all we have been through in our lives, together as well as separately, all I sincerely have left to say is that no matter the circumstances, 'Trust in the Lord with all your heart and lean not on your own understanding; in all your ways acknowledge him, and he will make your paths straight' (Proverbs 3:5–6 NIV)."

Epilogue

Life after the Huntington Hills Crimes

Much had happened at the O'Neal-McFarlan farm since everyone's return. For now, Amanda had closed her law office, making sure all her cases were handled with care by other knowledgeable attorneys. Her longtime legal assistant, Beatrice, had found another job immediately in the law office of one of Amanda's good legal friends, so she was as happy as pie. Plus, Beatrice was still involved with her new significant other, Lenard. Beatrice and Amanda missed working together, but life was about change. After all, they'd been a great legal team.

Amanda took a new appointed position at the Tampa Police Department as a legal case adviser and honorary detective, due to all her legal and investigative expertise. She just hoped her new career didn't get in the way of raising José and Ian, both of whom she had legally adopted. Besides, everyone always smiled while indicating that Soledad was really the one in charge at the farm anyway.

Ryan was working on a coffee table book of some of his outstanding photographs he'd taken all over the world. The whole family had a wonderful time voting on which pictures should be in the book. Ian, of course, always picked photographs of animals, especially those from Africa. Surprisingly, José and Soledad selected photos that showed the suffering of the oppressed from war, poverty, homelessness, human trafficking, and drugs. Amanda loved the landscape and nature photos. Ryan was also teaching some courses at Tampa University and University of South Florida, as well as doing guest speaking at various campuses.

From the day Ian arrived at the farm, he claimed José as his big brother, and he would hear of nothing else. It seemed the two of them were coming into their own. The years flew by, and Ian was soon to enter middle school, while José was graduating in a few months from high school. Ian told everyone he was going to be either an artist like his da or a detective like his ma. In contrast, José never strayed far from always wanting to be around animals. The family farm animals meant so much to him. He decided he wanted to be a veterinarian. Ryan and Amanda were proud of the boys. As for Soledad, she had so much pride in José and Ian that she often said if her buttons weren't buttoned tightly, they'd pop right off her blouse. She stood tall when talking about them, which she did often.

FBI agent Maxwell Davis had recently visited the O'Neal-McFarlan farm, and Soledad had spoiled him rotten. In Soledad's mind, Maxwell, a.k.a. Running Horse, needed some loving care. His stomach did anyway! She cooked as many of her famous tacos and fajitas as he wanted. Everyone at the farm sensed that something wasn't quite right with Maxwell, so Amanda and Ryan convinced him to go back home to the Cherokee reservation for rest and relaxation. He had been working too hard for too long. His soul was hurting.

Once back home, Running Horse took off his white-man clothes and put on the garments of his ancestors. His thick jet-black hair had begun to grow out longer, and he released it from its leather tie. Sitting at the top of the hill, he looked down toward the reservation—a beautiful view. The breeze softly blew, almost as if the trees were dancing, as the sunrise began its glorious blossom in the sky.

Running Horse knew he had to get his soul back in order so he could happily get back to his FBI duties, but he had seen so much pain, suffering, and pure evil that he felt as if he were in pieces. Somehow, he had to restore himself again. The next month on the Cherokee reservation where he had grown up would be good for him. He knew the white God and the spirits from his ancestors would help him. Inside, he felt his life was suffering; his soul was yearning for more. He needed to feel balanced again. He would take the time needed to rest and rely on his faith, placing his future in God's hands.

Printed in the United States
by Baker & Taylor Publisher Services